"Haunting and compulsively readable, *The Night Flowers* is
sible to put down. A novel that is as much ghost story as m
Herchenroether has crafted a truly original narrative that u
with a shocking array of twists and turns against the backdr
the Gila National Forest. Every voice in the chorus that mak
this novel sings a siren song of suspense you won't be able to
I devoured it."
　　　　　　　　　　　　　　　　　　　　　—KATY

author of *The Clo*

"Hypnotic, heart-wrenching, and harrowing, *The Night Flowe*
an exceptional debut. The twisted path of long-buried wrongs
ing to light will keep you on the edge of your seat. Still, it's
honest exploration of violence, trauma, and scars that never h
that will haunt you. Sara Herchenroether is a true talent."
　　　　　　　　　　　　　　　　　　　—HILARY DAVIDS

author of *Her Last Brea*

"Sara Herchenroether's astonishing, intricate debut is a deep
nuanced portrayal of those called to name the dead. A cold ca
detective and soon-to-be grandmother, a genealogist libraria
recovering from breast cancer, and the ghost of a murdered woma
are the unforgettable heroines of a novel about confronting—an
transcending—mortality. Like Tana French meets Ann Patchett
The Night Flowers begs to be raced through the first time and savored
the second. Sara Herchenroether is a fierce talent with much to say
about women's strength in their most vulnerable moments."
　　　　　　　　　　　　　　　　　　　—KATIE GUTIERREZ

author of *More Than You'll Ever Know*

"*The Night Flowers* is so many things: a murder mystery, a ghost
story, a meditation on violence and the fragility of the body. Com-
pelling, insightful, and evocative."　　　　　**—JANE PEK**,

author of *The Verifiers*

THE
NIGHT
FLOWERS

THE
NIGHT
FLOWERS

A NOVEL

SARA
HERCHENROETHER

TIN HOUSE / PORTLAND, OREGON

First US Edition 2023
Printed in the United States of America

Manufacturing by Lake Book Manufacturing
Interior design by Beth Steidle

Library of Congress Cataloging-in-Publication Data

Names: Herchenroether, Sara, 1983– author.
Title: The night flowers : a novel / Sara Herchenroether.
Description: Portland, Oregon : Tin House, [2023]
Identifiers: LCCN 2022060780 | ISBN 9781953534866 (hardcover) |
ISBN 9781953534941 (ebook)
Subjects: LCGFT: Thrillers (Fiction). | Novels.
Classification: LCC PS3608.E7326 N54 2023 | DDC 813/.6—dc23/eng/20221219
LC record available at https://lccn.loc.gov/2022060780

Tin House
2617 NW Thurman Street, Portland, OR 97210
www.tinhouse.com

DISTRIBUTED BY W. W. NORTON & COMPANY

1 2 3 4 5 6 7 8 9 0

For Ryan

Nothing remains except her bones and voice—
her voice continues, in the wilderness;
her bones have turned to stone. She lies concealed
in the wild woods . . .

—Ovid, *Metamorphoses*
Translated by J. Brookes More

AUGUST 31, 1983

ANDY BLAMED THE BOOTS. EASY TO DO SINCE THEY were no longer beneath him. He had a good view on his back, sliding headfirst, his shoulders scraping rough brush, into the canyon. The boots were Vasque Sundowners with leather the color of horses' saddles. Thick black soles. Wide cadmium-red laces that made the tops of his feet look like the crisscross lacing of a Swedish doll's dress. As he was falling down the eastern ridge of Reeds Peak, he had the distinct impression of being pulled from below. That invisible hands gripped him, dragging him into the canyon.

The hiking trip had started innocently enough. At the trailhead where they'd parked Andy's rusted Corolla, Elise had traced their route along the map of the Gila National Forest and Black Range mountains spread out on the hood, her finger running along the dots and dashes between their peaks: Moccasin John Mountain, Reeds Peak, Rocky Point. They signed their names in the register at the trailhead and were off. For the most part, they followed a rambling creek sandwiched between canyon walls. The farther north they went, the steeper the granite. Its face a blend of smudged newspaper gray and burnt apricot. The steeper the wall, the shorter the daylight hours.

They hiked for four hours a day, crossing the creek at the lowest points to follow the trail. They made so many trips back and forth across the water, there was no point taking off their boots each time. It didn't take long for a family of blisters to develop along Andy's heels. Didn't take long for those blisters to merge into two giant blobs, one per foot. They each felt like the sweaty top of a warm Jell-O cup that had been left sitting out on a hot summer day. Same color too: cherry red.

Each morning, Andy pulled his boots back on and strapped on the heavier pack—heavier because it carried the extra water and the last trail map. They had lost the first map on the first day, though they couldn't agree whose fault that was. On the morning of his fall, Andy didn't notice when the water began to leak because, rather than run down his leg, it found a bed in the remaining paper map. When Andy pulled the zipper open, his fingers found pulpy sludge.

When it became clear they no longer knew where they were, Elise thought it best to head east. There were cattle ranches in the area. Maybe they could find one. It would be safer than trying to retrace their steps. Instead of hiking parallel to the canyon walls, they'd climb one. They found a path leading to the canyon's peak. The climb started gradually, but soon Andy's chest and thighs began to burn.

At the top, he could see the eastern side hadn't been touched by whatever fire had cleared the western of its undergrowth. Here, charred trunks like telephone poles littered the mountain, devoid of any green. But on the east, he and Elise had to beat back branches in places. Andy wondered how one half of a mountain could be clear while the other remained dark and tangled and wild. Wind, maybe. Or something to do with the elevation. Or chance.

They descended into a valley. Another creek churned deep and wide across their path. They crossed without incident and climbed what should have been the last major ridge. Andy's boots slurped and squelched. Until a misjudged step along the crest. Loose dirt, maybe. Andy slid to the canyon's belly, stopping when his back slammed into something metal.

The impact of his body slamming into two steel barrels knocked one over, and Andy heard a popping sound. He pushed himself up and slid his pack off. His ankle hurt, but otherwise nothing was broken, he decided, and turned to get a better look at what had stopped his fall. Before Elise found him, he had a good two minutes to stare, agape, at what had slipped out of one of the barrels. A woman's bare arm stretched out from the black hole. How he could tell it was a woman's arm and not a man's, he couldn't say. He forced his jaw closed.

"It's a mannequin, right?" he said when Elise arrived, clambering down after Andy. But she knew, right away, even if Andy didn't. Andy tried to stand, but his ankle wouldn't hold his weight. They decided he would stay with the barrels while she went for help.

Elise's figure disappeared through the woods. He propped his pack under his ankle, an indigo firework exploding under his skin. Now that he had stopped moving, his sweat-soaked shirt clung to him as though someone had poured a glass of ice-cold water down his back.

He settled in with his back pressed against the nearest tree. The afternoon sun rotated above the canyon. Eating fistfuls of trail mix when his growling stomach demanded attention, he passed the afternoon waiting. When the sun slid behind the western ridge, another arm—or the sensation of another arm—cupped his shoulders. The way his older sister used to do to comfort him when they sat on the top step of the house they grew up in, listening to their parents fight in the kitchen. Their four bare knobby knees like marbles knocking, as they waited to see how it would end. Andy didn't move. Afraid the arm—or whatever it was—would leave. Or worse, that whoever it belonged to would grow angry.

All afternoon, the surrounding brush had scented the clearing with earthy pine. As the sun sank, florals replaced the pine. He scanned the ground. If there were flowers here, he couldn't see them.

He stopped waiting for Elise to return and began fearing what would happen if she didn't. The evening air tore at his exposed skin like the blade of a serrated knife. The floral scent intensified, filling the air with noxious perfume.

In the wind, Andy heard children's laughter.

His attention was split between listening for laughter, telling himself it was crazy—there weren't children out here—and watching the barrel, half expecting the lifeless woman to crawl out.

Later, when he read that the remains were skeletonized, he would swear that couldn't be right—he *had* seen a woman's bare arm, hadn't he?

THIRTY YEARS LATER

LAURA

LAURA MACDONALD HAD GOTTEN USED TO BEING naked, but this was a bit much. For the last ten minutes, she had watched as Dr. Fusaro walked back and forth along the long corridor separating two rows of beds in the surgical bay. His hard-soled shoes tapped the floor in rhythm with his staccato Italian as he chattered to himself.

Laura had wanted to call out, "I'm right here," but didn't. Maybe he had another patient to check on.

When Dr. Fusaro did find her, the anesthesia attending had been in the middle of introducing his team. He was standing with a resident and two surgical nurses when Dr. Fusaro entered, closing the privacy screen behind him, the metal rings screaming along the curtain rod.

"Pull down your gown please," Dr. Fusaro said. Not so much as a nod of acknowledgment to the people who would keep her alive while he cut and sewed. The anesthesia attending stood frozen in mid-sentence.

Laura hesitated. Showing your breasts to one doctor was one thing. This was another.

The seconds it took her to untie her gown were an eternity. While she stared at the ceiling, Dr. Fusaro scrawled dashes across her chest with a thin-tipped permanent marker, pausing to take a step back, examine his work, and make a few more. The others kept their eyes on the floor. The surgeon left. Laura closed her gown without looking at the sewing pattern scribbled across her chest. The anesthesia attending lifted his eyes after she was covered.

"Sorry," he said.

"It's okay," Laura said. She'd give anything to tuck herself into a ball and disappear. The anesthesia team left next, leaving Laura alone again, free to hide in the anonymity of her hospital bed, watching the surgical bay come to life.

Dr. Fusaro had been the latest in a long line of medical personnel to filter through the surgical wing of Smilow Cancer Hospital. A hospital within a hospital, Smilow was one peak within the larger Yale New Haven Hospital's towering conglomerate downtown. All morning, Laura had wanted to open her phone, check the crime site she read, but instead found herself drawn into the rhythms and movements of the nurses and doctors. They were an army. So accustomed to their routine they moved by muscle memory, unaware of the terror their presence registered in those who sat waiting in beds.

Each group wore a uniform color-coded for their role in taking her apart before putting her back together again. First, bright-faced nurses in teal scrubs. They took your temperature, blood pressure, and oxygen level with a little finger-grip thing. Laura had never learned the word. People skills over medical skills for this group. Their job was to make sure you hadn't eaten and to have you change. Laura had eyed the rubber-nubby-soled orange socks in a flimsy plastic bag. Single-serve. Like the ones from the roller-skating rink her mother took them to growing up. Laura remembered the time she stared at her naked toes in flip-flops, realizing her mistake. Someone pulled her over to a vending machine, where she found row after row of uniform white cotton socks, each pair in its own sealed baggie. A pair had fallen from the metal corkscrew, landing with a soft thud.

The next company were stone-faced surgical nurses in aquarium-green scrubs. Then came the anesthesia attendings in darker blue. Then the last group, sticking out in surgeons' street clothes. Ultralight L.L. Bean jackets over dark boxy jeans. Crisp monogrammed button-downs over creased chinos and leather loafers. Northeast moneyed prep.

Her breast surgeon, Dr. Choudhry, was the last to check in with Laura before surgery. She went full Chanel. Tweed blazer, matching skirt, and double-C earrings. French luxury on a five-foot-four woman in the basement surgical wing of a cancer hospital in Connecticut. The earrings looked painful, heavy.

Dr. Choudhry was too perky for five in the morning. Too perky to carve a woman's breasts out of her chest.

"How *are* you?" the surgeon said, as though this were brunch.

Once the surgeon left, Laura slipped out her phone, opened her regular crime site. There was a new post. The bodies of a woman and two children were found on this day, thirty years ago, in two steel barrels. Laura had time to read the first paragraph before her curtain slid open.

A new nurse stood before her. Hair capped, surgical mask bibbed, a cape-like scrub that billowed when she entered. Hospital superwoman.

"Sorry, I know you've done this a hundred times already," she said, pushing her pink-flecked glasses up. "I promise I'm the last one. Name and date of birth?"

Impolite elsewhere, this was the standard hospital hello.

"Laura MacDonald, 8-31-83."

The nurse did a quick double take, checking a phone pulled from a back pocket. "It's your birthday," she said, sliding the phone away again. "Don't worry. It's not TGI Fridays. We're not going to sing. What are you here for today?"

"Bilateral mastectomy for HER2-positive breast cancer and expanders," Laura said.

Since her diagnosis, Laura had mimicked the precise medical jargon of her doctors. She wanted to show them she got it, and more, she was no dummy. As if to say—by parroting them—*Please don't kill me. I'm as smart as you. I'm someone.* In nine months of treatment, she had confused a handful of nurses, who asked if she was in the medical field herself. *No*, she had wanted to say. *I pay attention. Wouldn't you?*

She scratched the prickly hair under her cotton cap, waiting for the nurse to finish. Laura's treatment plan called for chemo before surgery. Called neoadjuvant chemotherapy, it allowed her oncologist to track her tumor with regular scans to see if the chemo drugs were working. Twelve rounds of easy, weekly drugs, leaving her sluggish for a day but otherwise functional. Followed by four rounds of what Laura referred to as the heavy hitters, to be administered monthly. Each left her in bed for a week. One had sent her to the emergency department. She had seen her tumor disappear in MRIs, but the trade-off was going into surgery—a seven-hour surgery—a shell of her former self. She now had a heart condition. No hair to speak of. Mirrors were intolerable, her face a ghost. Skin school-glue-white, eyebrows barely there. She hadn't recognized herself in months.

The last nurse put out her hand, palm up as though asking Laura to dance. "We have you walk in," the nurse said. "Research says people have more positive outcomes if they walk into their operating room." She helped Laura get to her feet and held out her hand for Laura to hold.

There was no way Laura was holding this woman's hand.

"Just push the IV stand," she said.

Laura watched her orange-socked feet, convinced she would be the first person to trip on her way to the operating room, where, on her thirtieth birthday, she would lose her breasts. Her final thought, as she lay on the table counting backward from ten and not making it to seven, was of two steel barrels, hidden in the forest, waiting to be found.

WHEN LAURA WOKE UP, she thought nothing had happened—she had closed her eyes a moment ago. Maybe they had decided she didn't need surgery after all. Maybe she still had breasts. A violent shot of yellow bile into a flimsy plastic bedpan erased any confusion.

Afternoon light filtered through the recovery room blinds. She found the clock. Four p.m. The world had decided to keep spinning.

When she sat up in bed, her body felt wrong. Four drainage bulbs, the size of eggs, were filled with red stringy globs and bright pink liquid. These were attached to four skinny tubes pinned under her armpits like tangled Christmas lights to a thick white surgical bra. Taking a breath was like pushing against one of the thick purple elastics they used to bundle broccoli. She pulled the bra away from her skin, but the tightness remained, constricting her breathing. A row of staples, or stitches—she didn't know which—dug into her ribs where a shelf had been attached to hold up her expanders. A flap of pectoral muscle had been cut and sewn to the shelf to hold them in place. She couldn't feel this, exactly, but she knew that was what had happened. She had given her body to the doctors and had gotten back a different one.

Laura would have liked to sleep, but her door never stayed closed with the constant flow of doctors checking on her. She looked away when they examined her. It was during one of these vacant stares into the corner while a nurse emptied the globby fluid from her bulbs that Laura remembered the article. After the nurse left, Laura ran her fingers over the thin hospital blanket the texture of dried corn husks as she retrieved her phone from under her thigh.

Anniversary of 30-Year-Old Cold Case
Prompts New Investigation

On August 31, 1983, hikers found the bodies of a young woman and two children in a remote section of the Gila National Forest in New Mexico. The hikers weren't sure what they had found: two 55-gallon black steel barrels, hidden by brush. The top of one drum had opened to reveal a pink fitted sheet soaked in a foamy white liquid. Underneath, the skeletal remains of a woman.

The body of the adult female was in one barrel, and the two children in the other. Both were girls. The three bodies had experienced severe decomposition, but bone, teeth, and hair samples were collected. Forensics were unable to determine how long they had been left in the forest. Some experts estimated they sat undiscovered for 20 years. Detective Sergeant Jean Martinez, known throughout Sierra County for her work on major crimes, has transferred to cold cases and reopened the investigation. It is the county's oldest cold case. A spokesperson for the Sierra County Sheriff's Department says recent advances in DNA testing may afford new investigative avenues.

Laura read the article twice. Thirty years ago today, on the same day she had been born, a woman and two girls were found. And before they were discovered, their bodies may have been sitting there, in some forest, for another twenty years. Why hadn't anyone found them before? Why hadn't anyone looked for them?

Wishing she had her laptop, Laura was about to make another search when a hard knock startled her. A nurse entered, smashing a cart on the way in. Laura held out her hand automatically. The nurse spun the wristband around to scan the barcode as though Laura was a can of tuna at Stop & Shop.

"Name and date of birth?"

Another nurse, same hello.

"Laura MacDonald. 8-31-83."

"It's your birthday," the nurse said, smiling. "Anyone staying with you?" The nurse regarded the empty room. There wasn't much to see. The window overlooking the parking garage. The love seat devoid of a loved one's overnight bag.

"No. There's my sister but her kids are sick," Laura said, feeling the emptiness of the room like a solid mass.

The monitor beeped, and the nurse typed something in. "I'll be right back," she said.

Laura shifted in her bed. Maybe they would sing after all. She shuddered. Her phone burned in her hand. The faster this nurse left, the sooner she could get back to the article. A moment later, the nurse returned holding a small plastic cup.

"Happy birthday," she said, pushing the food tray over Laura's bed and making room for the off-brand lime-green gelatin. She scanned Laura's bracelet again, then placed two pain pills in a small white paper cup, leaving them on the tray with water.

After the nurse left, again crashing the cart on her way out, Laura waited a moment to be sure she wouldn't come back. Then she pulled off the gelatin's silver top and licked the little blob stuck to the inside of the foil. The nurse had forgotten a spoon. Laura squeezed the cup in her hand and shook jiggly chunks into her mouth. Then she made another search.

First: the facial reconstruction images. The first set from the '90s. Then a second from this year, ordered by the new detective. Jane Doe had a heart-shaped face, wide-set eyes, and a pinched mouth like she had taken a long drag from a cigarette. The older child had a square face, an upturned nose, wavy hair. The younger child had a rounder face and straight dark hair. They had given her bangs.

Deeper into the results came the crime scene photos. A dense valley of forest. Mountains in the distance. Two galvanized steel drums, one upright and one on its side. A pink fitted sheet spread out on a white counter with a red-lined ruler next to it for scale. Laura peered into her phone, thinking she could see the outline of a child's hand in the sheet.

No matching dental records. No matching missing-person report. Laura considered this. Maybe no one had filed a missing-person report—not officially, anyway.

Pulling up Ancestry, Laura found the message board titled "Missing family and friends." She knew every corner of the internet when it came to genealogical research. It was an outgrowth of her job as a research librarian at the New Haven Free Public Library. She worked primarily in local history, but she also worked with people who were trying to research their family trees. In her free time, she volunteered as a search angel, helping people locate missing biological family members.

The Ancestry message board was where people posted about how to find more information about a great-grandfather or how to locate records from a country with sketchy internet. But they also posted about their own missing family members. The posts started with the words "looking for": looking for lost father, looking for half sibling, looking for mother's brother, looking for something, anything—small, unofficial pleas cast into the internet void. Could someone have looked for Jane Doe here?

Somehow, Laura felt she knew the woman in the barrel. Every day during treatment, she lived with the shame of her body having failed her. Logically, she knew: no twenty-nine-year-old was to blame for getting breast cancer, of all things. It wasn't anything she'd admit to her sister or doctor. Friends, if she had any of those left. But the shame was there. The woman in the barrel would understand. A part of Jane Doe had to blame herself for what had happened—what had happened to those girls.

There was the other similarity. While time had erased Jane Doe's body, cancer had erased Laura. In the Gila Wilderness, Jane Doe had no name, no date of birth. Here, in the hospital wilderness, Laura was *only* her name and date of birth. She had no voice. No identity outside her diagnosis. Both had lost control of their bodies.

Laura's eyes traveled to the love seat, quickly. She thought for a moment that she'd seen a shadow. She returned to her phone, finding a map of the Gila National Forest. She studied the different lines and boundaries. The notations for elevation, the names of mountain ranges and creeks. The woman and two children were found in an unprotected section. An arbitrary slice ran down from the north, carving out a long triangular area where someone had decided the protected wilderness ended. They had been lost, and found, in the in-between. Running her finger along the inside of the gelatin cup, Laura licked it clean, wiped her hand on her blanket, and opened another search window.

JEAN

THE FLUORESCENT BULB BUZZED ABOVE THE ROOKIE patrol assigned to the front desk as Detective Sergeant Jean Martinez nodded a silent hello. The kid, a Midwestern transplant, was new. He had been slouched in his seat when she opened the door.

"Good morning, ma'am—err, sorry. I mean, Detective Martinez," he said, sitting forward and knocking his weak excuse for a coffee over.

Jean swallowed a retort and made her way to the back bullpen. If she ever supervised baby patrol, lesson number one would be: Don't do that. It was Detective Sergeant. Lesson number two? Don't go looking for trouble. She knew how these kids were trained these days. She'd gone nineteen years without discharging her weapon. There were a couple of times she'd thought it would come to that. Jean had found the second you sat down, thinking you had an easy day ahead of you—those were the days trouble found you.

Maybe next time. Jean had work to do.

There was no need for her to come in early, but she liked the early morning quiet. If you came in at six in the morning on a Friday, you'd find Thursday's third shift filling out the last of its paperwork. Same if you came in early on a Sunday. Saturday night high holy day for drunks' arguments, culminating, hopefully, in fists instead of guns. Once, a wooden bat pulled from a display case on a bar's wall. Some dead slugger's autograph imprinted onto the losing end of a shattered cheekbone. There was an unwritten rule that Sunday's third shift could submit their end-of-duty reports the following day, which meant Jean was the first to walk the halls, flipping each switch as she went.

Jean grabbed the stash of good coffee she kept hidden in her desk drawer. Anyone arriving early got Jean's Colombian dark roast. The rest, the station sludge. Guys she'd worked with for the past twenty years never put two and two together. They thought the pot she brewed in the morning was better because she had "a woman's touch" in the kitchen. She never told them it was different fucking coffee. Bunch of crack detectives around here. She also never bothered to tell them she didn't know how to cook, just how to eat. Only Detective Sergeant Billy Parker was privy to those details.

Jean took her dark roast to the small kitchenette and stood listening while the coffee brewed. The auto mechanic next door had opened. The large metal bay doors rolled up, clanging metal echoing into the empty street. She breathed in the coffee, already feeling more alert, and waited for a mug's worth before pulling the pot. Jean smoothed her pants. Maybe a size bigger and a smidge tighter than she would have liked. No one told you that past the age of forty you basically couldn't eat anything without blowing up. But she loved food, so she had made up her mind to stop beating herself up about her body. It was an argument she'd almost won. She filled her cup and went back to her office.

A row of pictures lined the wall opposite her desk. A career catalogued and framed in black matte. Her academy graduation class, accommodations. One family photo from Colleen's college graduation. A modern family: Irish American mom and

Mexican American dad. Kids were as much O'Hannigan as they were Martinez, but you'd never know it if you cut Jean out of the picture. They were RJ through and through. But they had her eyes. Her eyes and Irish names: Colleen and Seamus. Jean knew her mother-in-law had blanched at the names—especially with Shay—but she got Martinez.

The pictures weren't for her—they were for any brass who walked in. The pictures acted as a shield. That sort of thing mattered to the people who spent most of their day behind a desk. The only real opinion that counted for a damn belonged to the guy sitting next to you in a cruiser or across from you at your desk.

"Don't look up, look across, to the other white hats," Parker would say. Jean wasn't sure where he got that. A movie, probably.

One of her lights started to buzz, like the one out front, and she paused, waiting to see if it would burst. It held out, crackling every few minutes. She let the coffee cool a minute, its smell filling her office. She was expecting the labs for the DNA work she had ordered on her oldest cold case: the Sierra County Jane Doe. She wanted to review the file one more time before she got the results, should they lead her down a new path or throw up another brick wall.

Jean had arranged all the Jane Doe files into three two-inch-wide white binders. She had seen other triple homicides take over entire rooms, white binders stacked alongside each other, plastic-protected pages housing nightmares. Jean had started with the hardest case. Most people looked for low-hanging fruit; not her. She pulled the first binder.

The initial forensic report showed a lot of nothing. They may have dodged a forest fire, but time and heat had done their worst. The county had followed the best storage procedures they could—for the '80s—but sitting outside in twenty New Mexican summers had destroyed any soft tissue. Nothing left under fingernails, hair shafts but no follicles. At the time the remains were found, DNA analysis didn't exist. It was three years before Alec Jeffreys would solve fifteen-year-old Dawn Ashworth's rape and murder in Leicestershire, England, with DNA pattern recognition.

There hadn't been any other telltale clues. There was the pink sheet. Jean had tried to identify a pattern on the cloth and see if it was traceable to any company or manufacturer. It wasn't.

The only other item in the barrels was a filthy stuffed animal. A rabbit with a black-and-white-checked bow around one ear, untraceable to any store or company. Probably belonging to the younger girl, the rabbit was one of the only details the original investigator kept to himself—a detail only the person who put them in the barrels would know. Not much, but something. Maybe she could release that information now, but she wasn't sure it would do any good. What were the chances that a fifty-plus-year-old stuffed animal would be the key to solving a triple homicide?

Jean heard a truck careening down the street, something loose and metal jangling in its bed. In the truck's wake, the station's silence amplified. The light above her crackled. Her heartbeat drummed in her inner ear, and she had the sensation she wasn't alone. Her hands, holding the file pages in midair, felt exposed.

Keeping her head fixed, she turned her eyes, millimeter by millimeter, toward the door, certain she would find someone there, waiting. Maybe the rookie patrol with his Midwestern manners again. When the doorframe came up empty, she breathed out, her shoulders falling. But when she returned to the file, out of the corner of her eye, something moved. She looked once more, saw nothing. *You're being ridiculous*, she told herself.

Jean had ordered the same DNA test that had broken an old cold case in California. She used the same lab—the only lab that could do the work, currently—and if they kept their word, she'd have her results before lunch. There was a new technique that re-created autosomal DNA—the kind you find in soft tissue that can be run through genealogical databases—from mitochondrial DNA, the hardier stuff found in bones and teeth and nails. Mitochondrial DNA would tell you the mother's line, but not much else.

Jean had a tight window to work with. The case had hit its thirty-year anniversary, which meant a boost in media coverage. The case was getting attention because it was a white woman and her kids. As far as she was concerned, that was the media's fault, not hers. Media critics would say the police were only using resources because the Doe was white. Jean's daughter would make a similar argument, but seeing as she was about to give Jean and RJ their first grandbaby, Colleen could have all the opinions she wanted. Jean treated each case the same, each victim the same. People with a family and a story. They mattered and what happened to them mattered.

Jean hoped to use the anniversary to get more eyes on whatever the lab came back with. She wasn't buckling to media pressure; she was capitalizing on it. It only took one person to come forward. One person who remembered the girl they went to high school with, the girl next door who had moved away. The truth was, not many people cared about these old cold cases.

There were some other pages in the file, but after the land parcel information from the county auditor, she noticed something missing. There should have been correspondence with the Doe Network, and the National Center for Missing and Exploited Children, and NamUs, but it was gone. She flipped back and forth, searching for the pages. Then she ransacked her office until she found them, upside down and backward in a different binder, for an unrelated case. Had someone gone through her office? She put the pages back where they belonged.

Finally, the mitochondrial DNA workup the last cold case detective had ordered before retiring. It provided the most chilling detail of all: the younger child wasn't related to the mother.

This fact, more than any other, churned her stomach. Another little girl, from another mother, pointed to a pattern.

Jean looked up from her desk, quickly. She could have sworn she saw something outside her door. To be sure, she walked into the hall, listening by the door. A cold spot pooled around her doorway, as tangible as a solid block of ice. She put her hand out, feeling the cold press into her skin. Then she stepped through, freezing air spilling down her body. Outside, a tow truck was reversing; its telltale beeping punctuated the air.

She opened her mouth to call the rookie patrol. What was his name again?

"Officer?" she called.

There wasn't an answer. She walked out to the front desk but found it empty. Strange. Maybe he was in the bathroom. Returning to the bullpen, she shivered. The photocopier in the back flashed red, a little cry for help in the empty room. Someone had jammed it. Jean went over, opened the door, found the accordion paper blocking the feed, and reset the machine. She returned to her desk, passing through the frozen barrier. With her back turned, she heard footsteps in the doorway.

"Morning, partner. I mean, old partner. I mean, old like we worked together our whole careers before you dumped me. Not old, old. Even though, by some measuring sticks, you could be considered over the hill."

Jean swore loud enough for the mechanic next door to hear. Parker, long and wiry, crossed the room in two quick steps, placing a printout on her desk. Thin, wispy spiderweb wrinkles fanned out from the corner of each eye. They had been fixed in a semipermanent glare for as long as she knew him.

"Where did you come from?" she asked, eyeing the doorway behind him. She studied his face. She had spent twenty years knowing his every move, and now she hadn't talked to him in—actually, she couldn't remember the last time. He had a new partner, another kid. This one had just passed his detective exam. He was the only one to volunteer for her old job.

"The hall," he said, scratching his temple. "And before that, my car. And before that, my house."

"You're a certifiable ass, you know that, right?" She knew him better than anyone else in the building did. Better than his current girlfriend, Rayna, or his two ex-wives.

"No one knows that better than me," Parker said, pointing to his printout. "Fresh off the presses."

"I'm waiting for something too," she said. A quick look confirmed: it was a photo. Most likely a video still. She'd seen enough to know by first glance. "How'd you get your thing before I got mine?"

"It's all about who you know," he said.

"Uh-huh."

"This came in from an Australian task force. Grabbed a huge asshole. Number three guy on the dark web. Watching him for months. Hundreds of thousands of files. The original IP for this one comes up local to us. Look at that rug."

Jean turned to the photo. The light above her stopped crackling, returning to its full strength and erasing the murky dim. A child, half-dressed, sat on the edge of a bed. Her shoulders slumped, hair over her face. Her shoulders' curve bent her body into an unnaturally sharp angle for her young age.

"What do you think?" Parker asked.

Jean zoomed out. The bed had no headboard. Two black plastic milk crates stacked one on top of the other posed as a nightstand. A lamp that belonged on a college dorm desk sat on top. Some sort of round ottoman in the corner. As a child, Coll, not remembering the word, had called their own ottoman an "octopus," and the name stuck.

Parker pointed to the rug in the photo. "Doesn't that look familiar?"

Next door, the mechanic shouted something to a new truck that had rumbled up.

"Maybe," Jean said. The rug did look local. Black-and-white lines, rows of triangles—Navajo rip-off, like the ones you could pick up at any gift shop around town or the roadside stands outside Indian caves. "What about the guy? Any distinguishing features when he comes into the shot?" They loved tattoos, tattoos and birthmarks.

"Not that I've seen," he said.

Jean pointed behind the girl. "Look at that window. It's too low to the floor. Maybe a trailer?"

He nodded, rubbing a long finger along his top lip. "Could be. See, I knew you were the right person to ask."

Jean brushed him off. "Where's your new partner? Shouldn't you be babysitting? I mean, training?"

"Yeah, he'll be in soon," Parker said, smirking. "Poor guy's wife just had their first."

Jean knew what that meant. Not having kids of your own made you better armed for working child abuse, that's what Parker and Jean said. Parker had managed to marry and divorce two women without having kids. Jean told herself being a mom made her better able to talk to children. It didn't make it any easier.

"I said, leave it there!" the mechanic yelled.

Jean turned away from the picture, and slowly, the cold returned to the room.

"Do you feel that?" she asked Parker.

"Feel what?" he asked, his eyebrow creasing.

"Never mind."

Parker left, taking his picture with him. Her email dinged. She read the top line from the California lab and swore. Next door, the metal bay doors shuddered as it closed, slamming the ground with a hollow thud.

People tend to think of us as shadows. Blurred black mist. Often, it's "out of the corner of my eye." People sense the cold. I've heard of ghost hunters who use a tape measure, laying it on the ground to mark our boundaries. I don't want to be measured.

You can't measure a ghost any more than you can measure an echo.

The end of an echo isn't silence. Your ear, anticipating the pattern, fills in the gap. A missing final beat as real as the first crash, the first shatter. A thing your mind creates in the after. The same's true for feelings. They're all stories we tell ourselves. Like the stories I make up about that couple—Andy and Elise. In my current version, they've moved in together, in their first apartment, in a big, new city. They can't decide what shade of blue to paint the walls. When you're alive, these are the decisions that bind you into knots. When you're dead, these are the fights you miss.

Remember how I got so upset about robin's-egg blue?

Silly me.

You miss other things too.

I watch them eat by candlelight and make love on the bare floor. Fight about Elise's new job and whether they should move. I rewind the argument, finding the ill-fitting parts, and replay the scene in my head. In my version, there's always a happy ending. Stories are better that way.

The other benefit to storytelling? It distracts from what we'd rather ignore.

Like whoever is searching for me.

They should leave me alone.

The first officers were doing their job. Same for the next one. He was kind, at least. He'd come to the clearing with a picnic lunch. Turkey on rye. Even he left. Someone new must be looking for us again.

I know why people want to know. It's not for me. Dead or alive, people make the story about themselves. Me and Daisy and Jo. I can't forget to include them. It's their story too.

The thing is, we're fine. It's peaceful here. We've started a garden. The girls have room to play. Aside from the flowers, there's the creek nearby. The forest. The mountains and canyon walls, protecting us. This is where we're happiest. We leave, crossing over to the next ridge, when he comes back.

If they find me, I'll only be remembered by how I died. Would you want that?

My body can't speak for me. It's my ending—it can't tell the rest. It can't tell where I've been. Bodies like mine tell of brutality and pain. There was more.

Wasn't there?

I push the thought away and look for the girls.

They're by the flowers, playing tea party. Jo's rabbit sits in a circle of pine cones. Rather than join in, I sit near the creek, watching them. From behind me, a pebble rolls into the water. The water takes no notice. Something is different.

Usually, the creek's a quiet bed of gentle ripples. Today, there are patches glass-smooth, others jagged-edged. I lean forward.

Reflections of trees' undersides and blue sky cover the water, framing a face staring back at me.

"Hello," I say.

"Hello," she echoes.

Her voice startles me. It's hard to make out her features. I can see another woman beneath the surface, but her face is blurred. She must be my reflection—right?

"Who are you?" I ask.

"What came after," she says. "People are looking for you again."

"What people?" It's what I say, somewhat dishonestly. What I don't say: How does she know?

"You'll see," she says. "Tell me a story."

I want to ask more, but I'm afraid she'll leave. I haven't had some-one my own age to talk to in more years than I can count. "About what?"

"What happened to you."

"I don't like thinking about that," I say. Maybe this is a mistake. From behind, I hear the girls' tea party cut out.

"What is it?" Daisy asks her younger sister.

I sit up and turn to see Jo standing. Her stuffed rabbit, Mrs. Philip-Shandy, has toppled over. Good God, the lengths it took to get that damn rabbit back. The girls frightened Andy half to death. I did what I could to comfort him. I'd hate to be that kind of ghost.

Jo's little head cocks to the side, listening. Daisy hears it too. I know from Jo's face it isn't him. Confusion has rearranged her fea-tures, ready to tip into fear.

"Someone's coming," the woman in the water says. Her face dis-appears, and the water's surface once again reflects the underside of clouds.

Standing up, I hear it too. Snapping branches. Someone trips, swears. I was right—my reflection was right. Someone is looking for me.

LAURA

WHEN STANDSTILL TRAFFIC TRANSFORMED THREE-lane highways into parking lots, most people picked up their phones to check email, return a text, or scroll Instagram. Laura combed Ancestry.

I'm looking for my mother's sister, Judith Rae Walsh, born November 23, 1937 in Dayton, Ohio. She has three sisters: Gladys, Sarah Beth, and Connie (I'm Connie's daughter). She married Lawrence DeMarco April 12, 1953 in Annapolis, MD. She disappeared a few years later. My mother would love to find her. If you have any information, please email me.

Posted on 02 June 2006 12:00 AM by indygirl487

Looking for any information on Darla Gorman, born July 7, 1942, Worcester, MA, or her sister, Aileen, who married Joseph Grinnell. Anything you know would be greatly appreciated. Both sisters haven't been seen since 1979. We just want to know if they're okay. Thank you.

Posted on 14 October 2010 4:32 PM by stmarshall33

My name is Linda Gilbert (now Hughes) and I'm looking for Ellen Reynolds. I lived on Evergreen Avenue in Charlottesville, VA. Ellen lived next door. We were friends. She married a Bartholomew Garrett (who was in the service). Her sister is named Denise Reynolds. We think they moved to Florida in the early 1970s. I would love to get in touch with her again.

Posted on 03 May 2012 9:50 PM by linda_g87

Laura skimmed the messages in between letting her car idle forward and hitting the brake. Ancestry was a good idea, but there was a problem, specifically, with scale. "Missing daughter" turned up close to twenty thousand results. Some were innocuous. "Missing records from Delano County, circa 1922. Mapping my husband's family tree and can't find his great-grandmother's youngest daughter's birth certificate," for example. In others, there was violence hiding behind the half stories people posted. It would take years to sift through them all. Laura shivered, put her phone away, and focused on the road.

Across from her, a guy with wraparound sunglasses that made him look like he should be running alongside a presidential motorcade sat with one hand on the wheel and the other up his nose. She missed walking to work, from her little apartment off Whitney downtown to the library. When Laura had started treatment, she knew she couldn't live alone. She'd need someone to take care of her. Moving in with her sister and her family outside Hartford wouldn't have been her first choice, but there hadn't been another.

When the traffic lurched to a complete stop, Laura pulled up a message board that she regularly posted to, used mainly by other genealogists. Several threads covered the typical range of inquiry Laura was used to following.

"Anyone know a work-around for Cork records dating prior to 1940?"

"Did people fail to register church marriages with the state with any regularity post-WWII?"

"Americanized versions of Betz: Bentz, Pentz, Pence—am I missing one?"

She typed: "Anyone here have background searching for missing persons? Would like to pick someone's brain."

Laura felt confident Jane Doe's parents were long gone. She flicked back to Ancestry, trying different search terms. "Missing sister" returned thirteen thousand entries. Too many. The question nagged: Why hadn't anyone looked for her? People could go missing from all different sorts of families. Laura knew it from her work. But this kind of disappearance spoke to a family with a deep fissure running down the center. Laura tried "Missing half sister." Eight thousand results. A smaller haystack.

Laura opened up a second message board, this one used by web sleuths, and found the sub-thread on the Sierra County Jane Doe. She had been lurking on the board, reading without posting anything herself, but today she was ready to dive in.

She typed: "Are there any clues to suggest where Jane Doe could have been born? Working on a genealogical search but need ways to narrow my criteria."

Traffic began to move again. Thirty minutes and six miles later, Laura pulled into her sister's driveway. Kate and Doug's standard New England colonial had been given the Joanna Gaines farmhouse treatment. A wraparound porch with raw wooden columns had been added during a recent remodel. On his days off, Doug had been given the assignment of putting up shiplap on every free surface. Laura wasn't sure what he'd do with his free time once they ran out of accent walls. Her sister and brother-in-law might have to start having actual conversations with one another.

Kate was the type of person who kept her door locked when she was home. Laura figured it was from all the time her sister spent alone while Doug was flying—he was a commercial airline pilot—but it drove Laura crazy every time she ran out to her car to find herself locked out in her bare feet. Their house was set off in the woods with only a scattering of neighbors. Kate had cameras installed at the top of the driveway, the front door, side door, and back door.

"It's terrifying," her sister had said, slicing baby carrots into matchsticks for the twins.

"What is?" Laura asked, eyeing her sister's knife work.

"Sitting in your kitchen and looking up to see a man outside your window."

"But it's the Amazon guy. His truck's right there."

"Still."

Laura entered with her key and heard doomsday beeping from the keypad next to the door. Bella, Laura's red-nosed pit bull mix, found her owner after following her from window to window. The dog ran in circles around Laura while she struggled to type in the correct code.

"Kate?" Laura called into the house. She thought she heard water running from the upstairs. A fog descended on her ability to recall the correct code. She couldn't remember if the sequence was Kate's anniversary or the twins' birthday. There was definitely a six somewhere. Bella knocked into her knee, and Laura hit the wrong number of what was possibly the wrong combination. "Kate?" she tried again.

"Warning, alarm will sound in ten seconds," said an even-toned female voice, unaware of the dog and the memory loss.

A shrill alarm pierced the air a second before the only landline started to ring from the kitchen. The twins, Daphne and Cullen, emerged from the basement with confused faces and hands pressed to the sides of their matching heads. Laura ignored them and ran for the phone. The twins followed, elbows knocking into one another. Bella, thrilled with the new game, also followed. Her thin tail thwapped the wall under the high-pitched alarm.

Laura put the landline to her ear. "Hello?" There was no answer. How did you answer a landline? When was the last time she'd used a landline? Pushing Bella off her leg with one arm, Laura looked at the phone again. She had made an error in judgment and muscle memory. Laura tried to hit the green call button with her thumb, which didn't seem to be the right word though it did seem to be the right color. But her fingers went numb and the phone fell from her ineffectual hands, clattering to the counter.

A voice rose from the speckled granite. She cupped the phone with both hands, holding it to her ear like a seashell, waiting for the ocean.

"This is Atlas Insurance. We have an unauthorized entry at 1-6-4-2 Pleasant Avenue. Please confirm security passcode." The human female on the other end summoned a you're-wasting-my-time-you-idiot vibe and an I-can't-believe-this-is-my-job exasperation all at once. Laura may not have remembered the key code, but she remembered the security password.

"Lemonheads." Their favorite candy growing up, which left them with puckered faces and, later, cavities.

"Thank you. And who am I speaking with?"

"Laura MacDonald. It's my sister's house. They're—"

"Yes, I have your name."

The siren clicked off. The twins pulled their hands away from their ears, but only by an inch, expecting the sound to return. Laura's ears rang, filling in the silence with an imaginary alarm.

"Is there anything else I can do for you?" the voice asked.

Laura couldn't resist. "Like order Thai?"

Pause. "No."

"All set then. Thank you."

The twins, satisfied that whatever had happened was done happening, ran off without a hello or a hug.

"It's nice to see you too!" Laura called to their backs. Bella jumped for attention. "Yes, and you too," Laura said, rubbing the top of her head and behind her ears.

Somewhere in the house, water turned off. Bella ran off for a toy to bring back and show off. Laura rested her hands on the counter, studying their ineptness. They were curved like Barbie hands and, like the hands of the twiggy-legged blonde, unable to hold on to anything.

The phone rang again. Laura could feel the nerve pain in her fingers this time. *Fool me once*, she thought, pressing the call button before picking it up with both hands.

"Hello?"

"Laura?" Doug. Not the security lady changing her mind about the Thai. Shame. "I got a call that the alarm went off. Everything okay?"

"Yes." Laura felt immediately and immensely stupid. Kate appeared from behind her, wet and wrapped in a towel. Doubly stupid.

"What's the matter?" Kate asked, readjusting her slipping towel.

"It's my hands," Laura said.

"What?" Kate and Doug asked, from opposite ends of the phone, at the same time.

Laura didn't know who to answer first.

"Who's that?" Kate asked.

"It's Doug," Laura said.

"Yes?" Doug asked.

"Doug?" Kate asked.

"Yes," Laura said.

"Yes?" Doug asked.

"Oh my God," said Laura, pinching the space between her eyes. "My hands were bothering me from the neuropathy," she said to them both. She left out the part about not being able to remember the code. Copping to one permanent rewiring of her body from treatment was enough.

"You okay now?" Doug asked.

Kate and Doug had seen her enough to understand. The short-term side effects of chemo—loss of appetite, diarrhea, nausea, hair loss—had ended with the drugs. But the promised long-term side effects persisted: cognitive impairment, cardio-myopathy, neuropathy. Forgetting words was annoying, but the nerve pain was the most frustrating. The heart damage was, by all measure, scarier, but she couldn't feel her heart. Nerves were different. Laura dropped mugs, couldn't open jars, sometimes had to pull over if she lost her grip on the steering wheel. Once damaged, it had been explained to her, nerve pathways could become permanently rerouted.

"I'm fine," she answered.

Kate's face softened.

"Is Kate there?" Doug asked.

Laura turned to her sister. "Kate?" she asked. "I don't know. I can look."

Kate shook her head, her long wet hair remaining plastered to her shoulders.

"No, she's not home," Laura said, slipping this white lie into her back pocket to needle her older sister with later. "Do you want me to tell her to call you?"

"Don't worry about it. See you on Thursday."

Laura hung up the phone. "Why was the alarm on?" she asked, turning to her sister.

"I was in the shower."

"That's not an answer."

"How was the library?" Kate asked.

"Fine. Another person who thought their house was haunted."

"People come in asking you to find out if their house is haunted? Seriously?"

"It comes out at the end. Usually they come in wanting to research their property and find the past owners. Then, at the end, they'll mention funny noises they've been hearing."

Kate's towel slipped again. Laura tried not to look at the soft curves of her sister's breasts. Like an alcoholic counting their days of sobriety, Laura had gone her entire treatment plan without seeing a female breast. A knot clenched, deep in her stomach. Kate tightened the towel and moved her hair off her shoulders. The smell of her sister's shampoo—lavender and mint—filled the kitchen. There was a second when Kate knew something was wrong, but also didn't know what it was. A good MacDonald, Kate changed the subject rather than ask about feelings.

"I'm going out tonight, with friends. Did you remember? You said you'd watch the kids."

Laura had a vague memory of this. "When do you need to leave?" Her phone buzzed with a notification.

"Thirty minutes. Half an hour."

"You realize those are the same thing?"

Laura could tell Kate wanted to say something smart in return but turned on a wet heel in an apparent truce. She paused at the doorway. "Oh—I opened a bill of yours from the hospital. I thought it was for me. I left it on the counter."

Laura found the thick business-sized envelope by the blender.

"I don't know how you make sense of those things," Kate said.

"It's fun," Laura said, pulling out the pages.

"Fun?"

Laura shrugged. "The hospital tries to bill me for all I'm worth and a little more. I try and make insurance pay a small fraction of what they're worth. I pretend it's a game instead of my life." Kate's eyebrows were halfway up her forehead. Laura tried a different tack. "I like numbers."

"Glad someone does," Kate said, leaving the room.

Laura pulled out her phone and saw a new message. Before running to her room, she ransacked the fridge for leftover lasagna. She fed Bella while waiting for the microwave, and with a happily fed pit bull and an overheated plate, Laura took the stairs by two up to her bedroom. She slipped off her wig. It hit the comforter like shiny roadkill.

Laura turned on the three monitors on her desk while Bella pushed her way under her feet, finding a good spot to curl up.

From the hallway, Kate yelled for Daphne: "Did you take my nail polish again? I can't find anything in this house. Why does everything go missing around here?"

"Then you probably shouldn't have had children," Laura said to herself. Bella licked her exposed ankle.

A reply on the web sleuth board from k_bonesdoc84, in response to one of Laura's questions, lit up her first monitor: "My partner and I conducted isotopic testing on their mitochondrial DNA samples three years ago and the police never responded. Can't tell if they're hiding something or are generally negligent. Here's a link. I'm no longer at the lab, so I feel better about sharing this."

The address sent Laura to a University of Florida lab report. Laura was familiar with some of the terms but didn't want to make a mistake. Two names appeared at the top: Karen Schussler and Daniel Singh. Laura searched both names on the university website. She could only find Dr. Singh, a paleoclimatologist, which conjured images of both *Jurassic Park* and the local weather guy—*Heat is blazing its way across the state!* Laura assumed k_bonesdoc84 was Karen Schussler, but she wasn't responding to Laura's direct message. Impatient, Laura dialed the phone number listed for Dr. Singh's lab.

A man with a faintly British accent that sounded like perfumed Earl Grey in a porcelain teacup answered. After an awkward introduction during which Laura stated and repeated that she was a curious citizen and not operating in any official capacity, Dr. Singh proffered his side of the story.

"We couldn't figure out why the police didn't make our results public. I wondered, briefly, if they were hiding something. But you don't want to think the police aren't doing their jobs, do you? I hope they are keeping it from the public for some good reason."

Laura didn't know what to say. "I don't know," she said.

"It's no matter. I'm happy to share what we found. You see, normally, paleoclimatologists study atomic compositions of bones, soil, dirt, that sort of thing. Isotopes, which are one type of atom, have specific characteristics that can be linked to geographic regions. Typically, you find this work being done in archaeology."

Laura thought she heard a small spoon clink against a teacup rim on the other end. Her pen hovered over her yellow legal pad.

"Okay," she said.

"Karen, my partner, wanted me to see if isotopic testing could be applied to the Sierra County Jane Doe."

"Karen works with you?"

"She works on missing persons as a sort of hobby. She volunteered at Ground Zero identifying remains. Does it full-time now that she's no longer here. She got one of the DNA samples from a colleague in Santa Cruz. I believe they were doing the mitochondrial workup a few years ago. Karen proposed we test the samples ourselves."

British Indian Floridian dinosaur/weather scientists with crime junkie/humanitarian partners: a new category of people Laura hadn't known existed. "What did you find?" she asked.

"Isotopes are atoms with either too few or too many neutrons. Unlike other particles, they are quite stable—even Jane Doe's samples, which otherwise showed severe biologic degrading over time. Each element has one or more isotopes. One isotope, oxygen-18, can be linked to specific geographic regions, depending on how light or heavy the atom is. It can tell you how far away from the coast you lived, which coast, and at what time during your life. Certain carbon and strontium isotopes tell us a great deal about dietary habits. This allowed me to eliminate Canada and Mexico. In the end, I was able to pinpoint where Jane Doe and the two girls came from.

"Different parts of the body tell different stories. Your teeth, for example, represent a kind of childhood time capsule buried within the enamel. Another reason to brush twice a day."

He paused. Laura forced a laugh, and Dr. Singh continued.

"Isotopes from the dental remains told us that the adult female was born near the Pacific, most likely in Southern California. At around age five or six, she moved closer to the Atlantic Ocean, most likely in the Northeast. Specifically, southern New England. However, she moved back to the Pacific around the time her daughter was born."

Laura scribbled, fast.

"Hair, however, reflects a person's present, depending on how long the hair is. The longer the hair, the longer your time-line. She had long hair, thankfully. All that data gets stored in the shaft, not the follicle, which is far less resilient. Her hair confirmed she lived in Southern California before moving to the Southwest."

"What about the children?"

"Her daughter was born close to the Pacific, corroborating what we found in the mother's teeth and hair. At some point during her early childhood, they moved further inland to the Southwest. The other girl who was not her biological daughter has a different geographic profile. She was born somewhere close to the Gulf of Mexico, but not directly along the coast. If I had to guess, I would say Texas. Then, of course, she too ends up in the Southwest."

Laura repeated back what she had written to make sure she had the information correct. "Dr. Singh—I have one more question. Does anything point to how old the Sierra County Jane Doe was when she died?"

"It's difficult to say. She was fully grown. She had given birth. Anywhere between eighteen and fifty-five."

Laura sighed. The range was too large.

"I can tell you when she was born though," he said. "Not an exact year, unfortunately. But she was born before 1950."

"How do you know?" Laura asked.

"People born during the 1950s have dramatically higher levels of carbon-14 in their teeth enamel because of the raised carbon levels in the overall atmosphere. Later, it gradually leveled out. Her levels were what we consider pre-1950."

"Why—"

"Nuclear testing."

"Oh," she said. "Well, useful for some things I guess."

She hung up with Dr. Singh, offering more thanks. She reread her notes. She had a timeline. A decade plus some change for birth year made genealogical research feasible, right? The giant haystack shrank. She needed a map, a big one.

Another message on the genealogy site had popped up while she was on the phone: "As long as you have name, date of birth, and place of birth, you can work it like you normally would. DM with more questions."

Everything except her name, Laura thought.

She ran to the basement. Above the kids' Lego table was a giant map of the continental United States. She pulled it from the wall, taking the thumbtacks with it, then grabbed markers at the kids' art table.

Without warning, searing pain shot through her right arm from her shoulder, through her elbow, and into her pinky. Like she had hit her funny bone, but everywhere. She yelped, involuntarily, and the markers fell from her hands, rolling across the floor. She rubbed her arm and shook it off. The twins had a movie to watch. Laura had a map to color.

JEAN

MOST PEOPLE CAME TO TRUTH OR CONSEQUENCES— "T or C," to locals—for the mineral springs and spas. Originally named Hot Springs, T or C catered to couples' massage and soaks, tubs the size of rich people's dining room tables filled with mineral water. Plenty more passed through as part of a hiking tour of the Gila Wilderness. But no one made the drive out to Serrucho—not on purpose.

Serrucho was a verifiable ghost town. Forty minutes outside T or C, the place used to be home to thousands of miners, back when there was gold and silver in these mountains. The few people who did live here must work in the last mine another hour's drive west, Jean guessed.

A cattle guard announced the town line. A few single-story buildings that had forgotten to collapse announced the rest. Time had run an eraser down the middle, leaving a trail of empty dirt lots. One intact tin roof sat alone in an arroyo, separated from its lower half in a long-ago flash flood. Only two buildings remained along the abandoned half mile: an 1800s whitewashed Catholic church like a gothic painting of the Wild West, and the Old Serrucho Bar and Store.

Another cattle guard told her she'd left. The edge of town was also where her cell phone signal died. She hadn't made the trip out to the site because she had promised Colleen she'd stay close. A quick prayer that her grandchild wouldn't come today was the best she could do.

Jean had filled the front seat of her car with her notes, two water bottles, and a breakfast burrito from Carmela's. She was going to be hiking a mountain, she told herself. She needed the energy.

The Hail Mary DNA test hadn't worked. Their sample was too degraded. Jean decided to start at the beginning—back where the barrels were found.

Pulling off the highway an hour later, she found a smaller road used mainly by trucks as a cut-through from Ironside Mining. The company was the only anything within a five-mile radius of the barrel site, and it was the reason this area wasn't included in the national forest. The company had been around long before the land had been designated as a federally protected area. It was owned and run by the same family who founded it, last name Tellefsen.

She passed her next turn twice. According to the original maps from the '80s, there was supposed to be a road here, but when Jean pulled over, dirt and clay-colored sand covered any blacktop. Two tracks for tires led into the brush. Time to go on foot.

The clean scent of pine hit her lungs as soon as she stepped out of the car. She couldn't imagine anyone coming this way, but she locked her car anyway. With her map, .45, and notepad, she made her way into the forest. She left her food in the car. No need to draw the attention of any wildlife.

Ponderosas stood like tall spears on either side, thin at first, then denser farther in. The air was cooler here than back in town. She listened with her body, acutely aware of every branch that broke under her step, every rock she kicked loose. She knew a stream, small but not far off, ran to her left—the sound of water hummed underneath birdsong and insects' shrilling.

Ahead of her, a pair of trees darkened the trail, casting a shadow on the path. Most of the trees here were ancient pine, straight and narrow, their feathered branches combing the air. But these two were knotted and gnarled, twisting and curving, as though a giant had bound the trunks into a fumbled figure eight. Two bulging knots, conjoined where the trees met, looked like faces. Jean had the impression that someone was standing near her. Or standing in front of her.

There was a spot, a few feet from where she stood, where the tree knots' gaze intersected with the ground. Cold air stretched in front of her. Jean put her hand out. Something about the air felt deliberate. She froze, embarrassed to admit she was frightened. Of what, she couldn't say. The forest had grown too quiet, the air too still. Something her father had taught her when she was little: out in the bush, birds are nature's alarm system. When they take off, they're telling you—you're not alone.

The birds had gone quiet. She hadn't been listening carefully enough. Couldn't tell if they had flown off or were keeping mum. She could have been the one to scare them off. Or—

Jean listened, making up her mind.

No, she would not cross the place where the tree faces met. Every cell in her body told her to turn around and try a different path.

She backtracked to her car, checking over her shoulder every few steps until she was back in the sunlight and its warmth. The sight of her car gave her relief, and she got in, locked her doors, and scolded herself for being so spooked. Of what? A couple of trees? She started the engine and drove to a trailhead up the road. It would be a longer walk, but it would get her to the site all the same.

A few minutes later, Jean found the parking lot. There were two other cars parked in the small, sunbaked square of dirt: a Jeep Cherokee covered in bumper stickers of bands and mountain abbreviations and a beat-up brown pickup truck. Jean stopped to read the register at the trailhead. A Sam Custer and an Abby Ruiz had signed in together the day before. No one else for a few weeks. She didn't imagine day-trippers would take the added measure of registering before starting their hike.

Following the trail, she shifted her gaze between the map and her feet. At some point, she'd need to abandon the trail and cut deeper into the forest. Her breath took over and calmed the part of her brain flying red flags over tree knots. She paused when she saw another person ahead of her.

An older man, mid-seventies if she had to guess, was stooped over, fussing with his bootlaces. Mottled skin, patched with darker spots from age or sun or both. A backpack with the chest strap fastened, tightly. He heard Jean from much farther than she anticipated he would. His eyes narrowed on her before spreading into warm pools. By the time she reached him, he had removed his pack and tipped a scuffed water bottle to his mouth, a dribble of water running down his chin.

"Morning," Jean said.

"Morning," he returned, screwing his bottle cap on and wiping his face with his sleeve. He returned the bottle to his pack, then opened a small zipper on the front, reaching his hand in and scowling.

"I'll be damned," he said, like something out of a movie. "Forgot my keys. I'd forget my head if it weren't attached. Watch out for snakes, I saw two a little ways in." He shook his head and returned the backpack to his shoulders.

"Garter?" Jean asked.

"Black-tails, sorry to say. Keep an eye out." He headed back in the direction of the parking lot.

Great. Haunted trees and now this, she thought.

Jean followed the trail farther into the wilderness. People were surprised to learn New Mexico had the densest wilderness in the Southwest. They heard New Mexico and pictured desert mesas. She cut into the forest, bypassing the trail for woods.

For a second, she thought she could hear laughter. She paused, leaning her ear in its direction. It stopped as quickly as it had started. Maybe she *was* losing it. Pushing away some branches, she came to the site, tripping on a root and swearing as she caught herself.

She held the crime scene photo up to the mountaintops jutting like chimneys and church steeples above the tree line. The only difference between the photo and real life was the shape of the treetops. They had grown over the years. Otherwise, the two canyon backgrounds matched like a fingerprint. A ring of piñon flanked a dense patch of creosote. She pushed through the brush. There was a small clearing beyond the bush where sunlight cut the dark like a halo.

Jean knew she'd found the spot the moment she broke through to the clearing. The wind rustled the tree branches and died back down, silence filling its wake. A tangled mess of vine encircled the spot where the barrels had been found. Closed white petals, curled around themselves, hung at lazy angles between heart-shaped leaves. They reminded Jean of discarded wedding dresses, twisted into rope and hung from windows, a runaway bride's escape.

Jean had heard of flowers opening and closing each day like a barnacle following the tide. But shouldn't they be open during the day? Maybe these flowers waited for the dark to show their face. Jean had another thought. Maybe the flowers had closed because they knew she was coming. Like the birds, they had taken off, in their own way.

Studying the original photo, Jean saw nothing but forest. When had the flowers been planted? She had never seen flowers like this in the Gila. Wildflowers, sure. But these belonged in an English garden. Should be grown along a trellis.

The flowers hadn't been here when the barrels were found. She peered into the grainy four-by-six. They were growing in the exact spot the barrels had been. Vigil or mask, these night flowers came after. Had someone planted them here?

Jean dropped to a knee. The only flowers—especially white flowers—she came across were lilies filling funeral homes. She hated lilies. Cloying, overbearing. Trying too hard for attention. Jean moved closer to the closed flowers, inhaling deeply. All she got was pine.

She stood and scanned the area. In all the years she had lived in New Mexico, she had never seen a patch of forest so dense. How had it escaped wildfires?

A mother and two children, one her own, one not, had lain here for twenty years without anyone knowing. You got a sense for the psychology of a crime by how a body was found. This didn't feel random. Didn't feel impersonal. He could have stuck around. Taken his time. Whoever did this was an old man now. Old or dead. How had he gotten the barrels out this far on his own? She had needed to make the journey herself to see that there was a strong possibility he'd had help. She had been foolish, hoping DNA would blow this open. She should have come out here from the start. Reading a case file was one thing; walking the scene was another. Even with a four-wheeler, this was dense brush and those were impossibly cumbersome barrels. She imagined what the barrels had sounded like, thudding along with three bodies inside. He must have made this trip at night—he wouldn't have been able to risk moving them during the day. Even more reason to think he was local.

She pulled out her notebook and wrote *4-wheeler, local, help*.

But she didn't need to find the man—or men—who brought them out here. If by some slim chance the person was still alive, she'd be more than happy to put bracelets on his wrists. But her real reason for being out here was simple: Jane Doe and the two girls deserved their names back. A name meant you mattered. A name meant you were somebody to someone else. If to no one else, Jean wanted them to know they mattered to her.

Out in the forest, she patched together a picture of the man who did this. He'd be a chameleon, easily changing his personality and maybe his looks to fly under the radar. He would be good with his hands. He was young when he did this, younger than thirty-five, Jean would guess, given the physical demands of transporting the barrels. He probably had half a dozen aliases and addresses, changing names as he went. She wouldn't be surprised if he was responsible for the deaths of a long line of Jane Does across the country.

In the clearing, Jean sensed he was the type of perpetrator who snapped. There had come a moment, between him and this woman, when he lost control of her, of their relationship, of whatever con he was running. Maybe she threatened to leave. If he couldn't have her under his control, he'd have her here.

A gust of wind ripped through the clearing, rippling the leaves. She crossed herself. Old habits sat under your ribs, clawing.

Jean took a final look and left the clearing, taking what she thought was the trail back to the parking lot. But a wrong turn sent her into another clearing she didn't remember, smaller than the barrel site. Pulling out the map, she turned it like a steering wheel, trying to make sense of where she was. She read the mountain peaks' names again: Reeds Peak, Rocky Point, Moccasin John Mountain. No help there. When she lowered the weathered paper, she froze for the second time that morning.

A mountain lion stepped into the other side of the clearing. Its shoulders curved up while its back arched low. Something dead hung from its mouth. Jean's sense of calm surprised her, given the effect a couple of trees had had on her. Slipping her hand behind her, unclipping her .45 and flicking off the safety, she took a step back, keeping her focus on the mountain lion. Brunch would be one course, not two.

The mountain lion crouched to the ground, the dead thing fixed tightly in its mouth. Then, ignoring Jean, the lion pressed its paws into either side of the brown-furred body, clamped its mouth around the top, and pulled. The carcass tore in two, a puddle of organs spilling out from its opened middle. Jean walked backward slowly, waiting until she could no longer see the mountain lion, before turning her back and running as fast as she could in what she hoped was the right direction, listening for the sound of paws behind her over her own breath, her own footsteps pounding.

When she found the parking lot, she bent over, digging her hands into her knees and breathing hard. The other cars in the lot were gone. The old man had found his keys after all. Her own keys dug into her thigh as she bent over, sucking wind. She got in her car, this time forgetting about locking the door behind her, and pulled out.

SHE DROVE THE HOUR back into Serrucho to make sure she had a signal before pulling over. There was nothing friendly about the church. It sat sternly, its severe gaze on the empty road. But the Old Serrucho Bar and Store slumped at an odd angle, mimicking one of its patrons, cut off and stumbling to the curb, looking to hitch a ride home. Jean parked in front.

She got out to peek inside the building. A layer of dust covered the bar top like a thick-piled hallway runner. Small circular black stools, too tiny for human proportions, lined the bar. At the end, Jean could make out a cash register with one of those giant slot-machine handles. Pictures lined three of the walls. Peering up, Jean thought her eyes were playing tricks on her. A patchwork of viridescent tin plates coated the ceiling, undulating as though they could fall if someone so much as sneezed. If ghosts were real, they lived in the Old Serrucho Bar and Store.

She turned, studying the buildings across the street. A terra-cotta ranch baked in the sun behind a row of tall cottonwoods and dense bush. The two front windows each had a flower box, and someone was managing to keep pansies alive. They sat in neat alternating bursts of color—violet, crimson, sunlit yellow. Jean walked into the road to get a better view of the driveway. A dusty sedan sat out front.

The ghosts would have to wait. Jean might have found one of the thirty-five living souls claiming Serrucho as home.

A wind chime jingled as Jean approached the front door. She knocked and waited, examining the car again. A couple dozen dolls with porcelain smiles, uneven eyes, and checkered pinafores stared at her emptily, encased behind the dirty glass of the rear windshield. A woman wearing all white answered, her braceleted wrists silver like the chimes. Her hair was parted down the middle. She was in her early fifties, not coloring her grays. As she considered Jean through the dirty, flimsy screen, having opened only the inner door, her chest rose quickly, once, twice, and her cheeks flushed.

"Are you with the police?" she asked. She pressed a hand to her chest as though she had been called on to start the Pledge of Allegiance for the rest of the class.

"Yes. I'm Detective Sergeant Jean Martinez. I'm with the county," Jean said, retrieving her badge. "I'm out here—"

"Did you figure out her name?"

Jean hadn't expected the woman to beat her to it. But she had left out the girls. The woman corrected herself before Jean could clarify. "The mother and children?" she asked.

"That's what I'm out in the area about," Jean said.

The woman's chest spasmed. Jean couldn't tell if she was having a heart attack or a panic attack. Then she heard it. A hiccup rose from the woman's chest, throwing her shoulders up to her ears. Then another. And another. Jean had seen many reactions to having the police show up at your door. Hiccups were a first.

"Is it all right if I come in?" she asked. "I had a couple questions about the area."

"Yes, of course."

Jean opened the screen door and followed the woman inside.

"I'm Susan. Susan Waddell," she said, hiccupping again. "I was cleaning up. I run this bed-and-breakfast."

Jean scanned the room. She wasn't sure what claim this tiny house had to a bed-and-breakfast. They had aimed for 1950s retro but taken a couple of wrong turns. A coffee table held a stack of magazines with Elvis on the top cover. A canvas print depicted the Virgin Mary bowed in prayer. A record player sat next to an old TV. The tile floor throughout was a faded clay red, clashing with the lime-green walls. Jean had been in the room for less than a minute and wanted out. She resisted the urge to pull back the curtains; the room suffered from a lack of daylight.

"You get a lot of visitors out here?" Jean asked, straining to keep her face neutral.

"You'd be surprised," Susan called, disappearing into the kitchen. Jean could hear water running. The woman returned with two glasses of water and handed one to Jean. Before Jean could say anything, Susan, still standing, widened her stance. She put the farther rim of her glass to her top lip and bent over at the waist. One bracelet snagged on her sleeve, but the remaining stack slid down her arm. They weren't separate bracelets at all but a chain of interlocking circles, cutting her arm into silver-edged triangles.

Susan sucked down the water in a few long gulps. Standing upright, she returned one hand to her chest and paused for a minute, waiting. Her bracelets slid back into place. Satisfied that her acrobatics had stifled her hiccups, she smiled and sat opposite Jean. "All better," Susan said.

Jean forced a smile. "I work on our cold cases. I was looking into the Jane Doe found in the Gila. You've heard about the case?"

"I grew up here. I was still living at home when they found them. Everyone talked about it." As she gazed off into space, her pointer finger traced circles around her thumbnail.

Jean nodded. "I was wondering if you could tell me what the town was like back in the '80s. I'm not from around here. I'm trying to get a sense for what the area was like."

Susan took a breath, and Jean worried she was going to start hiccupping again. "All the jobs came from the mine. There used to be more people, more families. Some men came out to work for a season, then moved on. Like my dad. No one wants to move out here anymore. I mean—would you? It was an okay place to grow up, but I wouldn't want to raise kids here. Not that I have kids," she said, shaking her head. "As more businesses closed, more people moved away. Ironside was the only thing left, but a lot of people got laid off when I was in high school. By the time I moved back home, the place had turned into a ghost town."

"After college?"

Susan frowned. "Never went. I worked in meat processing for years. I miss my knives. My mom got sick. When she passed, I got the house. It was only me and her. She had me when she was young. This used to be her parents' house. My uncle's house is down the street. When she got sick, I moved back in. Now, I can't bring myself to sell it. I live out by the lake. I rent this place out, mostly weekend campers and hikers. It's good you're working on her case. It's not right they never got a proper burial, with a headstone and their names," Susan continued, her hand on her chest. "You know—kids used to make up ghost stories about a woman in white. That sort of thing."

"Your mother ever talk about the case?" Jean asked, deflecting the mention of ghost stories. The woman's mother would have been better to talk to, if she were alive. She would have been the right age—closer to Jane Doe.

"No, never," Susan said, shaking her head again. "I hated the idea she'd been out there all those years." The underside of her eyes flushed, rimming her eyes in a thin red line. Maybe the woman felt genuine grief for strangers. Maybe the memory had stoked something else. But Jean kept noticing that the woman referred to the three victims as "her" and "the woman," singular.

Jean let it pass, eyeing the window-ledge flower boxes visible from the inside. "There's a bunch of flowers growing around the spot where they were found. Couldn't tell you what kind they were, but it's not something you see out in the middle of the woods."

"I've never been out there. I refuse." Her eyes went big again, as though Jean were suggesting skydiving without a chute.

Jean couldn't think of anything else to ask. "I won't take any more of your time."

Susan led Jean out the door and pointed across the street to Jean's car, which, like everything else in Serrucho, was covered in dust. "Is that you?" Susan asked.

Jean nodded. The chimes trilled above her head.

"You wanna go in?"

"Excuse me?"

"The bar. A stay in the house also gets you a tour of the bar. Owners leave me a key, in case there's any trouble."

They crossed the street and Susan unlocked the Old Serrucho Bar and Store. Jean followed her inside as the woman lamented over the dust. Jean tried to take small breaths of the musty, stale air through her nose, but it didn't do much good. The floors creaked with every step, and Jean transferred her worry about the ceiling coming down on her head to her boot going through the floor.

Remembering the wall of photos, Jean searched the faces beneath dusty glass frames, hoping one would stand out. She pulled out the facial recognition pictures she kept in her back pocket, holding them up to the bar's ghosts. Friends toasting, glasses raised in the air. Lovers standing hand in hand. A mechanic bent over the popped hood of a mint-green Cadillac. Nothing. Jean noticed an old rotary phone sitting behind the register. She hadn't seen it from the window.

She went to the phone and ducked under the bar. There, below the phone, was a stack of leather-bound books, their spines smooth despite their age. *Serrucho and Kirkland 1939–1942*, *Serrucho and Kirkland 1942–1945*, *Serrucho and Kirkland 1945–1948*, and on until *Serrucho and Kirkland 1990–1993*. Jean pulled one of the older volumes from the bottom. Families listed with names, addresses, and the husband's occupation. Then, in a later volume, the occupation column had been dropped, and a phone number took its place.

"Do you mind if I take these back with me?"

"I can tell the owners you borrowed them."

"I'd appreciate that."

Susan helped Jean bring the directories to her car, stacking them neatly in the back seat. Jean pulled out of the Old Serrucho Bar and Store, heading east with the black knife of the Gila in her rearview. Jean watched the mountains grow smaller. They cut across the valley like the town's namesake—a handsaw, black and ragged, its serrated edge slouching toward heaven.

The footsteps get closer. Daisy's eyes go wild, and she crosses her arms over her chest, instinctively, forgetting she has no physical body left to protect. Jo stands in front of her, like she's ready to punch the school bully. She places Mrs. Philip-Shandy on the ground and closes her eyes. I don't know what she's doing. She takes a deep breath, and when she exhales, long and steady, her outer edges curl in on themselves like a leaf tossed into a fire. From the outside in, she erases herself from the meadow, and in a moment instantaneous and extended—she disappears. I've never seen her do this before.

The second she vanishes, time stops. A bird, having left its perch, hovers in midair, its wings raised in suspended flight. A cloud, drawing a slow line across our clearing, pauses in the sky, its vacuous shape freezing. I'm rooted to the ground, unable to move. Then Jo snaps back, the bird's wings beat, and the clouds resume their trip. Daisy's eyes dart back and forth, searching her sister's face.

"Is it him?" Daisy asks.

"No," says Jo.

"How do you know?" Daisy asks.

I have the same question, but I wait for my adopted daughter's answer.

"I saw her—it's a woman," Jo says. "She's coming here."

Sure enough, a woman enters our clearing. She's alone, carrying only a map and a notebook. Concentration carves her face. She's middle-aged, with graying blond hair pulled into a bun. She has a face like a cop. I've seen enough of them to know. She holds an old photo up to the sky, her eyes traveling between the small four-by-six and the mountains. It's here, I want to say. But I sense she's the type of person who needs to find answers on her own.

Satisfied, the woman puts the photo away and kneels by the flowers. I shield the girls, wrapping my body around theirs. Daisy's tiny fingers dig into my rib cage. Jo holds Mrs. Philip-Shandy at her side.

I bet she's hunting him. They're called whodunits for a reason—emphasis on the killer and the nightmare made real, not the woman on the wrong end of the knife. The detective says a prayer. Sweet, but unnecessary. There's no room for prayers here.

The woman stays a few more minutes. When she leaves, the girls go back to playing. Birdsong and insects return to the air.

I slip down against the tree trunk, pressing my hands into its solidness, wishing I could feel the bark cutting my hands. First my reflection, then this stranger. We've gone years without interruption. Today brings two breaks to our daily pattern.

Jo comes over, standing in front of me. Mrs. Philip-Shandy is tucked under her arm.

"You don't want her here, do you?" Jo asks. She has pulled a piece of her hair into her mouth, one of her sister's habits that she's trying on to see how it feels.

"No, I don't," I tell her.

"Daisy doesn't like her either. It's okay, I have an idea," she says. She swaps her wet strand of hair for her thumb and walks away. Mrs. Philip-Shandy's long, ragged bunny ears sway behind her.

I return to the creek, peering over the edge. "Are you there?" I ask the water, but whoever she is, she's gone. Like so many times before, I'm alone.

LAURA

LAURA SHOULD HAVE BEEN COLD, LYING NAKED FROM the waist up on Dr. Fusaro's exam table, but the room was warm. Still, she usually got a robe. Dr. Fusaro's office had the good ones. Deep mauve, waffle-knit, kimono sleeves. As though she were spending the day at a spa. Perks of a private practice; little details to distract you. The downside: Dr. Fusaro's office was typically overwhelmed. A good sign, she supposed. You wanted the most popular plastic surgeon. The packed waiting room, filled with women in headscarves, had meant Laura had time to check her message boards.

Someone had linked to a missing-person report they thought was the Sierra County Jane Doe. A NamUs page appeared. Laura was well versed in the site by now, along with the Doe Network and the National Center for Missing and Exploited Children. It was hard to believe there wasn't one centralized federal database for missing persons. Instead, there were three separate sites maintained by volunteers, constantly threatened by a lack of funding. Laura peered at the thumbnail picture next to the woman's name: Betty Jenson Sinclair.

Demographics came first: Missing for forty-three years. Age at disappearance: twenty-four. Height: five foot two; weight:

125 pounds; race: Caucasian. Then, the circumstances of her disappearance:

> Betty and her daughter were last seen at their home on Warner Rd. in Merrimack, New Hampshire, on the weekend of March 15, 1970. Betty was previously seen at her place of employment, the Nashua Shopping Plaza, where she worked at a women's clothing store. Her daughter was last seen in school the previous Friday. Her family is treating her disappearance as suspicious. Her daughter was six years old when she and her mother went missing.

A physical description followed: dark brown hair dyed strawberry blond, dimple on her left cheek, hazel eyes. Nails reliably well manicured. Ears pierced. Surgical scar from appendectomy. Tattoo of a red rose along her ankle.

"Laura MacDonald?" asked a nurse from the doorway.

"That's me," Laura said, sliding her phone away.

Laura folded her top on the chair and lay back on the exam table. Music played on the other side of the door. On the wall hung an Italian painting of a golden field lined with cypress trees, like a brochure for a wine tour. She studied the trees and the mountains behind them, wondering how many other women had lain in this spot, wishing they had visited Italy. The thought had never crossed her mind. But now she desperately wanted to go to Italy herself.

Dr. Fusaro stood on the opposite side of her door, talking to a nurse. As he entered, cool air from the hallway followed him. The hairs on her stomach stood up as the new air hit her abdomen, then nothing, then her shoulders. She had waited, once the air hit her stomach, for the feeling of her nipples getting hard, responding to the cold. But there had been nothing. No sensation at all. Her head had remembered, but her body hadn't.

"How are you today?"

Without preamble—most doctors asked permission before prodding her breast—Dr. Fusaro pressed his fingers around each expander. This was the last fill before they could be swapped for silicone implants.

"Looks good. Are you ready?" he asked.

Laura nodded.

Dr. Fusaro checked to make sure no air sat in the syringe. He stuck the needle into the port under her left breast and compressed the plunger. Her skin pulled, her muscles felt like they were tearing from the inside out. This was the last time, she told herself. But she couldn't ignore the feeling of being pulled apart from the inside out.

Laura tried to breathe. She opened her eyes and counted, turning her head to the painting. She studied the cypresses, like miniature cathedral spires, lined in a neat row. So different from how she imagined the Gila. Trees with names like something from a children's book: ponderosa, alligator juniper, silverleaf. Laura wondered if Jane Doe knew what was coming before it happened. Which would be worse? Knowing or not knowing—exactly as it's happening—you are going to die.

Dr. Fusaro moved to the other side of the table to repeat the process on her right.

The steel barrels. They must have been so heavy. The pink fitted sheet. Maybe they had been killed in bed, while they slept. They had been partners. He knew her. Maybe one of the girls was his own. As her skin and muscles stretched, Laura repeated over and over: *Ponderosa, alligator juniper, silverleaf.* Not fucking cypress. Then another thought, immediate and insane. *Not Italy, no—I should go to New Mexico.*

JEAN

"DIABLO."

"Anything else?"

"La Cumbre IPA and the chiles rellenos."

"I'll be right back with your drinks."

Jean didn't need to read the menu. Once she found a drink or meal she liked, she'd order the same thing over and over. At the Sierra Grande Grill, that meant the chiles rellenos and the chicken tostadas. She liked what she liked. A chile stuffed with cheese, battered, and fried came as close to perfection as Jean could figure. She hadn't eaten since breakfast—what was the harm?

Jean and RJ splurged on a meal at the Sierra Grande only when the weather meant they could sit on the patio. Out-of-towners came to the Sierra Grande for the spa, but the view was enough to make locals put up with the vacationers in their peach sundresses and turquoise jewelry, trying to blend in and overshooting the mark.

The Black Range sat to the west, framed by the patio's stucco columns. Banana leaves sprouted from potted plants. Thin wooden slats, the color of honey, covered the ceiling where fans helped a breeze move through the patio, and on the floor, warm-hued travertine echoed the sound of flip-flops finding their tables. Music coming from speakers inside the restaurant drifted out through open doors and windows. Someone had ordered steak fajitas at the next table, a cast-iron skillet sizzling behind her. Jean took a sip of her ice-cold water. The sweaty glass left a watery dark brown circle on the cardboard coaster.

The drinks arrived as RJ entered the arched doorway. He found his wife and paused, letting a busser carrying a large tray of empty glasses pass before making his way to their table. She liked watching him age. He said he liked watching them age together, but Jean would have hit the pause button if given a choice. With salt-and-pepper hair and dark tanned skin, RJ walked over.

"I ordered the chiles," she said.

"Of course you did."

RJ was one of the few people in her life outside her family of origin who had known her before she was a cop. She liked that he wasn't on the force. She couldn't imagine having to come home and talk shop over dinner. Most cops ended up with nurses or teachers—the salt of the earth tended to keep ranks. RJ was a real estate attorney, and Jean liked being able to leave work at work and keep home at home, where each belonged.

There was nothing as peaceful as the beginning of a meal. Before talk of the house or the yard or the car crept in, you could enjoy the idea of time together until someone screwed it up. After twenty-four years, they knew which land mines to avoid and danced around them, for the most part. Bringing up Jean's work had strong odds of derailing an otherwise idyllic evening. Investigative work wasn't a nine-to-five, not if you wanted to do it well. She'd done her best when the kids were little, but she'd had the feeling she had two full-time jobs and wasn't doing either well. When they got older—for the first time in her career—she could give the job the time it required. Friends would ask with pity-filled voices about being an empty nester. Jean knew the response people expected and played the part, but the truth was, she loved this time. RJ had had the impression that when the kids moved out and college loans were paid, they'd slow down too. Lately, this land mine had grown so large, she was never sure where to step.

The waitress returned with the chiles rellenos. Not caring if it would burn the top of her mouth, Jean pulled a pepper from the ceramic white plate. After a bite, melted cheese spilled from pepper and a crisp fried crust.

RJ opened the menu. "These are the good burgers, right?"

"Yes," she said. He asked the same question every time they came here. Maybe one day the answer would stick. "There's also a bison burger."

"There's also a kale bowl," he offered.

"Think I'll pass."

Jean's phone trilled in her pocket as the waitress returned.

"All set, or do you need a couple more minutes?"

"I'm ready," he said. "You?"

Jean slid out her phone and silenced it. "I'll do the chicken tostadas, please."

"Bison burger, medium, with cheddar and jalapeño," RJ said.

"Fries?" the waitress asked.

"Could I do a side salad instead?"

"Sure thing."

A text message came in. Then another. As the waitress left, Jean folded her napkin on the table.

"Side salad is almost like a kale bowl," she said.

"Almost." He smiled.

"Bathroom. Be right back."

She walked into the empty dining room. Apparently, everyone had the same idea to sit outside. Jean pulled out her phone in the bathroom. *Crap*, she thought, reading the message. She sent a text back and washed her hands. A grandmother came in with a girl, maybe six or seven. Making eye contact with Jean, she smiled, quickly, without moving her eyes, as she guided the child into the larger end stall.

Jean left, passing the matching grandfather at a table with a toddler boy. The scaffolding of his face sank with the exhaustion only young children can wreak upon a person. They were coloring. The grandfather had sketched a black dog. The boy dragged an emerald-green crayon across the paper, ignoring the lines.

"Those poor people," Jean said, sitting down and returning the napkin to her lap.

"What's the matter?"

"There's a couple grandparents here. They're raising their grandkids. I would not want to be running around after a toddler right now."

"What makes you say that?" RJ took a sip of his beer. "Maybe they're taking them out to dinner."

"Not the impression I get."

Jean peered out over the veranda, hoping they would find something else to talk about. Milky-white yucca bloomed like fireworks exploding over knifelike leaves. Laughter rose from a table in the corner, followed by the sound of clinking glasses. A runner passed by. Jean handed him her empty glass, nodding that she'd take another.

"Maybe they help out with their grandkids through the week," he said, exposing another trap. She shouldn't have brought it up in the first place. While she saw dark corners, he tried to see the good. She should move on. Eat their meal, count their blessings.

"I could be wrong," Jean said. She watched the yucca sway in the dry wind. She knew she wasn't.

"I nearly forgot," RJ said, reaching into his back pocket, unfazed by the invisible stone wall between them. He pulled out a brochure. RJ window-shopped for real estate listings the way some people went to the mall "just to look." According to the glossy page promoting Desert Pines, the housing development promised maintenance-free, custom-built, single-level living for empty nesters. *Downsize and upgrade!*

"They're breaking ground now," he said. "You can pick all your finishes. We would come out ahead on the house. No mortgage. And with your pension, we'll be more than fine."

"People with jobs don't collect a pension." She didn't know which to react to first: retirement in the guise of her pension, or selling their house, an idea they had talked about only in passing. Not "Let's stick a yard sign out front tomorrow." It hit her: he wanted to *talk about* the land mine, not avoid it.

"You only need another six months before you've maximized your benefits. What's the point of staying longer?"

The fact that he knew her pension details better than she did confirmed both that he had been the more responsible financial partner in their marriage and that, while she was pushing off retirement, he was closing in on it.

"I'm not ready to quit my job," she said and took a sip of beer. Then she twisted the sweaty glass around in a circle with one hand while holding the coaster in place with the other.

"You've had a long, successful career. You've served with distinction."

Her eyes told him this wasn't an answer, at least not the answer she wanted to hear. Another server arrived with their food. The interruption a brief detente.

The server left, and RJ tried again. "We've all sacrificed for your job. This place," he said, pointing to the brochure, "this is five minutes away from Coll. They're not getting married. You and I both know it. The kid, he's nice enough, but I don't see him doing the right thing. She'll never say it, but she needs us. How is she going to go back to work with a newborn?"

"You want me to retire so I can raise my grandchild?"

"No, I want us both to retire so we can help our daughter raise our grandchild together."

"You're going to retire?" Jean should have paid more attention when RJ explained their various retirement accounts. Looking at rows of pluses and minuses made her dizzy. Numbers were never her thing.

"It's not fair to ask you to slow down and not slow down myself." Jean hadn't seen this coming. She hated it when RJ proved to be a decent man.

This was what she was supposed to do. Support her about-to-be-a-single-mother daughter. Her whole life, Jean had lived by the consequences of her actions. Some would call it a sense of obligation. An army brat with a serious case of Catholic guilt. Or maybe living in this town for the past thirty years, it was in her DNA. A thought struck her while she gazed out to the Black Range, and farther in the distance, out of view, the Gila. Then a second thought. Each connected like a string of lights heading into the mountains and the valley where the barrels were found. They lit the way to a grand bargain.

"I want to close this case first."

RJ nodded. "How long do you need?"

Studying the terra-cotta-colored mountains scattered with brush, Jean did her own rough math. "Six months, like you said." No one else had done it in thirty years. Then she turned away from the mountains to her husband. "I have a question." For the first time in her career, there was something her husband could do to help.

Daisy and Jo play with the squirrels. When they run off, the girls turn their attention to a family of baby foxes, while the mother goes out to hunt. I sit by the river and listen to their laughter and small voices, never allowed to age.

I nestle into the tall grass beside the creek, picking up my story where I left off. Andy and Elise have settled on a color for the walls— bluebell. I follow them to restaurants, order them fried calamari and braised lamb shanks. They take a trip to the lake house, strip, and go for a swim. The water as salty as the ocean. The sun sets, painting the tawny desert coral and rose.

In the middle of my story, a golden glow appears at the bottom of the creek, like a light affixed to the bottom of a pool. The creek bed is deeper than I thought—much deeper. The glow intensifies as the light comes to the surface; beneath the light, my reflection reappears.

"Are you there?" the woman calls.

I hesitate, curious about why she has returned.

"Are you there?" she calls again.

I lean over. Another woman's face stares back at me from below the water. Neither of us smiles.

"There you are," she says. "I've been waiting to hear the rest of your story."

"It's not a happy one."

"The true ones usually aren't. You know—you might feel better if you talk about it."

There's a chance she's right. "What happened, happened," I say. I pick my head up, realizing I can't hear the girls anymore, and scan the woods.

"Where are you going?" she asks.

"Hold on," I say, standing.

Small footsteps dance through the clearing. Daisy's yellow dress flits among the flowers. I wait another minute, but Jo doesn't appear by her side. Daisy is alone.

"I have to go," I say.

"Don't go," the woman echoes.

I find Daisy in the clearing. A loose scattering of rocks surrounds her.

"Where is Jo?" I ask, peering into the woods' shade.

Daisy chews the inside of her cheek, twisting a strand of hair around a finger.

"Daisy," I try again. "Where's your sister?"

"She went to look for someone," Daisy says, keeping her eyes on the ground.

"What?" My heart should race, my stomach should turn somersaults.

"She always comes back."

"She's done this before?" I remember the image of Jo curling into a ball and disappearing. But she went a few hundred yards away. Can she go farther? What are the rules? The truth pummels me—my daughter has left before, and I haven't noticed. "Where did she go? Back home?"

"No."

"Not our home," I say. "Her other home."

I don't say the one he stole her from. Three generations of women, a mother, grandmother, and daughter, living alone, far outside town. Her mother worked during the day, while Jo stayed home with her grandmother. Until he showed up in town. Within days, her mother and grandmother were gone. He had told her he was her father now.

"No. I don't think so. She said she had to check something," Daisy says.

I don't know what to do with this information. The girl I have raised as my own since the day she showed up at my front door—small, quiet Jo—can . . . what would you call it? Travel? Fly? Without knowing where she is or how to find her, all I can do is wait for her to return.

"What are you playing?" I ask, sitting down where Daisy was setting up another game.

I can't remember the last time we played, the two of us. A squirrel crosses her pile of rocks, something small and brown in its mouth. I watch Daisy, smiling. I should do this more, and I promise myself I will. Daisy details an elaborate story of a castle and a prince and princess. They're being hunted by an evil wizard who comes in through their window at night and traps them in their bedroom with the queen. I play along, pretending not to notice the parallels.

Jo returns before the prince and princess can be rescued by the king, reappearing beyond the clearing. She has Mrs. Philip-Shandy under her arm.

"Where did you go?" I ask, keeping my voice light. If I'm not angry, maybe she'll tell me the truth.

"To a friend's house. We played make-believe," Jo says, kneeling and joining our game. She sits Mrs. Philip-Shandy next to her. A wolf howls in the distance, and I turn away for a moment, startled. When I turn back around, the pile of rocks is stacked into a neat pyramid.

"How did you do that?" I ask, pointing to the symmetry.

Jo shrugs. "I don't know. I saw it that way." Then she sits Mrs. Philip-Shandy on top, a conquering hero.

The girls pick up their game, and I stay with them. I can't lose them again. Until I remember: I lost them years ago. I'm the one who is playing make-believe. Maybe it is time to write a new story.

LAURA

"READY OR NOT, HERE I COME!"

Laura could hear her nephew leave his counting place at the bottom of the stairs. Daphne had excluded Cullen from her sleepover in the basement, so Laura had agreed to play hide-and-seek. Hiding on the second floor with her door closed and the light off broke two hiding-spot rules, but Laura had found someone she liked.

Brenda Janowitz had posted a message for her missing half sister, Wendy Slocum. Wendy had disappeared right before her divorce was to be finalized, and her family never heard from her again. In the years since, Wendy had never opened a credit card, never purchased a car, never applied for a mortgage, and never died, officially. Brenda had been searching for her older half sister for the past thirty-plus years. They shared the same father but had different mothers. The more Laura learned about Wendy's story, the more she let herself believe this could be the one. Maybe Wendy had changed her name or lived outside the mainstream with its requirements of Social Security numbers and credit checks. Or she was the Sierra County Jane Doe. Or another Jane Doe.

"I don't think she's in the kitchen! Maybe you should check upstairs!"

Laura heard the edge to Kate's voice. Before she could feel any guiltier, Cullen's dark outline stood in the light-filled doorway.

"Found you! Why are you in the dark?"

Cullen climbed up into Laura's bed, and Bella, who had been helping Cullen search though she knew where Laura was, jumped into bed with them.

"What are you doing?" he asked. If there was the possibility of putting his face in front of a screen, Cullen didn't miss it. His excitement quickly diminished when he saw his aunt was scanning vital records, not building new worlds in *Minecraft*. "This is boring," he said after a minute.

"A lot about life is boring."

"But what are you doing?" he asked.

"Looking for someone."

"Like in hide-and-seek?"

"Yes and no."

He watched for another minute. "Can we go downstairs now?"

"Sure, go ahead."

"But I want you to come."

Laura sighed. "Come on." She brought her laptop.

An open bottle of red sat on the counter along with three pizza boxes. Kate always bought more food than they needed, baffling Doug. When the twins turned five, an extra two dozen cupcakes had sat on their counter for the next week until Kate threw them out. A childhood spent with their mother bouncing checks at the grocery store had left her with a particular anxiety about not having enough. The *what* didn't matter. Enough cupcakes, pizza, milk, hand soap, paper towels. Kate steeled herself in quantity.

Laura planted herself at the kitchen table, wishing she had brought a sweatshirt. She refreshed her page on Franklin

County vital records. What she wouldn't give for a good family Bible—passed down from one generation to the other, names and dates listed on blank pages in the back in sweeping, fine cursive, the kind taught by nuns threatening to rap uncompliant knuckles with a ruler.

"Have another slice, there's plenty to go around," Doug said, pouring himself a glass of wine. After a two-week shift, this was his first weekend home in a while. Doug had that all-American cookie-cutter look belonging solely to pilots and Eagle Scouts. In addition to his high and tight hairline, he had a compact frame, as though his body had been compressed into cockpit dimensions. Even in sweatpants, Doug looked like a walking ad for flying the friendly skies.

"Can I get you a glass?" Doug asked.

"Maybe in a minute, thanks," Laura said.

Kate stood at the sink rinsing plates, her mouth fixed in a firm line, while Doug scrolled on his phone. Laura had stepped into the lull of an argument. Maybe she could extricate herself without them noticing. She decided to hide behind her laptop instead.

"If you're done playing hide-and-seek, why don't you go play Legos in your room?" Kate asked Cullen, who stood at the kitchen counter, barely tall enough to see over the edge, peeking into the pizza boxes one by one. "Or have more pizza, whatever. Just use a plate."

Unsatisfied, Cullen bounded out of the room, stomping to make his point. Whatever it was.

"I only said I was thinking about it," Kate said, after another minute of silence.

Laura was sure this wasn't intended for her and crouched down lower, trying the next Ohio county vital records page.

"I didn't say it was a bad idea, I only said I wasn't sure it was something you needed to take on," Doug said, rocking a knot in his lower back against the counter's edge.

"It's only thirty hours a week. I wouldn't need before- or after-school care."

Wendy Slocum had never lived in Ohio. On to Illinois.

"I don't see why you'd want to."

Kate was about to say something when the sound of two girls screaming "Cullen!" rose from the basement. Kate turned to referee, but Doug was closer to the door. She stopped herself before running into her husband's back.

"What's up?" Laura asked from behind the laptop. If she looked distracted by her laptop, which she was, she could get the debrief without losing her place in Cook County records.

"I found a job at the middle school. Doug thinks it's too much."

"What do you mean, too much? Or—what does he mean?" While Laura couldn't imagine spending the day with middle schoolers, she knew Kate's happy place was micromanaging people.

"He feels guilty about being away so much and me having the twins full-time and doesn't want me to have to work on top of it."

"Do you need the money?"

"It's not about the money. They're in school full-time now. I want to go back to work."

"Tell him that," Laura said.

Kate made a face like Laura had asked to borrow her favorite shirt in high school. Laura went back to her laptop. Kate did what she did best—she changed the subject. "What do you need from me for your next surgery?"

"Nothing. It's not as bad as the first one. I can take a car there, but you have to pick me up."

Doug emerged from the basement. "Cullen interrupted a game of Fancy Nancy with rules I couldn't begin to understand relayed in accents that, by my best guess, were French Canadian."

"How does French Canadian sound different from regular French?" Kate asked.

"It's funnier?"

"Fancy Nancy is American, but she explains things in French."

"Who's the British one?"

"The pig."

"The one with the tutu?" Doug asked.

"Olivia has the tutu. Peppa has the rain boots," Laura offered from the table. She had lived in the house long enough to know the difference between Olivia from the books and Peppa from Channel 5, originally, and Nick Jr. here, across the pond.

"Then who's the rabbit?"

"I don't know a rabbit," Laura said, returning to her screen.

"I don't know, the rabbit also sounded British. Also, there's some sort of disagreement about an invisible friend who is supposed to sit next to Daphne. I have no idea. Cullen's playing the engineering game with the impossible pieces."

"I threw that one out," Kate said.

"Then he's playing the other engineering game with the other impossible pieces. If it's that important to you, you should do it. I just worry about all the extra work."

"I'll be fine."

Laura could tell there was more Kate wanted to say. She'd been on the receiving end of her sister's glare enough times to know when she was simmering on a low boil, ready to blow.

The wind outside picked up. From the kitchen, Laura could hear a dog bark in the distance. She returned to her laptop. Maybe they wouldn't see her if she ducked a bit lower behind her screen. Another "Cullen!" erupted from the basement. This time Kate beat Doug to the door.

In the minute or two it took Kate to lure Cullen away from the girls, Laura pretended not to watch Doug as he ambled around the kitchen, purposeless.

"It's freezing down there," Kate said when she returned. "I turned up the heat. Anyway, Cullen can't play that game alone, it's too hard. I gave in and let him have the Nintendo."

Doug hovered by the sink. Laura had noticed that when someone else took her spot, Kate paced the island like an agitated and caged tiger. If nothing else, Laura could move Doug from her sister's default position.

"Doug, I'll take a glass of pizza now."

Kate and Doug turned, their heads tilted, eyebrows furrowed.

Laura scrunched her face. "Wine. Glass of wine."

Doug poured her a glass. "I'll go play with Cullen." Without another word, Doug disappeared into the basement.

"He doesn't get it isn't about him," Kate said. Laura could see her sister's shoulders dropping from across the room.

Laura found a Cook County marriage license for Wendy Slocum to Peter Nowak on November 8, 1979. Wendy, happily ever after. Or not happily married. It was anyone's guess. Laura took a big sip of wine. She copied the information and was about to forward it to Wendy's sister when she paused. Like it or not, Wendy had left her family, changed her name, and apparently made a new life for herself. It wasn't Laura's place to out her. Laura deleted the file as Kate side-eyed her from across the kitchen. Crossing off Wendy's name, Laura moved on to the next on her list and took another gulp of wine.

She wouldn't know what to say to herself either.

JEAN

WHEN JEAN PULLED INTO THE PARKING LOT OF FINA'S
Diner early next morning, she saw Eli's 2007 white Ford Focus
in the back, a University of New Mexico sticker on the rear
window, and went inside. The place had just opened. Carol,
who had started when Fina's was Tony's, pointed her chin at
the corner table. There, Jean found Eli Johnson: not the name
he was born with, but the name he had taken when he was
sixteen. He wore a tight-fitting shirt hugging his thinly piped
arms and had recently cut his hair short around the sides, keeping the top longer. Jean remembered the floppy light brown
curls he had as a child.

Every few months they'd meet for coffee or breakfast. Jean
hadn't been careful. She'd let herself get too close to Eli and his
sister, Ally. Together, they were her first major case after making
detective. All cops have a first—one that crawls deep inside you
and sticks. She had been Jean to the boy. Detective Martinez
had seemed too imposing for him at six. Carol met Jean at the
table with a cup of coffee, sliding it in front of her and leaving
without fanfare. The thick ceramic mug was hello.

"Sorry for bothering you," he said. He had covered his plate
with hot sauce, the plate rim painted red with Cholula.

73

"You're never a bother," she said, adding two sugars to her coffee. The seats around them were empty. Police departments should be required to pay rent to diners. Jean had had nearly as many conversations here as she had in interrogation rooms. A table was a table. The walls mattered. Food mattered too. The station was the place for people you needed to lean on. The diner, for making people feel like they were being taken care of.

Jean picked up where they had left off over text. "When's the last time you saw her?"

"I couldn't get hold of her this week, so I kind of freaked out. I haven't talked to her in like—three weeks? We normally don't go more than two. Maybe her phone died, or she turned it off, or it got turned off. I don't know." He pushed some home fries around his plate, smearing more of the plate red. "I didn't know what else to do."

"You need to get back for classes?" The last time they spoke, he had been considering whether to major in psychology. No surprise there.

"Yeah. I emailed my professors. I'm okay for today, but I have a shift at the student center tonight."

Jean nodded and pulled out her phone. "Where has she been working?"

"Her friend Destiny said over by the big truck stop off 25. But she'd also met some new people down in El Paso. She was moving around a lot. I drove around all day yesterday but couldn't find her." His teenage existence had been organized around keeping track of his older sister, Ally—a reversal from how they had spent their childhood.

"I'll call some people," Jean said. She made a couple of notes in her phone, then put it away. "How about you? How's school?"

"Good," he said, leaning over to pull something out of his back pocket and handing it to her. A printout of his midterm exam results. For a second, he was seven again, showing her how he had tied his laces on his own for the first time. She remembered his gap-toothed smile on full display. Jean had slipped him two fives: one for the laces, one for the teeth.

"You should be proud of yourself," Jean said, reading the grades.

"Thanks."

"I mean it."

Eli focused on his plate, blushing slightly.

"Have you gone to see your mom recently?" she asked.

"No."

"You should go see her. Bring the transcript. She'd be proud too."

He gave her eyes like he was humoring her. "Maybe."

"And don't worry about your sister. Like I said, I'll call some people. I'll take a couple drives myself. I promise."

They talked for a while like two people separated by time. When children form relationships with adults and keep those relationships as they grow into adults themselves, a part of them stays the age they were when they first met. Despite the years, Eli would always be the small child asking for ice cream. But if given the option, Jean would have preferred to remain a memory in the boy's life. She was afraid her current incarnation would never live up to the first version.

"I have to get going," he said after they had run through their familiar checkpoints: classes, friends, annoying roommates.

"I'll call when I know something," Jean said and waited a beat, deciding to ask the question anyway. "Have you talked to him lately?"

"No."

Jean knew he was picking his cuticles under the table. "What about Ally?"

"She swore if she ever saw him again, she'd kill him."

"So that's a no."

"Hopefully."

Eli tried to leave money, but Carol waved him off. "Your money's no good here. Never has been, never will be." Carol waited until after he had left to slip Jean the bill and a breakfast to go. She had charged Jean for two coffees. Jean left two twenties on the table.

✳

JEAN TEXTED ALL HER cop friends in the surrounding counties, putting out an informal APB before heading to work. She cut a straight shot to the Serrucho and Kirkland directories once she got to her office. The problem was, they weren't on her desk where she had left them, even though she had locked the door.

"What the hell?" she said to herself. She checked each of the offices around hers. Nothing. Then the interrogation rooms, in case by some chance they had ended up there. Now she was pissed. She went out to the front desk. Miguel Garcia, the regular desk sergeant, held the post today. He'd had a desk job since his knee surgery, and a face immune to other people's problems.

"Has anyone been back there this morning before me?" she asked.

"No one I've seen," Garcia said. "The photocopier is down again."

"What does that have to do with me?"

"You're the only one who knows how to fix it."

Jean shook her head. "Pass me the visitor log—please," she said, tacking her manners on at the end.

Running through the names of everyone who had been through the back bullpen, she saw nothing that stood out to her. She headed to storage.

Most buildings in town weren't built with basements. No need. Plenty of space to build out rather than down. But this building did have a basement, and while the county kept most of its old files in an off-site facility, there was some dedicated room down below.

Jean turned on every light she could find, half expecting someone to jump out from behind a stack. She wove through each shelf, pushing boxes out of the way, searching for her stack of directories. In the final aisle, they sat on the bottom shelf, next to a bag of golf clubs, of all things.

She brought them back up to her office, placing them on her desk. First the missing-person files, now these. What was going on?

"Does anyone know how to fix a jam in E7? It's telling me to open G2 to access E5, and I can't figure out which little green tab it's talking about," a voice called, playing up the helpless routine.

Jean swore under her breath and went over to the photo-copier, opening its underbelly and resetting the latches, tabs, and pulls.

By the time Jean had fixed the machine, Ruben Moreno, her commanding supervisor, had made his way to the office. He'd been out for the past two weeks, using vacation time he hadn't wanted to because if he hadn't, his wife would have sent him to work in the wrong side of a body bag.

Jean pored through the directories while finishing the breakfast from Carol, confirming a working theory she had. More and more, she surmised someone from the mining opera-tion nearby—Ironside—had to be involved. The current owner was named Reed Cortez Yates, grandson of Bjorn Tellefsen. There were other Tellefsens in the directories. No Yateses, but maybe there was a way to track people who worked at the mine through the directories. Plus, she had some employee records to work with. They weren't complete by any means, but with the directories, maybe there was something to go on. Once she was sure what she wanted was physically possible, she headed in Moreno's direction.

People liked Moreno as a commander because, generally, he got out of people's way and let them do their jobs. As far as supervisors went, Jean had done worse. Over the years, she'd seen people get excited when someone new moved up. But she'd take the devil she knew over the devil she didn't any day of the week. She knew where Moreno kept his skeletons. Two in interrogation room B and one in his right-hand file cabinet. He waved Jean in.

"What's up?" he asked. "You see these new budget numbers?"

Jean didn't know what he was talking about and her face showed it. She took a seat opposite him. A pile of mail sat on his desk.

"Never mind, my mistake. Looks like you didn't burn the place down while I was gone. Thank you for that."

She gave him a half smile. "How was the cruise?"

Moreno waved his hands in front of him. "Never again. Floating coffins—cruise ships are floating coffins."

"You're preaching to the choir here."

"How's the new job? You settled in? Need anything?"

"I could use some help. I'm working a theory on our Jane Doe."

"You started with the Jane Doe and the two kids?"

Jean nodded, waiting to see where he was going.

"You never make things easy on yourself, do you? What about the Diaz girl? Or the Randall homicide? Something smaller to start?"

"I like the Doe case. Have anyone I could grab?"

"Sure. But—" He stopped himself. "What smells good?"

"Fina's." God, did she smell like breakfast?

"What brought you out there?"

"Eli. He hasn't talked to Ally in a while."

Moreno nodded. "You want guys for Ally too?"

"No," Jean said, though his offer to send a couple of patrol after a victim from a case closed over fifteen years ago made her respect him a little more. "I know a sergeant I can ask about

Ally. Just need help for the Jane Doe. I want to track down some people who were local at the time the woman and children went missing—people connected to the mine nearby."

"Is that enough to go on?"

"For now."

"And nothing useful came out of the DNA you ordered? The very, very expensive DNA?"

"Nothing," she said. "They were too degraded to re-create the autosomal."

Moreno sighed. "You check in with Paul lately? He'd want to know about the lab report."

Jean had heard that the retired cold case detective, Paul Henderson, wasn't doing well. If she remembered, he was about to move to hospice. She should go see him—and soon.

"No, I haven't. He at home?" she asked.

"I think he's at Memorial."

"I'll go see him."

"I should too. Anyway, how many people you want? There's two guys in patrol with nothing to do. Your pick."

Jean stood. Two kids sat at a couple of desks in the corner, trying their best to look busy. They couldn't have been older than her son, Shay. What they needed was to get out into the world. Unfortunately, that wasn't what Jean had in mind.

"Blondie and the square?" she asked Moreno. The blond kid was the one who had been staffed to the front desk when her lab report came in.

"They're all yours."

"Thanks," she said.

"You may want to learn their names while you're at it. One of them is family, after all."

Jean had no idea what he meant but didn't want to ask.

"And Martinez?" Moreno asked.

"Yeah?"

"Ask Carol to send two next time."

Jean shook her head. "You paying?"

Ten minutes later, Jean had the two newbies carrying old desktop computers up from storage into the spare room next to her office. She didn't need anything fancy, only basic Windows programs. They glanced at each other like they had gotten picked first for kickball. She knew those expressions would melt like butter left next to a hot stove once she gave them their assignment.

"You want us to read what?" said the square.

Jean explained about the directories.

"And you want us to do what?" said blondie.

Jean explained about the need for a timeline.

She wanted to track down members of the family who owned and operated Ironside Mining, as many as possible. She wrote the columns she wanted on the board: dates they were working, last name, first name, street address. Didn't seem hard—she wasn't asking for the phone numbers; *that* would be ridiculous. It's not like anyone had landlines anymore. Once they had the immediate family down and Jean could track their movements over time, they could move on to known Ironside employees from the other records.

The young officers looked at each other, glanced at the directories, shrugged, and got to work.

Jean went to find Parker. He was in his office with Hernandez. The new father had black circles under his eyes. Ah, the joys of new parenthood. She wouldn't touch them with a yardstick. She was excited to be a grandmother, because then you could hand them back once you got your fill.

"Can I borrow you for a minute?" she asked.

Hernandez pushed back his chair, addle-minded, until Parker tapped his arm. "When she's talking to you, you'll know it. Get another cup of coffee. I'll be right back."

As Hernandez sat, a bit crestfallen, Jean couldn't help but smile.

"You smell like huevos rancheros," Parker said in the hall.

"What is wrong with everyone today?" she asked.

"All I'm saying is, if you're gonna go to Fina's, the least you could do is let us put orders in first."

"Does anyone do anything around here besides think of food?" At least it wasn't only her.

"What's up?" he asked.

She told him what Eli had said, and he listened, rubbing his chin and kicking an invisible spot on the beige carpet, worn thin from years of pacing.

"I'm waiting to hear back from the El Paso patrol sergeant I know," she said. "There anyone you can call?"

"Yeah. I used to play basketball with a detective in Las Cruces."

"When did you play basketball?"

"Everyone's got their secrets."

"Fine," Jean said as Parker turned back to his office. "Wait," she said, stopping him. Jean put her hand on his arm, remembering how close to the skin his muscles ran. "Want your opinion on something else. Need you to play devil's advocate."

He smiled. "My kind of job."

Jean led him past her newly appointed kiddie-pool transcription team to her office, where she had spread the case file photos, notes, and documents across two whiteboards. She loved whiteboards. Was considering getting a few for her dining room, to make it feel more homey.

"You've been busy, haven't you?" Parker said. He gestured to the aerial map and the crime scene photos. "This your site?"

"That's it."

He paused by the picture of one of the barrels, a temporary steel tomb. Then he studied the map of the surrounding mountains and valley. She knew he was taking a picture and making it 3D in his mind, walking the same path in his head as she had a few days earlier.

"I've read this file a hundred times. It's not like they seriously screwed up when they first caught this case—they just didn't follow every lead. They did their due diligence with NCMEC and NamUs, but there weren't any matches. Then there's this." She rested her hand on the employee records. "These records are a nightmare. Nothing lines up. Chunks are missing. I don't know if it was intentional. Lately, things have been developing legs around here and walking off."

"What do you mean?"

Jean wasn't sure of the answer. "Things keep going missing. There's personnel files for some people but no 1099s, and vice versa. There's years where no one's earning anything. I can't tell if the discrepancies are because Ironside deliberately didn't provide everything or if they got lost over time. I found a set of directories, like a first iteration of a phone book, and so far, it's the only complete anything I've got."

"You never were one for bookkeeping," Parker said.

"Give it a rest. It's not me. I'm not sure what it is," Jean said.

Parker stepped toward the parcel maps on the far-right board. RJ had told her where to find the information she wanted from the county auditor. She had pulled a complete history of the area in terms of who owned what around the barrel site.

"Was it Bring Your Husband to Work Day?" he asked.

Jean scowled.

"Don't give yourself a hard time, you've only been here a couple months since you ditched me," Parker said.

"And you seem to be doing fine without me."

"That's because I'm an expert at masking my true feelings."

Jean ignored him. "It's all the land around the barrel site. What's owned outright, what's leased. The mine expanded in the '40s, then shrunk again in the '70s. They were selling off everything not nailed down. I can't tell if there's something there—not yet. Look, this is where you come in. Tell me if I'm crazy. I've been wondering—maybe I have to work this thing backwards."

"How so?"

Jean had been kicking around an idea in her head. She wanted to see if Parker would bite.

"Maybe I have to work it like a homicide. Find the murderer, and from there, name the victim."

"You looking to put someone away? You got a solid chance this guy's dead, sitting in some old folks' home, or living in his daughter's guest room."

"I know that. There's never going to be enough for the DA—even if he is alive. But this may be how I name Jane Doe."

"So you want to solve a murder without the victim's name, without a murder weapon, without any forensic or any eye witnesses, and you want to solve it forty—maybe fifty years after the fact? While we're at it, can you pick a couple Powerball numbers for me?" His skepticism filled the room.

"Look, everyone around here knows about the woman and children in the barrels. We know the woman wasn't from around here. Her family would have come forward. But this guy, this guy had to be local. You don't wander into that valley passing through. I'm betting the guy who did this worked at the mine."

"That's plausible enough. What do you want me for?" Parker asked.

"Your sunny disposition."

Parker glared.

"Take a drive out to Ironside with me," she said. "Tell me if I'm missing something. Believe it or not, I miss working with someone." There was another clue—could be something, could be nothing—she wasn't telling Parker about. A name written in the margin of the original detective's notes. She'd wait and see if the Ironside owner knew anything about it.

"Now you're making me blush."

Jean pulled her car keys from the desk.

"You wanna do this now?" Parker asked, arms crossed against his chest.

"You got something else you need to do?" she asked.

"I suppose not." He thought for a moment. "Though if you didn't get me Fina's, the least you could do is bring some snacks. Snacks *and* coffee. If you want to drag a guy into the wilderness and all."

Jean smirked and pulled the in-case-of-emergency honey-roasted peanuts from her desk. She tossed the slim plastic bag at him, and he caught it without looking.

"These'll do," he said, stuffing the bag into his back pocket. "Let me check in with Hernandez, then I'm all yours."

Parker left, and Jean poked her head around the door where the newbies had begun going through the directories. "These don't leave this room."

For a few days and nights, I won't take my eyes off Jo. I play with the girls, and if I step away, I watch from afar, hiding behind a tree or bush, waiting for her to disappear. I stay away from the creek, avoiding distractions. Then it happens. One morning when she thinks I'm not looking, Jo curls herself up into a ball and disappears. I pace the clearing while she's gone, watching a rock pyramid's shadow crawl across the ground, trying to guess how much time has passed. Later, she reappears, spreading out like a glass of spilled milk. After a few more days of this, I catch the pattern: every three days, at the same time, Jo disappears.

One afternoon, I ask her. Mrs. Philip-Shandy hangs upside down from a low branch while Jo watches an anthill. I squat next to her, eyeing the minuscule lines of frenzied movement.

"I have a question," I say, easing in. "I noticed how you—" I weigh the next word carefully. "Travel—like the day the detective came here. Could you teach me how?"

"Sure," Jo says. I didn't think it would be that easy. She stares at me blankly.

"Great," I say. "How do I start?"

"First, you have to know where you want to go."

"Does it have to be somewhere you've been before? Or can you go to a new place?"

"Either."

The range of possibilities of where she has been visiting spools out in an infinite string. Also, I'm certain she couldn't have learned how to do this on her own. Who has taught her?

"What if I wanted to go out to the edge of the woods?" I ask, leaving my questions for another time.

"Close your eyes," she says. I do. "Try and think about the spot you want to go to. Pick one thing. And make it a picture in your head. Like you're watching a movie."

I remember the spot where someone would have to turn off the gravel road into the woods. There's a cluster of pine, dense, like something out of a fairy tale. The two in front have bulging knots, but one in the back is thicker than the rest, and even though its center is eaten out by rot, it stands among its brothers, unwilling to leave the group. I picture myself standing in the middle of the hollow tree, the smell of decay and rich dirt. I feel the coolness surround me, touch the damp wood. There's a crack running through its middle, wide enough for a person to step through. I imagine myself inside, peering up into the tree's center, not knowing where the dark ends and the rot begins.

"Can you see it?" Jo asks.

"Yes."

"Now puff out your chest," she says.

"You mean breathe in?"

"Yes," she says. "Now blow out bubbles."

I half open one eye to glance at Jo, then I follow her directions, blowing hard and fast. As I do, I feel her two little hands on my chest, pushing, hard. My arms coil into the spot, and my legs spiral in on themselves through a hole in my stomach. My body folds into a ball—a memory from that night arises, and for a second, I'm certain I'll throw up. I've contained my body in this origami before. Before I have time to remember, I find myself standing in the hollow tree, peering out from the dark.

It takes a minute for my head to stop spinning. The wood smells of rot, even though, to the touch, the wood is dry. From inside the hollow tree, I hear footsteps coming up the trail. Soft grunting, a cough. I step out from the tree's hollow center, and I feel him before I see him—like a window left open in December. The air crackles with silence—the birds and insects sense him too, tucking wings around their unsubstantial bodies, hiding.

I wait, knowing where he's headed, but find myself unable to move. When he cuts into the woods, I force myself to study him. Worn leather gloves. A thermos. A backpack with a sleeping bag rolled and tied to the bottom. I know the pack holds a tent, a small gas stove, extra water. He's planning a longer visit.

I try to do the picture thing, closing my eyes and re-creating the clearing in my head. But I'm wasting time—I can't jump myself back home. I take off running. Branches slice through my invisible arms as I race back to our clearing. I run as fast as I can, but there isn't enough time. When I return, I can tell: Jo already knows. She grips Daisy's hand, the whites of her knuckles gleaming.

"Ouch," Daisy says, trying to shake off her sister's grip. When they lock eyes—Daisy knows too. Daisy's eyes water, while Jo's face steels itself—her hands knot, her neck lines with thin metal rods. She could set the place on fire.

"Girls," I say.

"Girls," I say again. Neither of them meets my eyes. I can hear him behind us.

"Girls," I say a third time, this time realizing I don't actually have a plan. They peer at me. "He's coming. We'll go to the far side of the mountain," I say, taking their hands and leading them away.

"It's not far enough," Jo says, speaking for them both. She has tugged her hand out of mine.

With every second we delay, he gets closer. I haven't let him get this close to the girls before. I'm usually vigilant, but the woman in the creek, discovering Jo has been leaving—I've let my guard down.

Another old man moving through these woods would trip and stumble. He knows the path so well he could run it at night, without the moon. I close my eyes and can see him moving closer, though I don't know how. He's rounded the second bend. His breath has quickened. Same for his pulse. But not from effort. If you were next to him, you'd hear a low murmur from the back of his throat, moaning.

He could be here for a few days. Even for someone who measured their time in eternity, it would be forever. Because while we waited, each of us would be picturing exactly what he was doing, here in the clearing. Or worse—we'd be picturing exactly what he did while we were alive. No amount of distraction can stave off those stories. I switch tracks.

"Let's go," I say, improvising. "Let's go, not to the far side of the canyon. Let's really leave. We don't need to be here. Jo—take us back home. Daisy, do you remember our house? You need to picture it in your head, right, Jo? The floors were wide wooden planks. I painted the walls sky blue. There was a black-and-white rug with zigzags and lines. The fireplace—"

"I remember," Daisy says.

Jo nods.

"Daisy, do you know how to travel—like Jo does?"

"I taught her," Jo answers for her sister.

I hear a branch snapping behind us. He isn't being careful. He has been fast. I didn't want to look, but I can't stop myself. He has already unzipped his pants, making room for himself.

"Mom!" I hear Jo shout as she tugs my arm. "We have to go now."

"Home," I say, turning and blocking the girls from him. "We go home."

Daisy catches a glimpse of him. A glimpse is enough. Her eyes could have swallowed us whole.

"Home," I say again. A command, not a question.

They close their eyes. I feel the hole opening inside my chest, and we pull through the air together, out of the woods—together. Together and gone.

LAURA

LATER, LAURA WOULD REMEMBER THE MOMENT SHE found Jane Doe as clearly as the moment she got the call from the radiologist that the biopsy was positive. The day the radiologist called, she had been standing in her old apartment, leaning against the counter with a pint of ice cream in one hand and her phone in the other. Her spoon resting upside down in her mouth. It took her a minute to put together that "cancer" combined with the metastatic tumor in her breast meant she had "breast cancer." Her first thought, after she did the math: *I don't want to be one of those people. Those people with the pink ribbons.*

This moment struck differently, though it left her dumbfounded all the same. Kate was vacuuming for the third time that week. Laura scrolled to the next post, the next pebble dropped into the internet, by someone looking for a stranger's help. She read the post a second time, then a third. Then she ran for her bedroom, hurdling Kate's vacuum at the stair's base.

Margaret Ann Washington hadn't been seen since a family Christmas party. From the sketchy details on the Ancestry message board and the known geographic markers, Margaret's story fit. She had grown up in Southern California before moving to Connecticut. The person who left the message was a half sister who lived in Massachusetts. She was younger than Margaret—a lot younger. She was only six when Margaret left for college and never came back.

Something about the details demanded Laura's attention. It wasn't only the dates and the matching geography, it was three short sentences—"My name is Cynthia Walsh. I know it's unlikely, but I am looking for my missing half sister, Margaret. She had a little girl named Daisy." When she read it a fifth time, Laura pinpointed the part that turned her stomach—*a* little girl. The second girl in the barrel wasn't biologically her own—perhaps the family never knew about her.

She had already found Margaret's birth certificate. Margaret Ann Washington, born to Gloria Mary Russo and Joseph Charles Washington in Port Hueneme, California. There was a naval base there. There were naval bases in New Hampshire and Rhode Island and one in Groton, Connecticut. Then, hospital records from Memorial Hospital in New London, Connecticut. A high school diploma from St. Mary's, a private, all-girls Catholic school near the base. College records from Regis in Weston, Massachusetts. Another all-girls establishment. But only for one semester. What caused her to drop out? *The baby*. She remembered the known movement from the isotope testing. The daughter had been born in California. Jane Doe must have been sent away when she became pregnant.

She allowed herself to check out west. Laura searched California's online records for the Department of Motor Vehicles, the Employment Development Department, the Department of Education. There was nothing. She searched marriage records, death certificates, court records. Then she remembered the baby. She might have been born in Southern California. Starting with the largest county—Los Angeles—Laura checked hospitals, one by one. Methodist, USC, Van Nuys, another Memorial—every city, it seems, has its own Memorial—and farther south, Mission Hospital. Laura held her breath. A birth certificate for Daisy Marie Flaherty, born to Margaret Ann Washington and Francis Flaherty.

Laura's heart hammered her ribs. *Was it you?* she asked, peering at the screen. It was always the husband, the partner. *Did you do this?*

The same process, one by one, city by city, in New Mexico. Sifting for needles in a different haystack. This one came faster than the others. Like it was scolding her for not checking New Mexico first.

A driver's license issued from the state. And not in the name of Margaret Ann Washington but a Margaret Washington Crown. Laura yelled out, a shriek more than discernible words, before covering her mouth, remembering the time. What was the time, anyway?

She found the half sister, Cynthia, on Facebook. Why didn't people set their pages to private? Cynthia Walsh, retired Mass General nurse, was now living in Chautauqua, New York. She had moved. Lots of photos of baked goods. She sent Cynthia a message, and within an hour, received a response.

Laura plugged in the city on her phone. Four-hundred-sixty-something miles, seven hours.

Bet I can make it in six, she thought.

She had enough. A record of live birth, a possible driver's license, a date to meet the sister tomorrow out in Chautauqua. But she sensed there was more.

There were over eleven hundred churches in the city of Los Angeles, hundreds more if one included greater Los Angeles County. It was hard to tell from name alone if the churches were Catholic. She narrowed the list by geographic markers, staying within five miles of the hospital where the baby was born. Then ten miles, then fifteen, then twenty-five. One by one, searching for any online databases, scanned microfiche, scanned pictures of swooping cursive. Her eyes killed.

Then, payoff: Daisy Marie Flaherty was baptized at All Saints Catholic Church in Long Beach. God bless the Catholics with all their paper-trailing sacraments.

HER FINGER HOVERED OVER the doorbell to 172 Sycamore Lane, a yellow Cape with gabled windows jutting out of the roof like binoculared eyes. Laura studied her finger, transfixed by the small, weathered button. She pulled the word apart. *Trans*, across, beyond. *Fixed*, stationary. It seemed a perfect word. She was going to ring the doorbell to 172 Sycamore Lane in Chautauqua, New York. This doorbell belonged to the house that belonged to Jane Doe's sister. She let it ring for a solid two seconds—*one Mississippi, two Mississippi*—before letting go.

Cynthia Walsh answered. She had practical short gray hair that framed her face. Laura would have pegged her as a nurse or, in this case, a retired nurse, even if she hadn't found the information on the woman's profile. Cynthia smiled easily and broadly when she opened the door. A two-person couch, a coffee table, and trinkets and knickknacks lining a shelf filled the cottage living room—like someone's grandma's house. The tightness around Laura's chest lessened with the offer of muffins and iced tea.

"You post something on the internet, and you don't expect anyone to actually read it. Let alone do something." Cynthia smiled again and directed her to the couch. Three leather photo albums sat on the table, next to a plate of cinnamon crumble muffins.

The love seat forced intimacy among their crowded legs. Cynthia opened the top photo album. A picture of an older couple, standing outside this same house.

"These were my grandparents on my mother's side. We've kept this house in the family for four generations now. This was before I was born, but my parents came every year, even when it was just the big girls. Then we all came together."

"The big girls?" Laura asked.

"Catherine and Margaret. Every summer, they'd go out to see their mother and other sisters in California, then we'd all come here. You see, my father and his first wife had five daughters. Originally, they were all living in California, where she was from. He was on a base there. He was a navy man, his whole career. But then he got transferred to the East Coast. When they were in Connecticut, they divorced. The wife took the three youngest daughters back to California, and the oldest two stayed with him."

Laura's stomach flipped as though she had hit the top of a swing's arc and, in another second, would fall to the ground.

"That must have been hard."

"Missing their mother?"

"Feeling like you've been abandoned."

"When they would come back from California, it would take them a few days to act like themselves again. They'd be real quiet, like they were lost in thought."

"Did they get along with your mother?"

"As far as I could tell," Cynthia said, flipping to another page. Now the older couple had been joined by four girls. "My father, he only had daughters. I was lucky number seven." She pointed to one of the older girls sitting on the porch step. "There, that's Margaret. It's strange. I remembered her saying she was moving to Canada."

"Canada," Laura said fast, doubting herself. Then she countered: people lie all the time.

Laura studied Margaret's face. It had been one thing to imagine this person she had thought about for so long now. Jane

Doe had filled nearly all her waking hours. Laura had spent hundreds of hours imagining what her life might have looked like, her last movements, her last minutes. She had studied the facial reconstruction photos over and over. To look at, potentially, her actual face. This wasn't a story anymore. This was a person. Her left hand traveled to the spot on her breast where her tumor had been. Sometimes she could feel a twinge of pain there, in the muscle. Her body's way of remembering. She rubbed it now. "She was so young," was all Laura could manage.

Margaret had bangs in the photo, cut long and straight across her forehead just above her eyebrows. She looked to be sandy blond, with broad features, wide-set eyes, a narrow chin. Cynthia flipped through the rest of the album, but they were all pictures from Chautauqua: dinners, parties, speakers at the pavilion Laura had passed on her way here. She worried for a moment that there weren't any other pictures of Margaret. Then Cynthia pulled out a second album—a veritable deluge.

Margaret swimming at the lake. Margaret riding a bike. Margaret sitting on a checkered blanket, her knees tucked under her skirt, a wicker basket next to her. Laura searched Margaret's face as she grew older, page by page. *Did you know what would happen to you? Were you happy?* She looked for the picture when something had changed, when the course of her life had ricocheted, sending her on a trajectory ending in the mountains. But she couldn't find it. People smile for pictures. A picture can be worth a thousand words—but words, like people, lie.

"I saw she graduated from St. Mary's, then went to Regis for college. Why did she stop after her first semester?"

"She got pregnant. The father wanted to get married. His parents wanted them to get married. I overheard my parents talking about it—when they thought we were asleep. He was calling the house at all hours of the day, trying to get her to talk to him. Then somehow the decision was made that she should go out to California with her mother. My father was furious with her for getting pregnant. He wouldn't say the word. But he called her awful names—a tramp—that's what I remember most. He said she couldn't stay with us like that. Didn't want me and Patty thinking it was okay, what she did. But I'll never understand why he wouldn't want her to marry the father."

"Was the father of the baby—Francis Flaherty—was he violent with Margaret at all?"

"I can't be sure. I was so young at the time."

"Did Margaret ever legally change her name?"

"Not that I know of," she said, returning her gaze to the photo album. "Here, this is the last one we have of Margaret. We all flew out to California for Christmas after the baby was born."

Margaret had parted her hair in the middle here. It hung straight, framing her face. She wore a red sweater. The rolled-up sleeves revealed a stack of bracelets. She held the baby up against her chest, facing out to the camera. Daisy wore a tiny Christmas dress, a thick black velvet bow across her middle. Beside her stood a man, square jaw, checkered collared shirt, half smiling for the camera. Darker hair, dark eyebrows, but light eyes—probably blue. Laura tried to put herself in the picture and imagine Margaret laughing, imagine the baby crawling, sitting up and looking around. What did she see?

"Who's this?" Laura said, pointing to the man.

"I don't remember his name. He came to the Christmas party. It was the last time anyone saw her. She got into a fight over something with my father."

"This isn't Francis? Daisy's father?"

Cynthia shook her head. "No—he isn't. He was a new boyfriend."

Laura searched the photo for clues, then the page. One image captured a young Cynthia and another girl on a mauve velvet couch. They were dressed up, for a special occasion. "Is this from the same day?" Laura asked.

"Yes," Cynthia said.

There weren't any other photos from that Christmas. Laura pointed to the picture of Margaret. "May I?" she asked.

Cynthia nodded, and Laura picked at the corner with her thumbnail, pulling back the plastic sheet with a loud tearing sound. She lifted the photo off the thick, sticky cardboard album page. On the back someone had written, *Christmas, 1960. Margaret, Daisy, and C—*. The rest of the name had blurred, as though someone had wiped their thumb across the letters before the ink had dried. Although the last letter could be a *G*. Laura couldn't be sure.

"You sure you don't remember his name?"

Cynthia thought about it, then shook her head, tears beginning to well. It caught Laura off guard. She had never seen a nurse, even a retired, plainclothes nurse, cry.

"I think about her every day. The day I got married, the day my daughter was born, the day my grandson was born. I wonder what she's doing. She was so young. I'll never understand what happened. It never goes away. The not knowing, that's the worst part."

Laura thought the best thing was to say nothing and sit with her for a moment. Once Cynthia dried her face and eyes, Laura asked, "You said she got into a fight with your father at Christmas?"

"Yes. I remember them yelling. Then everyone got quiet. By dessert, it was like nothing had happened."

Laura looked at the picture again. Four white knuckles were set off against Margaret's Christmas sweater as the man gripped her shoulder.

"I never knew for sure what happened," Cynthia said. "My sister Patricia and I—we've talked about it over and over. We all assumed it had to do with him." She pointed to the man. "My mother always said she got a funny feeling from him. She asked him about where he grew up—she thought she recognized his accent—and she said it was like a light going off, watching his face change. He said he didn't like to talk about his past and it wasn't her business. Then he flipped right back, complimented her on her shoes. It's a weird thing for a man to notice. You said in your message you may know what happened to her. What have you found?"

This was the moment Laura had worried about. She had played it out in her mind but still wasn't sure what she should say—or shouldn't say. She hadn't brought up the possibility that Margaret could be a Jane Doe, let alone one who had sat in a barrel for years without anyone knowing. But she decided it was better to tell Cynthia the truth. Even if it wasn't what she wanted to hear—it might be what she needed to hear.

"Do you know where Sierra County is?"

"No."

"It's in New Mexico, east of the Gila National Forest. Not a lot of people live there, now or then." Laura told her what she knew, what she had found, what she thought. She showed Cynthia the facial reconstruction images, showed her the color-coded map, and summarized, as best she could, the isotopic testing. The knot that had been contracting the muscles throughout her chest and stomach began to ease up—Cynthia, rather than dissolve into a puddle, had seamlessly slipped into nurse mode with the less-than-sunny theory. Laura hesitated before laying down her finger on the spot where the barrels were found.

"I could be wrong, but there's a chance that the Sierra County Doe is your sister. She was found with one girl who they know is her daughter. And another little girl who isn't. I haven't figured out who she is. Not yet."

"Another girl?"

Laura nodded.

"But Margaret went to Canada. How would she have ended up in New Mexico?" As if she were asking another nurse whether a patient needed more pain meds, she kept her voice and her head steady, focused on the problem at hand. Maybe she'd deal with the fallout once Laura left.

"That's what we need to figure out." Laura showed her the driver's license record—but there wasn't an image. She hadn't been able to find a marriage certificate explaining the new last name, Crown. But Cynthia agreed, the name Margaret Washington was enough to follow.

"How else can I help? What do you need from me?"

"I have a surgery tomorrow. It's nothing major," she added when Cynthia's face showed a trace of concern. "I can figure out our next steps after that. But in the meantime," she said, picking up the Christmas photo, "do you mind if I take this one?"

JEAN

THE HIGHWAY UNFURLED HOT AND EMPTY LIKE A THIN sliver of hell ahead of Jean and Parker. She drove while he rotated between coffee and handfuls of honey-roasted peanuts. In Jean's mind, those two things didn't go together, but she had gotten used to his eating idiosyncrasies over the years. French fries with hot sauce or a ketchup-mayo blend, never plain ketchup. Pancakes with butter, not syrup. Coffee, dark and bitter, or none at all. Besides, she liked the quiet. They both did. She knew Parker preferred the sound of wind ripping through open windows to music or the news, though he nodded to himself as if playing a song in his head. Jean wouldn't dare try small talk with Parker. Wouldn't go near it with a ten-foot pole. He did things all the way or not at all. But she supposed Colleen didn't count as small.

"Coll's due any day now," Jean said, louder than normal to compensate for the wind.

"She know if it's a boy or girl?"

"Girl."

"She gonna get that kid to marry her or what?" Parker asked.

"Doesn't look like it. I don't want to push it, but I'm surprised his family isn't jumping on his back."

"I bet." Parker studied the valley dotted with creosote outside the window. "You're gonna be a grandma."

"Yes I am."

"This going to be your last blaze of glory before you go riding into the sunset, pushing a stroller on Tuesdays, Thursdays, and every other Wednesday?"

Jean could have sunk a knife in his side, a good flesh wound. "When have I given you the impression I'd be retiring to babysit?"

"Thinking about how your family must be jumping on your back," Parker said. "What's RJ have to say?"

"He wants my shield handed in yesterday."

"He tell you why?"

"Something about our golden years. Though I have to tell you, I don't feel very golden."

Parker looked relieved. "Still dark and twisty then?"

"Something like that."

The vista opened as they left the last trace of civilization in the form of a lone gas station for the open desert, and then the mountains. Jean continued, "I may be a grandma, but last time I checked, you got as many days on your card as I do. If anyone should be retiring, you make a strong case."

"What would I do? Take up golf? Maybe start giving tours around the canyons? I wouldn't know what to do with myself."

"You could keep busy."

"Bullshit and you know it. I was messing with you. I know you're not any closer to retiring than me. People like us, we are the job. You take that away from me, I kid you not, I don't know what I'd do. Retirement is two steps closer to the grave. Besides, I know you'd never leave me. Oh wait, never mind, you did leave me, didn't you?" He tossed another handful of peanuts into his mouth before brushing his hands off out the window and folding the now-empty plastic sleeve into his back pocket. She waited for him to return her gaze, but his eyes never left the rising black ridge.

Jean didn't respond. She wasn't sure how to. Outside her window, the evergreen mountains stood with black ridges running through like veins. With no open valley for the wind to cut through, the car got quiet. The faint smell of pine came through the window. The temperature had dropped since they left town.

The ground changed when they pulled into the lot. Whatever mineral ores ran deep underneath the mountains came to the surface here like the devil had pressed his thumb down on the spot, burning out any chance of life. The lot was a bone-dry wasteland of beige and sand walled by verdant forest along the perimeter. One single-story cement-block building sat in the center of the lot. Metal signs made dull with dust pointed to a truckers' entrance and a main sales door, and they followed the latter, parking out front next to a handful of dustier pickup trucks. One shiny truck stood out as though it had been through a car wash that morning and dropped miraculously onto the asphalt. Jean pointed to the clean Chevy.

"Boss is home," she said.

Parker glanced over. "Probably right. How many people have we interviewed together? Well, grandma, we're too old to play Beauty and the Beast in there. You got any other ideas?"

"You're a certifiable ass."

"Yeah, but tell me this: Who's better than me?"

No one, she thought.

Then, she corrected herself: *Me, dummy.*

"You warm him up. I'll play second."

"You got it," Parker said, opening the door.

The office was sparse. Some old magazines sat on a table between two metal chairs. The top of the stack had a front cover short one corner where an address label had been cut off in a neat rectangle. A water cooler, half-empty, sat in the corner. You'd have to pay Jean good money to take a drink from that. But the first thing she noticed about the space was its temperature.

Someone in here liked the air-conditioning on full blast. But she could hear no vent swirling, could feel no draft moving through the reception area. Instead, it was as though they had stepped into a frozen block of pudding, the cold fixed solidly around them. A shiver rose up from her middle, through her stomach, rolling in waves, like something alive.

"You want my jacket?" Parker asked, noticing her discomfort.

She shook her head, trying to shake off the cold. The receptionist, whose nameplate read *Ms. Shirley* in an embellished script out of place in the barren office, gave every indication to the two detectives that they had interrupted a busy morning working on a jumbo-sized crossword puzzle she made no attempt at covering up when they entered. She wore a wool sweater.

"Can I help you?" Ms. Shirley said as though the dust covering the trucks outside also covered her throat. Her light yellow hair, clearly dyed, washed out her olive-toned features.

"We're with the county. We were hoping to speak with Mr. Yates."

Ms. Shirley sighed low and baritone as she pushed her chair away from her desk. The chair legs groaned against the linoleum. Pausing halfway to the only other door in the room, Ms. Shirley turned.

"What did you say this was about?"

"An old case," Jean said.

Ms. Shirley grew two inches, her spine doing a shimmy her body could neither control nor cover. Jean wasn't sure it had anything to do with the temperature. The woman walked faster on the back end of her cross-room trip than on the front, only poking her head into the door briefly, saying something Jean couldn't hear, before motioning for Jean and Parker to enter.

The man sitting behind a metal desk could have been the woman's grandson, he was so young. Parker stepped forward first. Jean paused before crossing the threshold into his office, the snaking feeling through her middle growing in intensity. *Yes, something alive*, she thought, but where the thought came from, she couldn't tell. She was unpleasantly nauseous. Focusing on Parker's shoulders, she followed him, and then all three sat as if on cue for their roles in a high school play.

"Reed Yates," the young man said. "Pleased to meet you. Ms. Shirley says you're here about some barrels?"

Three thoughts struck Jean as she watched this young man sit and fold his hands carefully, resting them on his desk. While Ms. Shirley was bundled in a thick sweater, this man carried on in a thin button-down as though he weren't sitting in a meat freezer. Second, when he said "Ms. Shirley," it sounded as though he were speaking about an old elementary school teacher, not his secretary. Third, Jean had never used the word "barrel" with the woman.

"Have you ever heard about the Sierra County Jane Doe and the two young girls found with her?" Jean asked.

"Only a little. I remember my grandmother talking about it once or twice." He was in his late thirties, by Jean's best guess. He had light hazel eyes with flecks of gold in them and darker hair, cut short, like he was embarrassed by the curls trying to grow out.

"In 1983, a couple hikers stumbled onto the barrels outside your property line. The bodies of a woman and two girls, one of whom was her biological daughter and the other, not. Given Ironside's proximity to the site, the original detective came around and asked a few questions, but there wasn't enough to go on. The case went cold fast. We're trying again," she said.

Parker leaned forward and smiled. "Busy guy like yourself, we don't want to take much of your time. Just a couple routine questions, seeing as the deceased were found nearby Ironside property." This was why Jean had brought him. No one played a better good ol' boy than Parker. "Now, I know you weren't old enough to remember anything from when the bodies were found," Parker continued.

"Yes sir." Reed nodded, happy to have gotten an answer right. "Or I guess no sir, you're right. But it's sad. No one ever claiming them."

"That's the truth," Parker said, crossing an ankle over his knee. In ten years, their cues hadn't changed.

"Bjorn Tellefsen—he's your grandfather?" Jean asked, already knowing the answer.

"Yes, ma'am. He came out of the war, finished his degree, and moved back here to work at the mine. He could have gotten permission to stay in college when the war started, but he dropped out to fly B-52s over Germany. He was a ball turret gunner. Have you heard of them? I didn't know what it was until I looked it up one time. Pretty crazy. Anyway, he started his degree at Stanford, if you can believe it, but when he came back, he moved out here to New Mexico. Finished his degree at the University of New Mexico on the GI Bill."

"What degree was that?"

"Engineering."

"How would you say the company's changed over time?" Parker asked.

"It used to be bigger," Reed said. "There were a lot more guys back then. We can do a lot more with the machines we have today."

"What a blessing," Parker said. Jean knew he was lying.

"It sure is."

"Paint a picture for us—if you could. What kind of guys worked at Ironside back in the day?" Parker asked.

"Most of the workers, they'd only stay for a couple years before heading to another job. Not itinerant guys, but kind of drifters, you could say. That's how I remember my uncle talking about it. As long as they didn't unionize, he didn't mind."

"Sure, sure," Parker said. "Must be pretty common given this type of work. It must be hard raising a family out here."

"Yes," Reed said. "The only elementary school's an hour away. They only graduate one or two kids—every other year. Didn't used to be. I love it out here. It's quiet."

"Your uncle, what was his name?" Jean asked, reading her notes.

"Gerry. Gerry Tellefsen. He ran the company after my grandfather. First as CFO, then the whole shebang."

"And now it's up to you."

"Yes."

"A bit odd, isn't it? Your uncle Gerry passed it on to you? Your uncle didn't have any of his own kids?" Parker asked.

"Never had a family. I was happy to take it on."

"So it would have been Gerry running the company when those barrels were found?"

"I guess that's right."

Jean ignored the creeping cold filling her stomach. "Your parents still live around here?"

"No, ma'am. My mother left us when we were little."

"I'm sorry," Jean said. The chill intensified, and she resisted the urge to rub her hands together. "Is your father still alive?"

"Yes. He lives over in Elephant Butte."

"What about your uncle?"

"He passed, two years ago."

"And your mom"—Jean knew this from the directories already—"her name was Nancy?"

Reed nodded once.

"Any other siblings?"

"One. My brother, John."

"Your father raise you, then?"

"Yes, ma'am."

"Sorry—I didn't catch his name."

"Tom Yates."

Everything was lining up with what she had found in the directories. Bjorn and Anete Tellefsen listed as having two children, Gerry and Nancy. When they were adults, Gerry's name alone listed at a separate address. Nancy's name had disappeared, Jean surmised because Nancy had married and moved out. But Jean had never found her new married name listed in the directories, concluding Nancy must have moved farther away.

"Your middle name is Cortez, I have that right?" she asked.

"Yes, that's me."

"I hope you'll excuse the question. Where'd the Cortez come from? Someone on your father's side?"

"It's a family name."

"Got it," she said, crossing her legs.

Parker picked up her cue, asking the next question. "You have a family of your own?"

At the mention of family, Reed adjusted his position in his chair. He placed a smile on his face like a sticker. "No sir, not yet. Someday I hope, God willing."

Like a linebacker watching for a running back to shift his weight back into his heels, Jean jumped back in, pivoting. "Our best estimates say the barrels were placed anywhere between 1960 and 1975. I was curious about the location itself. I pulled up the property history. When the barrels were found, the property wasn't owned by Ironside Mining. But that's only because Bjorn sold that parcel back to the county in 1972. Any idea why your grandfather would have wanted to get rid of that land?"

Reed's forehead creased. "Can't think of any myself. Hard to ask him, he passed a few years ago."

"Couple other things, then we'll get out of your hair," Jean said, pulling out the notes from the first investigation. "There are a handful of notes from the original officer assigned to the case—Detective Carl Pendergast—about who he questioned back in the '80s." She pushed the notepad toward Reed. "There's some chicken scratch in the margins. At first I thought it said—well, it's enough to make a girl blush, I can tell you that. I thought it said 'need BJ ok.' Sounded more like a teenage kid passing notes in class. Then I realized 'BJ' could mean Bjorn. Or that uppercase *J* is a messy *T*. Either way, it seems the detective wanted Bjorn Tellefsen's approval before talking to someone. See right next to it? 'Curtis.' 'Ask about Curtis.' Any idea who that could be?"

It took him a moment. Reed glanced at Parker before answering. "No, definitely no relation to me. Not sure who that could be."

Jean made eye contact with Parker, who stood as if on command, shaking the young man's hand. "Thank you for your time," Parker said. He kept his hand clasped over Reed's and ended with the question Jean had set him up for. "The Ironside records we have seem to be missing a few pages. We were hoping you'd have the originals that we could double-check. See if something got lost in the photocopier, so to speak." Parker released Reed's hand, then smiled at him, wide and phony.

Or floated away, Jean thought to herself.

"Gosh. I don't know what we'd have. I can ask Ms. Shirley. I would like to help in any way I can. Whatever we do have might be a little sketchy."

"Sketchy?" Jean asked.

"May not be complete is what I was trying to say."

"We get that," Parker said. "Anything you have, anything at all, would be real helpful. We can speak to Ms. Shirley on our way out about those files. Don't want to take any more of your time."

"Not a problem. Anything else, you know where to find me."

Jean smiled and followed Parker out of the office, closing the door behind them. But Ms. Shirley wasn't at her desk. They heard a car door slamming shut. Parker opened the front door to see Ms. Shirley struggling under the weight of two Bankers Boxes. As soon as they stepped out of the building into the parking lot, the arm reaching up through Jean's insides released its grip, and the warm air splayed itself across her skin. Ms. Shirley's voice snapped her attention back.

"Come here, young fella, and help with these, please," the older woman called.

Parker didn't jog for many people, but Ms. Shirley got him moving.

"The minute they found that woman and her little girls, I photocopied every piece of paper I could find in this place, thinking things tend to go missing once the police get involved. With the bodies being so close, I guessed it was a matter of time before someone came knocking on our door. I made two copies when the police first came around. Gave one to them, kept one on me."

"You naturally helpful or—"

"I got it in my head Nancy was the one in the barrel, but they would have figured that out right away, wouldn't they?"

Jean was mentally flipping through state and federal law, trying to determine whether Ms. Shirley had committed a crime by taking the files and then deciding she didn't care. The point wasn't privacy, it was that Ms. Shirley suspected Nancy Tellefsen had been murdered. "You don't believe Nancy ran off?"

"She loved those boys. She'd throw herself in front of a train for them."

"Was there trouble at home?"

"I never heard of any, but I wouldn't know—would I?"

"She and her husband, Tom Yates, you have any idea where they were living?"

"I think up on some pecan ranch, north of here."

"Hold on a second," Parker said, breaking in to their exchange. "You're telling me you've had these files sitting in your trunk all this time?"

Ms. Shirley turned back to Jean, staring her down, hard. "Would you leave them inside?"

Jean didn't know where the thought came from, but she was certain that Ms. Shirley knew about the creeping cold, the thing moving through her insides.

"We were about to ask you if you had old personnel files," Parker said, ignorant of the silent exchange.

"Fancy that," said Ms. Shirley, smiling.

They finished loading the boxes into Jean's trunk. Ms. Shirley straightened her dress and adjusted her sleeves.

"You like your boss—Mr. Yates?" Jean asked.

"He's decent enough. He tries hard, anyway. He takes it personal that this is his family's company. He puts a lot of stock in that. I started under his uncle. Now, his uncle was another story."

"How so?" Jean asked.

"Gerry wasn't what you'd call a realist. Everything was 'fabulous' or 'fantastic' with him. Like he only saw what he wanted to see instead of what was sitting right in front of him. I saw more than a few people take advantage of him, in that respect. He expected the best out of people, and when they didn't meet his expectations, he sort of let it slide rather than hold them accountable."

"He get that from his father?"

"God no—Bjorn? Bjorn Tellefsen did not play, let me tell you. Even after he technically retired, he was still around, keeping his nose in everyone's business. You did not want to get on the wrong side of Mr. Tellefsen. You did not question what he said. He did not tolerate anything less than your full effort. He was of his generation, in that sense. He was a hard man with an unforgiving yardstick that he measured people by. But I got the sense that he felt guilty about something."

"What makes you say that?"

"Well, you'd think—the kind of man he was—he'd be harder on Gerry. He was certainly hard on Nancy, that much was clear.

But Gerry—his son could do no wrong. Complete opposite of Nancy. She couldn't have weighed more than ninety pounds, soaking wet. Small little thing. She was a beautiful woman. Hair so golden it looked like a halo. When she left those boys, it about broke her father. Bjorn was never the same after."

"Anyone ever suspect that something happened to Nancy? Anyone file a missing-person report?"

"Oh no, nothing like that."

"Anyone suspect her husband—Tom Yates—of her disappearance?" Parker asked.

"Tom? He was a quiet man. Kept to himself mostly. Did a few odd jobs here and there. But he has my respect, raising those boys all on his own. They moved back down here, him and his boys, once Nancy had left. To be closer to family."

"What about the name Curtis?" Jean tried. "Do you remember someone by that name who worked at the mine?"

"No. But it doesn't mean he's not in there somewhere," she said, pointing to the boxes. "You go ahead and look yourself, but you let me know. Time for me to get back to work. Best of luck to you." Ms. Shirley disappeared back into the building.

Jean met Parker's gaze. "I know what you're thinking," she said.

"A missing daughter, a brother with no family of his own, and another woman and kids whose bodies show up within spitting distance of the front door? Doesn't pass the smell test."

"No shit."

They got in the car, and Jean started the engine.

"This is the only job in town for a lot of folks. Seems to me no one would mind if an old cold case got forgotten about," Parker offered. "Show me those notes again from the first set of guys?"

Jean passed him Detective Carl Pendergast's notes. "I was thinking the same thing," she said, considering how a town might benefit from ignoring the murder of one of its own if it was connected to the company putting dinner on the table.

"Or could be a former employee, using the old company land as a dump site." She pulled out of the parking lot, heading back toward Truth or Consequences.

"What do you make of this?" Parker asked, pointing again to the note to *ask about Curtis*.

"It seems strange it's so informal," Jean said. "Makes me think the detective knew whoever it was personally. Thing is, I can't find anyone named Curtis anywhere else."

❄

WHEN THEY GOT BACK to the station after a ride spent in comfortable quiet, carrying the boxes into Jean's office, they passed a file cabinet that had been moved out into the hall-way. The right side had been smashed in. No way the drawers would open again. It stood next to the photocopier, which had jammed—again.

"What's this?" Jean asked a detective nearby.

He turned around from his desk. "That? Oh, Hernandez. He's okay now."

"He jam the machine again too?" Jean said, crouching, repeating the steps to find the crumpled page.

Parker shook his head. "I had him go through some evidence while we were gone. There's a thumbnail drive that needed to be summarized for court. From that case we had last spring."

"Jesus, you didn't want to be here with him? Has he done it before?"

"Hernandez said he wanted to be alone, for his first time. I'll go back and double-check his work." Parker's face lost its earlier light. "Let me check in with the kid. But your case. I think you have something. Let me know if you need anything else."

"Thanks," she said. There was nothing left to say to Parker. She knew what he'd have to do when he returned to his office.

Another kid, bearing the worst of what the world offered. She had put in a request to transfer off child abuse the next day. She didn't have the space to bear witness to those acts anymore. It meant Parker had to carry it himself. And now Hernandez. She should apologize. Instead, she unjammed the photocopier.

When she returned to the spare room where she had left the younger officers on transcription duty, she found two empty chairs. Before she could find them to tear them apart, she heard Moreno call her name. She knew what he was going to say before she sat down.

"Did you seriously ask those guys to copy out directories?" he asked.

"They weren't—"

"I'll give you that they aren't much more qualified to do anything but copy—what—some old phone books? But I have to say, you're wasting your time. I know you're wasting theirs. And that's hard to do given how little their time matters around here."

Jean was ready to take her scolding and get back to work when Moreno started in again.

"There's one more thing. I should have brought it up earlier," he said, glancing at his hands. "The new budget for next year. We had to move some people around. This wasn't my choice, but they want to make the cold case position part-time."

"What are you talking about?"

"The sheriff's gearing up for reelection. He's reallocating funds. There isn't a need to put a full-time position on a couple old cases. Not when we could use the help elsewhere." He slid a thick, stapled packet in front of her.

"Looks like you don't have a problem with the copier," she muttered, picking it up. The county budget. Pages and pages of revenue, cost of operation by department, shift—even gender. A few pages highlighting the K9 division. She found her own position with cold cases on a page titled "Personnel Cutbacks." Her job had been reduced to one little red bar. For someone who was used to turning on a dime, she was caught off guard. "I don't get it. Where's the money going?"

"Drugs. Your position, effective immediately, will go down to twenty hours a week. I checked your card. If you go part-time, you won't earn your full pension for another two years. I think you should take your old job back."

"What about Hernandez?"

"You have seniority. Hernandez is young, we can find somewhere else for him. Look, we all want to clear our cold cases, but honestly, DNA was going to be the only thing that cracked this open. It'd be nice to ID the vic, but she's long gone and so is any family of hers, most likely. You should be doing what you're good at."

"You telling me that I'm not good at this?"

"I mean, directories? Martinez, come on. Don't make me say it."

She stood before she answered him. "I'm not taking someone else's job. Pay me what you want, but I'm clearing this case." She knew she was being self-righteous but didn't care. It felt good.

She went back to her office and stared at the stacks of directories and Ms. Shirley's records. From down the hall, she heard Hernandez swearing.

Welcome to the club, she thought.

She checked her watch. On another day, she'd grab a cup of coffee. Begin organizing her ideas. Call for takeout. Instead, she pulled her jacket from the hook, turned off the lights, and closed the door behind her.

THE DRIVE NORTH ALONG 25 gave good views of the mountains on either side of the highway, following her. Those guys back in the '50s had named the town right—Truth or Conse-quences. She pushed that small word between her lips. *Or.*

A little while later, she pulled into the cemetery. It wasn't much to look at. Most of the graves were simple white wooden crosses banged into the ground. There was a big farmhouse badly in need of repair, sitting a ways off in the distance next to a similarly banged-up barn, but she'd never seen anyone come in or out. Jean crossed over to the side, to the plot she had picked out over a decade before.

Brushing off the marble slab, Jean knelt and crossed herself. "How you doing?" she asked the air. The air didn't reply.

She ran her fingers through the engraved letters—Lisa A. Fulbright—pulling dust out of each crevice and curve. Eli and Ally had decided to bury their mother up north in Socorro County where she grew up rather than somewhere closer to them.

"It's been a while since I've visited. I apologize for that. Eli's good. He's doing great in school. All As, if you don't count a C+ in poli-sci. He sends his love. I'm not sure about Ally, though. I think she's in trouble. Eli's worried. Keep an eye on her—if you can. I'm going to try and find her though, I promise."

She stayed a few minutes at Eli's mother's grave before push-ing herself up from the ground, cursing her knees. She'd try to find Ally, and she'd try to name Jane Doe. There would never be consequences, but maybe she could find the truth.

We reappear in the middle of our old living room. The floors have aged, darker in some places. A bright white line cuts across the middle where an old rug used to be. A flurry of voices surrounds us—the same voices I remember, hazily, from that night.

"Sylvia!" a man's gruff voice bellows.

I spin around to find an old man sitting in his reclining chair, glaring at us. I remember him, vaguely. I met him only once when we were both alive. The first day we moved to the ranch, I remember him meeting us at the front door, handing off the keys. Ernesto. We had lived here for only a handful of years, renting the house from him. I pause, realizing I've never let myself remember.

A woman appears in the doorway, an apron tied around her waist, her gray hair in a neatly coiled bun at the base of her neck. With her hands on her hips, she's ready to admonish someone. When she sees us, her face softens, her mouth spreads into a smile.

"It's the girls!" she says. I remember her voice. I remember what she whispered to me the night I found him.

"My eyes still work, Sylvia," Ernesto says as he pushes himself up from his easy chair. Other ghosts—aunts, uncles, cousins—emerge from different corners of the house. Five Chihuahuas yip at our ankles.

"Is everything all right?"

"What girls?"

"Hector! No barking!"

I haven't been around this many people in years. I haven't been in a room with four walls in forever. My head spins from the different voices, and I feel trapped, caged. The girls, overwhelmed, hide behind my legs; their little hands dig into my thigh and tug on my shirt. The woman named Sylvia sees this.

"Out! Everyone out!" As though someone has snapped their fingers, the group disappears. *"I'm Sylvia,"* she says. Her eyes tell me she's remembering something, though I have no idea what it could be. She smiles and tries to see around me to the girls, bending down to their level. *"I used to watch you while you lived here,"* she says to them. *"I remember you liked the big tree swing out in the back. Do you remember the tree swing?"*

Daisy's head emerges first, nodding. Then, slowly, Jo peers around from behind my legs.

"Come," Sylvia says. *"I'll show you and your mom the swing."* We follow her to the kitchen in back.

The only living person left in the house stands at the stove, a black spatula in his hand. He's wearing overalls better suited for a child. Butter cackles around the edges of a fried egg on a pan. He pauses, screwing his caterpillar eyebrows. Tufts of white hair sprout over each ear. While he scans the kitchen, Sylvia inspects the pan. *"Breakfast for dinner now,"* she says, glancing at the clock. She scowls. *"He's let it go too long. Blair, didn't you ever teach your children how to fry an egg properly?"* she calls into the house. Then she leads us outside.

A single swing hangs from an ancient, thick rope tied to an enormous cottonwood next to the barn.

"Go ahead," Sylvia tells the girls, who, once given permission, take off at a run. *"I haven't seen you in a long time,"* she says to me once they're out of earshot. *"How are you all doing?"*

"Fine, I suppose." I don't know what else to say.

"What brings you back?"

When I stare at the ground, she offers an answer. *"He came back, didn't he?"*

"Yes."

"You could have come back before," she says. When I don't answer, she continues. *"I never liked him. From the moment I saw him, I knew something was wrong."*

Lucky you, *I think.*

Sylvia opens her mouth as if to say something. Sylvia opens her mouth as if to say something then changes her mind.

"Thanks for getting the girls outside. They're not used to houses. Or people. You stay as long as you want. I'll make sure the girls can have their old rooms."

"You don't have to do that."

"It's no trouble. Let me go tell Blair and Dorothea," she says, and retreats into the house.

One of the Chihuahuas finds the girls and rolls on the ground between them with his front paws up. Jo rubs his potbelly while he wiggles. Daisy pushes the ends of her hair into her mouth. I go kneel next to them, happily distracted by a happy, fat dog. Even a dead one.

"What's the matter?" I ask Daisy. She does better if you give her feelings a name, like opening a door for her to explain herself. "Are you feeling upset? Scared?"

"Maybe both," Daisy says, now pulling the spit-matted strand from her mouth. The Chihuahua continues to wriggle under Jo's fingers.

I try again. "What are you thinking about?"

"He seems older than the last time," Daisy says, studying her hair.

I know where she's going, but I don't want to lead her there myself.

"Old people die," she says.

I dodge the unstated question. "And sometimes young people die."

I half smile at her.

"She wants to know where he'll go when he dies," Jo says. She has stopped petting the dog, who flips back onto his paws and trots away slowly under the weight of his belly. Daisy stares at the spot on the ground where the dog was, seconds ago.

"He was a bad man, he'll go someplace bad," I say, grasping for an answer.

"How do you know?" Daisy asks.

"I just do," I lie.

Daisy's eyes meet my own. "He'll come to the clearing. He could come every day."

"He won't," I say, but this time, my voice catches. I try to smile. I don't think any of us believes it.

"Come on, Daisy. It's your turn on the swing," Jo says, leading her sister away.

I watch the girls play. Normally, I'd return to the young couple. Andy would get a promotion at work, while Elise stalled out. So she'd start an affair with a coworker. Or, if I was feeling kind, they'd go on vacation to the lake house. Instead, I try to see ahead of myself— the same way I saw him moving through the woods. I search for the detective, closing my eyes and trying to re-create her face in my mind. I don't know how, but I see her, kneeling again, as though I could reach out and touch her. She's thinking about someone else who has passed—but not us.

Because I know the truth: there aren't bad places for bad people because there aren't good places for good people. There's only before and after. And in his after, he will come for us. Of course he will. But this time will be different. This time, I'll be ready.

LAURA

LAURA WOKE AT FOUR IN THE MORNING FOR HER SUR-gery. Today her plastic surgeon would swap her expanders for silicone implants. She had to arrive at five. Rolling over in bed, she checked her car reservation on her phone. Her room was too dark. She hadn't been up this early since her first surgery. Laura told herself that this wouldn't be like the last time. She'd be back hunting for more of Margaret's story by this evening.

She dressed and slipped the overnight bag over her shoulder before heading to the kitchen. There, Kate waited for her at the sink, putting away pots that had been left out to dry. "You didn't need to get up," Laura said, rubbing sleep from her eyes.

"I know. Still." Kate struck the counter's edge with a pot, sending a hollow metal clang echoing through the dark kitchen. They both stood frozen, waiting, listening to see if the twins would wake up, but no one stirred.

Laura knew that any other morning, the first thing Kate would do was make herself a cup of coffee. But her sister was too conscientious to drink or eat in front of her. Laura had made sure not to swallow any water when she brushed her teeth. She wished she had the courage to ask why the fasting was necessary. It wasn't as though gunshot victims had to wait to finish digesting a large lunch before heading into surgery.

"Are you sure I can't drive you?"

"I have a car coming. It's fine."

"You sure? Doug's home. He doesn't leave until four."

"It's okay."

"Are you—"

"I'll be fine."

✻

WHEN SHE WOKE AFTER the surgery, the two spots where the ports had been attached to her ribs were sore, the stitches having been removed. Aside from those spots, it wasn't nearly as bad as her first surgery. They watched her for a few hours, gave her instructions about the bandages, and sent her home. Mostly, she was a little tired, a little sore. Kate checked on her, bringing her water and reminding her to take Motrin. Laura heard her say goodbye to Doug downstairs. He had a ten-day workweek coming up. She wondered where they stood on the argument about whether Kate would return to the classroom. By the evening, she had come through the worst of it and sat in bed, searching Ancestry lists. She planned to spend the following day in bed, having taken it off from work. Thinking of all the work she could get done on the Doe case, Laura allowed herself to smile.

✻

THE NEXT MORNING, LAURA woke up not feeling right. For a moment, she thought it was the chemo. But she hadn't been on chemo—not for months. Her symptoms: she was sluggish, achy, light-headed. She went back to bed, only to wake up a few hours later violently shaking with chills. She knew this feeling. When they switched her chemo to the hard drugs, she had gotten neutropenic. Chemo took out people's white blood cells.

They pushed drugs to prevent your counts from going so low, but it was a delicate balance. They should come up after a few days, buying a person's body the time it needed to recover. Neutropenia, however, was when a person's white blood cell count didn't course-correct and instead got worse. People who were neutropenic had, essentially, no immune system. No white blood cells at all.

Laura knew she wasn't neutropenic now—it didn't make sense—but it was the same feeling, the same terror: the knowledge that she could not take care of herself. She needed help. It was a simple fact. As simple as knowing her name. She would die if she stayed in this bed.

She pulled herself onto the floor, wrapping her comforter around her, and crawled to the door.

"Kate?" she called.

As she waited for a response, her teeth started to chatter against each other. Her arms spasmed while trying to hold the comforter around her chest. Every part of her body hurt. She touched her forehead.

"Kate?" she tried again. She must be at the grocery store. *I need help*, Laura thought. Crawling back into her bedroom, she pulled her phone off the nightstand by the charging cord. It hit the floor, and she pulled it in like a lifeboat. Shaking, she tried to hit Kate's number but kept pressing the wrong buttons involuntarily, her body working against itself. She swore, then got it right, holding the phone to her head. Kate answered on the second ring.

"I need you to come home."

Once she knew Kate was on her way, Laura ran through what else she was supposed to do. The instructions were on a paper somewhere. If she had a temperature over—what was it?

Forcing herself up from the floor, but keeping the comforter wrapped around her, she fought her way to the bathroom.

She had to pause to sit down twice. She held the thermometer against her head until it beeped: 102.5. Fuck. *Fuck*. She tried a second time: 102.7. The confirmation that something was wrong made it worse. She immediately felt sicker.

When Kate got home, she found Laura in the bathroom, balled up on the tiled floor, shaking under her comforter, thermometer in hand.

LAURA'S FIRST TRIP TO the emergency department, during her neutropenia episode, had left her resolved not to make a second. They had asked her stupid questions, like if the cancer had spread to her brain, and did she know her stage. During that visit, she remembered, she had returned from the bathroom, dragging her IV line and stand with her, when a young nurse with curly red hair had added another bag to her IV. The nurse hadn't worn gloves when she unscrewed the cap of the access port to her IV. She hadn't swabbed the port with an alcohol wipe first, the same line Laura had dragged through the hall to a public bathroom. Laura had wanted to say something, but it was over before she could find the words. They weren't oncology people; they seemed marginally competent.

This time, Dr. Fusaro had her come straight to his office in the hospital instead of the emergency department.

As the same two nurses who had walked her through the steps of reconstruction took her vitals, Laura watched them struggle to operate the blood pressure cuff correctly. She wondered when they had practiced real medicine; they were adept at talking through the emotional loss of one's breasts, but it looked like they hadn't drawn blood in years. They had none of the capable swiftness her regular nurses had with needles and gloves and rubbing alcohol. They stepped into the hallway briefly, returning a few minutes later.

"We are going to admit you. It looks like you are in sepsis. We're waiting on a bed."

The next time they left, Laura pulled out her phone. She knew sepsis was bad. It was a word they used on *Grey's Anatomy* before a favorite new quirky patient with an unrequited love died on the way to surgery. She knew she shouldn't—she Googled it anyway.

The Mayo Clinic confirmed. "Sepsis is a potentially life-threatening condition caused by the body's response to an infection. The body normally releases chemicals into the bloodstream to fight an infection. Sepsis occurs when the body's response to these chemicals is out of balance, triggering changes that can damage multiple organ systems. Symptoms include high fever, high heart rate, fast breathing, and in more severe cases, low blood pressure." She knew she shouldn't scroll further, but she did anyway. "Mortality rate between 20 and 40 percent." Forty was a lot. Forty was nearly fifty.

Laura had all those symptoms. Kate told her not to worry, then went quiet. Normally Kate couldn't stop talking, becoming fast friends with all Laura's nurses. But now, Kate's silence hammered the room. Laura tried to sleep. The muffled footsteps and voices outside the door were the only sounds making their way into the room, interrupted every twenty minutes or so when the door opened and nurses came in to check on her. Laura and Kate stayed in the exam room for what seemed like hours. Laura stared at the painting of the cypress trees on the wall, thinking of the last time she sat on this table.

I am not here, she thought. *This isn't happening to me.*

Dr. Fusaro entered sometime later, apologizing for the wait. He also had an expression Laura couldn't place.

"They're getting your room ready now. There wasn't a bed for you. I had to email the hospital CEO." Laura couldn't tell why Dr. Fusaro had revealed this detail to her.

Laura ran to the bathroom, hoping she would make it in time. When she emerged, Dr. Fusaro said to her, "That should be tested." He paused, adjusting his glasses.

"Unfortunately, I am leaving for a conference in London tomorrow morning," he continued. "My colleague, Dr. Welsh, will take care of you. You'll be in good hands."

✳

AFTER A BRIEF STINT in the Smilow wing, Laura was transferred to the surgical intensive care unit—SICU. An acronym whose pronunciation did not inspire confidence. Upon being wheeled in, Laura realized: this room did not have a bathroom. She had never been in a hospital room without its own bathroom, and immediately, she knew exactly what it meant.

"There's no bathroom," Laura said to the orderly and nurse who brought her in, as though it were an accusation.

"There's a bedpan."

"I can't use that." There were certain lines Laura was unwilling to cross. A bedpan was one of them.

"We can bring in a chair."

The orderly wheeled her up alongside a new bed. He and the nurse moved to help her make the transfer.

"I can do it myself," she said. Another line.

"You sure?"

"Yes." She glanced at the IV in her right arm, the other IV in her left arm, and doubted herself. The nurse followed her gaze and went to the IV stand, holding up the thin plastic tubing over her forearm, allowing Laura to switch beds without getting tangled.

Once they got Laura in bed, Kate left to feed the twins. They had spent the day with a neighbor. Laura was relieved when her sister left. Now she didn't have to worry about shielding Kate from how sick she really was.

After a shift change, a new nurse came in to introduce herself. Laura couldn't keep track of how many nurses she had seen since she was admitted. The nurse put in another IV line, "Just in case." Then she strapped cuffs the length of Laura's shins on either leg, "To prevent blood clots." Then she strapped a blood pressure cuff to her arm, no explanation needed. The cuffs on her legs squeezed her legs up and down—a small, calf-specific massage chair. The blood pressure cuff went off on a timer every half hour. Laura couldn't roll over, couldn't move her arms without pulling off one of her IVs, couldn't adjust her legs. With her body tethered to her bed, she was caged.

"I found you!" The woman who entered the room introduced herself as Dr. Welsh. Delicately framed, even under her boxy white doctor's coat, the substitute plastic surgeon fluttered her long, slender fingers as she spoke.

"Took me a while. I haven't been to this part of the hospital before," she said. After examining the surgical site, Dr. Welsh declared the implants "looked excellent." It seemed Laura was supposed to take comfort in this statement.

A general surgeon attending came in next to examine her with residents trailing behind. Then the SICU attending introduced himself. Dr. Agarwal-Ray, unkempt and with a five o'clock shadow to match, was the first doctor Laura had met who didn't look like he ran five miles a day. His appearance didn't inspire confidence. Neither did the sheer number of doctors who were taking care of Laura, as counterintuitive as it seemed. With three doctors rounding on her and the SICU nurses coming in and out, Laura had the impression none of them knew exactly what was causing her infection. That she had one wasn't in dispute. The nameless general surgeon seemed to think the infection came from the implants themselves. The rumpled SICU attending agreed—"I saw this same thing during my residency." Dr. Welsh, however, did not.

That none of these doctors had been her actual surgeon or doctor raised alarms. As did the actual alarms in her room. Like clockwork, every three hours, Laura's fever would spike; she'd be uncontrollably cold, begging for blankets and shaking violently. She could feel it coming on, the subtle rumbling of a train station floor. Six nurses surrounded her, and as she peered into each one's face, she realized—they were scared. Laura blurted out orders in between her clattering teeth.

First: "Blankets."

Then: "Hot."

Then: "Ice pack."

She was like a wild animal. The monitor beside her flashed. She glanced at it. Her heart rate was in the 180s, her blood pressure in the 60s. There were other numbers she couldn't place. She couldn't distinguish the difference between her own body shaking and the screen screaming. With all the wires, they were one. She was on fire.

Then, her last command, more a plea than an order: "Can't breathe."

Laura couldn't get air in, her heart was racing so fast. She might as well have been sprinting in place. Her arms thrashed; her legs pulled against the cuffs. And her teeth kept smashing. The nurses moved around her bed in a blur. The SICU attending stepped to Laura's side.

"No, I'll do it," he said to the nurse, who moved out of the way as though on command. Then he said to Laura: "We are going to put in an A-line. *A* for artery. It will get medicine to your heart more quickly. And it will continuously monitor your blood pressure, so we can take your cuff off."

He studied her arm through his smudged glasses. "But if I miss, your arterial blood will shoot up to the ceiling—like a fountain."

Laura didn't know why the doctor told her this as he held the pencil-thick needle over her forearm. She pictured her blood blanketing the ceiling. Laura studied his face. He was nervous. The doctor was nervous.

"You can do this," she said with wild fever eyes. She willed him not to miss.

He got the needle in, took a breath of relief, and connected another bag of medicine to her new line. She had lost count of how many times she had been pierced to make a new IV.

But she still couldn't control her breathing. She couldn't distinguish between the real physical symptoms wrecking her body, her organs, her already chemo-weakened heart, and the knowledge that her doctors did not know what was wrong with her. They did not know what was making her sick. They could not make her better.

Surrounded by nurses, Laura felt more alone than she had in the weeks spent by herself in bed during chemo. She couldn't focus on any one face. They all merged into one. She could die, and there wasn't a single thing she could do about it. Her own death slid into bed next to her. As simple as swimming out in the ocean, fifty yards away from shore in a strong undertow, looking back at the beach where everyone seemed so small and far away. The waterline circled her face. She could let herself go under. She could stop fighting. It would be easy.

She pinched her eyes closed, then blinked, scanning the room.

You are not here, she told herself.

While her body failed her, her mind had to focus. She had to separate the two. She put her heaving chest in a box. Put her shaking arms there too. Her chattering teeth went in after. She closed it, locked it. She couldn't let her body pull her under. She could do this. They needed more time. *Focus.*

Laura picked a spot on the wall. There was a white dry-erase board that no one seemed to use. A spot for her nurse's name, today's date, which, left blank, looked ominous. A spectrum of faces from happy to sad to help her gauge how she was feeling. There was no face for this.

Below the faces was a graphic of a fork and spoon crossed over one another. Probably for today's lunch special. Laura picked the fork and the spoon. She tried not to look at the monitor behind her. The numbers were so far from normal she could no longer recognize which ones were which. As her body lay strapped, racing, sinking, Laura focused all her attention on the fork and spoon.

The rest of the room disappeared as she fixed on that spot.

You are not here, she told herself.

You can do this.

Breathe.

And she started, slowly. Counting to two up, two down. It seemed impossible, but she tried anyway. She forced herself to pause at the top of a breath and forced the air out on the way down. She fought for each inhale. When counting to two was a little easier, she went up to three. Then four. Gradually, she could feel the tightness in her chest subsiding. She took it out of its box. After a few minutes, she could take regular breaths. She allowed herself to feel her arms again. She came back into her body. The small pinpoint holding all her focus relaxed, and the room came back into view. For the first time in over an hour, the nurses' faces had softened. The attending took a moment to push his glasses back up his nose. The monitors beeped a regular rhythm.

"It's okay," she told them.

❈

THAT EVENING, HER NIGHT nurse explained the crux of the argument the attendings had been conducting outside her room, out of earshot. If the implants were causing the infection and they were removed, she would remain flat for the rest of her life.

They wouldn't be able to put new implants in right away: the site would need time to heal, and during that time, the skin would tighten and couldn't be stretched again. But the plastic surgeon was convinced it wasn't the implants. The surgical site showed no signs of infection and appeared perfectly healthy.

Through her exhaustion, in the dark as the nurse rolled her over to wipe her body down and change her sweat-soaked gown, Laura told her: "If I spike again, I don't think I'll come through it. Tell them I don't care. They can take the implants out. I don't care anymore."

⁂

THE NEXT MORNING, THE hospital came to life again. Three rounds of nurses and interns from three surgical departments came to check on her. Surgery to remove the implants was scheduled.

Another shift change brought in another new nurse, who walked into her room, turned around, and walked back out. She didn't need a test to know. The sickly sweet scent of her diarrhea was all the nurse needed to diagnose Laura. *C. diff*: *Clostridioides difficile.* The new nurse told the attending that she was sure, and he ordered the drugs before the labs came back to confirm. Once they kicked in, the fever eased. Surgery was canceled.

After forty-eight hours in the SICU, her numbers started to stabilize.

After forty-eight hours, a nurse starting her shift had found what three attendings from three separate departments had missed: the most common hospital-stay-related infection.

It didn't take Laura long to figure out what had happened, though she doubted anyone would admit to the mistake. Either Dr. Fusaro had never put in the order to send her stool sample to the lab, or a nurse had never followed the order. A glitch. An error. Laura wondered if the same chain reaction would have transpired if she had gone to the emergency department in the first place.

Until the smallest of things: a new nurse. That was all it took. Laura never found out her name. Never put a face to the one who diagnosed her. She would have liked to thank her. But she was too angry now. Her life had been saved, not by science but by chance. By a shift change. What would have happened if that nurse hadn't walked into her room that morning?

Later, when Laura recounted the story to a different nurse at a different hospital, when her hair was long and her appointments came every six months instead of every week, the woman said, "See there? That was your guardian angel."

Fury colored Laura's face.

"I don't believe in angels."

AFTER SHE RETURNED FROM the hospital, Laura stood in the kitchen to get a glass of water. She was thirsty. She had realized up in her bedroom, when her throat was scratchy, that she could get a glass of water herself—she didn't have to page a nurse, didn't have to ask someone to fill her cup for her. Laura stood in front of the kitchen cabinet, about to retrieve a glass, her fingers hovering over the brushed nickel knob, when she stopped midair, paralyzed.

I get to get water.

The little silver knob seemed, suddenly, profound.

On the way back to her room, the twins were wrestling in the hall when they were supposed to be packing their book bags. Their laughter filled the house. From the kitchen doorway, the sight of her niece's cheek, round with the last of her baby fat, stunned Laura. She was beautiful. Laura ran to her room before the twins could see her crying.

She opened her laptop and booked a ticket to Albuquerque.

�֍

THE NEXT DAY, LAURA had to pick up her prescription to finish her course of antibiotics. She hadn't left the house since she'd
come back from the hospital. Standing in line, she considered the
people around her. Did they get it? She studied the pharmacist.
Did he? She wanted to tell them, *You get to be alive today.* She knew
there were two types of people: people who knew they got to be
alive and people who expected it. Who took for granted that their
hearts beat regularly, their lungs filled with air, that their bodies
would keep doing what they were meant to do, all on their own.

The euphoria was exhausting, physically and mentally, but
she knew it would pass over time. She reminded herself to
remember this moment for the future, when she was bored,
annoyed, frustrated.

You get to be alive.

Until you don't.

✖

SHE COULDN'T GET COMFORTABLE in the airplane seat, not
with the wig. Every time Laura put her head back, the inner
netting shifted, pushing bangs into her eyes. She had enough
hair that she didn't need to wear it anymore. The man next to
her had fallen asleep, and the people across the aisle seemed
safely ensconced in earbuds and screens. Laura had noted two
men wearing honest-to-God cowboy hats on her flight. They
disappeared, probably to the men's laps, once the plane departed.
Laura ran her fingers along her neck, scratching.

Fuck it.

She pulled the wig off and folded it under her leg, running
her hands through her short hair to unflatten the little she had.

The flight attendant came by with a white trash bag.

"Trash?" She wore a standard-issue flight attendant smile.
The man in the window seat leaned over Laura. He didn't open

his eyes to drop his balled-up napkin and cup into the bag—frequent-flier somnambulism.

Laura pulled the wig out from under her leg and threw it in the bag, fast. The attendant's face froze as she fought to control her reaction. Her neatly lined eyes glanced at Laura, down into the bag, and back at Laura.

"Have a good day," the attendant said, smiling and moving on to the next row.

Laura panicked, doubting herself. She turned to see an untouched cup of cranberry juice go in. She should go get it back, pull it out, dripping in discarded liquids. What if she had to start up chemo again? She had let herself forget the possibilities; it was a mistake. She was about to get up when the seat belt light dinged overhead.

Laura leaned into her seat back and told herself to breathe.

After the plane landed and taxied to the gate, Laura stood, awkwardly half crouching under the baggage rack, waiting for her turn. As she pulled her carry-on down, a hand cupped her shoulder. She turned to see an older woman with short gray hair. She smiled warmly at Laura.

"Good for you."

"Thanks," Laura said. Any other gathering of words failed her. But as she rolled her bag out the hall and into the airport's stale air, past overpriced bags of nuts and rows of paperbacks, she smiled to herself. She passed a jewelry stand called Turquoise Dreams, another shop offering all Native-made gifts. The floors were smoothed brick, and the wheels of her bag clicked behind her. Above her, a sign read *Welcome to Albuquerque*. Over the airport speakers, a woman's recorded voice offered an addendum: "Welcome to New Mexico, the Land of Enchantment."

Laura had given herself a week to devote to finding Jane Doe. A week, starting now.

When she stepped out onto the curb and into the sun, the dry heat rolled over her skin. There wasn't a trace of humidity in the air. If she were in Connecticut, she'd be cold. She wasn't supposed to expose her skin to sunlight during chemo, but now, she closed her eyes, tilting her head back, letting the sunlight sink in. She pulled off her sweatshirt.

I'm here, she thought, nearly giddy. *I get to be here.*

JEAN

THERE WAS NO DISTINGUISHING THE ROAD FROM THE lots on Mesa Drive except for the chain-link fences separating one plot from the next. A row of fifth-wheels and single-wides lined the street. Some of the nicer trailers had makeshift porches in the form of sheet metal attached to the roof and propped up with sticks.

Jean parked outside George Wayne Shaw's trailer. Under one small square of corrugated shade sat two nylon lawn chairs, each with a busted strip of webbing hanging underneath the seat, whipping in the wind. She had spent more time than she cared to admit reading the Ironside personnel files and cross-referencing her list to police databases. George Wayne Shaw was one name fitting her criteria: alive and local.

According to Ms. Shirley's records, employment at the mine fit one of two patterns. Some people worked regularly, collecting a biweekly paycheck for years at a time. Plenty more came and went, itinerant and inconsistent. Reed's father, Tom Yates, had fit into this second category, collecting a paycheck or two along the way under the name John Thomas Yates. Gerry Tellefsen, the son and heir apparent, was on the payroll from sixteen to retirement. Jean hadn't been able to find any Curtis matching the name from the detective's notes.

Jean had also looked up Detective Carl Pendergast. The investigator hadn't been a rookie after all, as Jean had assumed. He had started his career on patrol in the neighboring county to the north, Socorro, working there for six years before transferring to Sierra County. He should have known better than to scratch a note to himself in the margin and not follow up properly.

A dog started barking from inside the trailer as Jean got out of the car. She waited a minute for someone to quell the barking and, when no one did, crossed the yard. Streets like this were made for people who came out to the desert to die, or those who, once here, realized they had no other choice in the matter.

Jean let herself into the screeching chain-link gate, stepped past a crumpled beer can, and knocked hard on the door.

"Who is it?" came a voice from inside, unfazed by the dog.

"Detective Sergeant Martinez with the Sierra County Sheriff's Department. I'm looking for George Wayne Shaw."

"Whatever it is, I didn't do it." Then, words for the dog. Maybe the promise of a treat.

"No sir. Have a couple questions about Ironside Mining." Jean couldn't be sure how much he heard. "Could you come outside for a few minutes to talk?"

Someone moved the dog, paws clawing the floor. After a minute, a man emerged. A stained white tank top hung over a lean frame with a back stooped like a question mark; loose-fitting jeans were held up by a taut leather belt.

"What you say your name was?"

"Detective Sergeant Martinez." She showed him her badge. "I work cold cases for the county."

"Hmm," was all she got in response. Before she could say anything else, he stepped out, closing the door behind him. The man walked over to the two lawn chairs, brushing them off, though Jean was sure any dust was baked in by now. Sitting down in the more damaged of the two, he motioned for Jean to take the other chair. He stretched his long legs out in front of him.

"You're George Wayne Shaw? You worked at Ironside from 1980 to 1997?"

"That's me. Or what's left of me. You said cold cases. I'm assuming you're here because of those people they found."

"Yes sir, I am. I had a few questions about what you remember."

"You been over there lately? Ms. Shirley still alive?"

"Yes sir, she is."

"That cunt," he said, shaking his head, though he said it more as a compliment. "Excuse my French. She was a ballbuster."

Jean let it lie. "What sort of work did you do at Ironside?"

"I was an engineer. Know it don't look like it. Ex-wife took everything," he said, gesturing to his trailer. "I maintained the machines over there, kept everything running."

"That sounds like an important job."

"You could say that."

"The remains were found in two steel fifty-five-gallon drums. Were barrels like that ever used at Ironside?"

"A few. For storing different coolants."

"You remember anyone talking about barrels that went missing? Inventory being off?"

"No, nothing like that. It wouldn't be hard to take a couple without people noticing them, though."

"After they were found—or before they were found—you remember anyone talking about a wife or girlfriend they had a problem with?"

"Plenty of people, sure. You can't throw a dead cat without hitting someone who's pissed at someone else, and usually that someone else happens to be the person you share a bed with at night. But doing what that person did to those poor people?"

George Wayne Shaw shook his head. "I don't know anyone capable of that. No—there were a few guys who said they would have liked to find the sumbitch who did it. That's what people were talking about. Lots of guys had young families then. Don't know where they all are now. Probably half of them are dead or about to be."

"Any one of the guys seem to talk about it more than others?"

"Not that I can remember, but boy, the bosses sure didn't like all that activity. Can't blame them. You want something to drink?" Then he got up from his seat, pushing himself up with his rail-thin arms. He had a gray hue to his exposed arms, like his heart had given up trying to lug blood that far. He went inside and came back a minute later with two cold beers, sweating in the morning heat. Jean normally didn't drink before noon, definitely didn't drink on the job, and absolutely didn't drink when interviewing someone, but decided demurring would do more harm than good. It was hot, she figured. The alcohol would metabolize fast.

"Thank you. Just don't tell my supervisor."

"Your secret's safe with me." George Wayne Shaw took a long drink and considered his response. "There were a few guys who kept quiet during the investigation. More than one, I think, maybe put their hands on their own women. Those bodies made them wonder if they had it in them to do the same. Detectives came by to talk to us individually. Boss said it was interrupting our work. Think they made a little stink about it."

"Your boss was Gerry Tellefsen?"

"Gerry and his old man."

"Bjorn Tellefsen was still around?" Bjorn hadn't been collecting paychecks in the '80s. He retired in 1970 at the same time that Gerry, his son, got a title change and a salary bump.

"That devil," he said, shaking his head. "Haven't thought about Bjorn Tellefsen in years. Had bright white hair. He was a big guy, even in his eighties. Giant of a man. Like he was born to move mountains. Even when he handed the keys to his son, he ran things, more or less."

"Did they ever seem to disagree about anything?"

George Wayne Shaw's eyes lit up a little. "You know, before I started working there, Bjorn had sold off a chunk of land. Mr. Tellefsen—Bjorn—said he didn't want to pay taxes on something he wasn't using. He went off about wasting resources or something like it. But it also put some fellas in a bind. No one told them it was off-limits anymore. They had hauled out some machinery to this area. A backhoe that needed repairing, except I had to fabricate the part. They were trying to move it out of the way until I could get to it. Well, Bjorn—he about blew up. Saw it out there and asked who gave them permission to use the area. No one knew we weren't supposed to."

Jean took notes as he spoke. He paused to take another drink. "What about Bjorn's daughter, Nancy—did you ever see her around?"

"Nancy? God no. Women weren't welcome. Ms. Shirley didn't count because Ms. Shirley would cut your balls off before you got two words in sideways. You know, with most men, having a daughter softens them up. But not Bjorn. The way he talked to his daughter—the one time I saw her anyway—she had the brightest golden hair I'd ever seen—I couldn't believe a father could be that mean to his own blood. Don't remember what it was about, something small. Now if his son screwed up, that was a different story. His shit didn't stink. But his daughter—when she took off, I didn't blame her. Course, how a woman leaves her children is something I'll never wrap my head around."

"You ever meet Nancy's husband—Tom Yates?"

"You mean John? He was around, worked part-time."

"I had a question about that. His son said his name was Tom Yates, but all his pay stubs were for John Thomas Yates. You know why he went by his middle name sometimes?"

"I only knew him as John. Never heard anyone call him by his middle name. Maybe it was a family nickname."

Jean chewed on this, unsure. "What was he like?"

"Real friendly. Super nice guy. Smart as heck too. Helped me with a generator I couldn't figure out. He'd go out of his way to be helpful. But gosh, you get him started on a subject—you couldn't get him to shut up. Set a timer for twenty minutes, you were going to be there for a while."

That didn't sound like the same person Ms. Shirley had described. To Ms. Shirley, he had been quiet, reserved. "Is that right?"

"That's how I remember him."

"I have some old notes from the first investigator, Detective Pendergast," she said. "He mentioned someone named Curtis. You know anyone going by that name?"

George Wayne Shaw thought for a moment, finishing his beer. "Nope."

"Were you still around when Bjorn's grandson, Reed, took over?"

"No, that was after my time. Though I did hear this one story."

"What's that?"

"Something I heard from this one buddy of mine. I guess Reed lost some money in a bet. Downright blew up. Took a bat to someone's truck. But who knows, could be just people talking."

That also didn't match the image Jean had of the young man. "All right," she said, finishing her own beer. Leaving a half-finished one would be impolite. It only took two gulps. "That's all I have. You think of anything else—I'll leave you my card."

"I better remember fast then," he said.

"Sir?"

"Diabetes. Type 1."

"I'm sorry to hear that," she said. She wasn't sure why he was telling her.

"I wasn't going to die in a hospital. That's for damn sure."

"I don't blame you."

"My daughter comes by when she gets off work. I'll be all right."

Jean couldn't tell if he was talking to her or to himself. The sun had risen higher in the sky and sat directly above them.

"It's good to have good people around you," she said.

"She is good people. It's a shame she can't take my dog though. They aren't allowed in her building. You know anyone who could take a good dog?"

WHEN JEAN RETURNED TO the station, she was surprised to find her office door already open. Maybe she'd catch the person moving her files around. Ready to sling a refrain of invectives, Jean stopped herself when she saw a young woman with startlingly short hair, waiting. No one out front had told her there was someone here to see her. A stack of papers and folders sat in front of her on the desk. Jean watched as she picked her cuticles, one of her knees bouncing in place, and wondered, for the briefest of moments, if this woman was the ghost haunting her office. Feeling foolish, Jean went in.

"I'm Detective Sergeant Jean Martinez," she said, putting out her hand. "I'm sorry, did we have an appointment? No one told me you were waiting."

The young woman stood—her eyes as large as cue balls. From the front, her hair appeared shorter. Her eyebrows were faint, her skin pale, almost hollow in places. They shook hands. Thin, but solid and firm. Still—for an alive person, she was pretty ghostly.

"No, I don't have an appointment," the woman said. "I'm here about Jane Doe. I think I know who she is."

Sylvia finds me in front of the house where I've been sitting on the cluttered porch, piecing together a plan. The girls play with the fat Chihuahua, who has brought along one of his skinnier friends for belly rubs. The two girls, two dogs, and one stuffed rabbit disappear around the corner, probably heading to the tire swing.

"Dorothea and Blair, two grown women, mad at their mother for kicking them out of their bedrooms. Can you believe that?" she asks. I don't think I'm supposed to answer. "Blair says she's going to Paris."

"Paris, France?"

"Well, certainly not Paris, Texas. Yes, France," Sylvia says, clucking her tongue.

"I'm sorry," I say.

"It's not a problem. I mean, we don't sleep, do we? More of a habit."

I have a question I want to ask Sylvia, but don't want to ask at the same time. I haven't wanted to, but more memories seem to be returning lately. Better to get it over with. "I've been wondering."

"Go on, spit it out," Sylvia says, sitting down next to me.

"When we rented the house from Ernesto, he said he was a widower."

"That's right."

"He was on his way to Colorado, to live with one of his daughters. Where were you? Were you here? The whole time we lived here, all of us, were you here too?"

Sylvia lets out a deep sigh. "I was going to follow Ernesto. It was Dorothea he was going to move in with. I thought I'd go with him. But when I saw you and your daughter, I—" Her voice catches. "Yes, I stayed here."

"So you stayed here, to—what? Haunt us?"

"Did you ever feel haunted?"

I think about this. "No, I suppose not. Not by you, anyway." I pause, studying the dirt and ashamed to meet her eye. "I'm sorry for everything that happened here."

Sylvia's voice changes; she's resolute. "That wasn't your fault. You were doing your best, trying to raise those two girls."

I like her version better than my own. "I should have done more."

"What more would you have done?"

"Known what was going on?" I ask.

"You couldn't—he made sure. If you did, it all would have come down sooner."

I run my hand back and forth across the top of my stomach, a muscle memory triggered by being back in this house, where for the briefest of times, I was happy. "I wish it was only me he—I wish I didn't have to—"

Sylvia puts her hand on my arm. "You tried."

I nod, willing her certainty to sink in. It won't take. "Could I ask a favor?" I say. "Could you watch the girls for me?"

"Sure. You headed somewhere?"

"I want to check on something." I pull my hand from my stomach, smoothing my hair.

Sylvia eyes me, her chin lifting an inch. "Of course, not a problem," she says, relaxing. "After all, what's the worst that can happen?" Her laughter bends her in two. When I don't join in, she offers, "The worst has happened already, don't you think?" Wiping her eyes, she asks, "Swing?" and when I nod, she stands and goes around the corner.

I don't have Jo to guide me, but there is no place I can re-create in my mind more easily than the clearing. I didn't protect them before. I wouldn't make that mistake again.

I pick a spot close to the next ridge, so I can make my way in, slowly. I pinch my eyes closed. Take a deep breath. Then, I disappear. When I open my eyes, piñon surrounds me. The air hums with insects. I move like a hunter, careful and quiet, in the direction of the clearing.

When I'm close, birdcalls stop. The insects, too, have shuttered their wings. An orange tent, big enough for two, sits a few feet away from our flowers. I pause, distracted by a single leaf caught by a spider thread. It's brown and dead and belongs with the other dead things on the forest floor but hangs suspended in midair, turning cartwheels, over and over.

He has strung up a black bag he kept food in farther away from the tent. The small camp stove sits in a space he has cleared of pine needles and brush. He's inside—I can make out his dark figure underneath the orange screen.

The sound of a zipper purring breaks the silence, and he emerges from the tent, standing a few feet in front of me. Then he walks toward me, before pausing. I could have touched his face if I had hands. He looks straight through me. His skin slouches like aged leather, all creases and wrinkles; his eyes have the same dead, sapphire knife to them. He cocks his ear. His jaw grinds methodically on the piece of gum between his teeth.

He's hunting—but not for me.

LAURA

THE NAUSEA THAT COURSED UP THROUGH LAURA'S MID-
dle was scarily similar to anticipatory chemo nausea. On her way
to the police station, Laura reminded herself: *This is, you know,
your civic duty.* Though she couldn't help suspecting that her
sense of civic duty bordered on delusions of grandeur.

Laura tried not to fidget when she had been brought to the
detective's office. The guy at the front desk—who didn't seem to
notice he sat under a very loud, very about-to-explode-at-any-
minute fluorescent light—had brought her back to wait, saying
he didn't know how long Detective Sergeant Martinez would be.
Laura had gotten up to sneak a peek at the pictures on the wall
before planting herself back in the chair. She was in the middle
of running through her dialogue for the seven-hundredth time
when she heard a voice—a woman's voice—behind her.

Laura heard her ask about an appointment and kicked herself. Of course, she should have made an appointment—she
hadn't realized that was something you could do. This wasn't,
you know, the dentist.

"No, I don't have an appointment," Laura said. "I'm here
about Jane Doe. I think I know who she is."

"Please, sit down," the detective said, moving around her desk and sitting opposite Laura. Okay, positive. She hadn't kicked her out. "What brings you in?"

"My name is Laura MacDonald. I'm a librarian, I live in New Haven." *You just lied to a police detective.* "Used to live in New Haven." *Is New Haven large enough that people know where it is?* "I live in Connecticut with my sister." *Get a grip, Laura.* "I work a lot with people who are looking for people. I found this dinosaur-climate doctor online—"

The swelling nausea now firmly gripped her esophagus.

"I'm sorry, can I start again?" Laura asked.

"Of course."

Laura couldn't be sure if the detective was humoring her. She took a breath. *You know this,* she reminded herself.

"For the past few months, I have been working off of the results of a University of Florida lab report that details the isotopic markers present in Jane Doe's DNA." Laura unfolded the twins' map, which she had color-coded by person, time, and area, along with her copy of the lab report.

"According to Drs. Schussler and Singh, the isotopes present in Jane Doe's hair and tooth enamel indicate that she was born in Southern California, moved to the Northeast as a child, returned to Southern California around the time of her daughter's birth, and then moved inland to the Southwest. The eldest daughter was born in Southern California before they moved to the Southwest, and the younger girl lived along the Gulf of Mexico before moving to the Southwest. I used these details to sort through entries posted on an Ancestry message board, using the possible years of her disappearance and death as a secondary filter."

"Where did you find this lab report?" the detective asked, frowning.

"The internet?"

When the detective didn't follow up, Laura kept going.

"Two years ago, a woman named Cynthia Walsh posted that she was looking for her missing half sister, Margaret Ann Washington. They shared the same father but had different mothers. Margaret was one of five daughters from her father's first marriage. She was born in Los Angeles County, California. When her parents divorced, the two oldest girls, Catherine and Margaret, stayed in Connecticut with their father, while the three youngest moved back to California with their mother. The father remarried and had two more daughters, Cynthia and Patricia. This new family stayed in Groton, Connecticut, where their father worked at a naval station. Base. Station or base, I don't know the difference."

Nope, you got this, keep going.

She laid out the copies of Margaret's birth certificate and school records.

"Margaret attended Regis College for a semester but dropped out in the middle of her freshman year when she became pregnant. She was then sent to California to live with her mother to have the baby, Daisy Marie Flaherty, who was born at Mission Hospital in Los Angeles County." Laura pulled out Daisy's records. "The father was Francis Flaherty of Boston. According to Cynthia, Francis had no contact with Margaret once she left for California, though he did try to phone her on numerous occasions. Margaret and Daisy lived with Margaret's mother and her three younger sisters—her younger full sisters—until the following Christmas. Then there was a family Christmas party."

Laura placed the photo of Margaret, Daisy, and the unidentified man in front of the detective.

"Her father and stepmother came out to California to meet the new baby. Margaret had invited a new boyfriend. Cynthia remembered some sort of fight between Margaret and her father, probably over the new boyfriend. Then Margaret announced she and the boyfriend were moving to Canada, and Margaret was never heard from again."

For the first time, the detective spoke. "Canada is not New Mexico."

"True."

"But people don't always tell the truth."

"That's what I think too. There are no records in New Mexico's Bureau of Vital Records for a Margaret Ann Washington. But in 1960, a Margaret Washington Crown received a driver's license from the state of New Mexico. It's not much, but women often take their maiden name as a new middle name when they marry."

"Are there any marriage records for a Margaret Ann Washington?"

"Not that I found." Laura noticed the detective's phone kept lighting up on her desk. "Daisy Marie Flaherty was baptized at All Saints Catholic Church in Long Beach. If she was baptized, then it's possible she received First Communion, and based on her geographic markers, that would have taken place here. I came here to start checking church records. It's possible there may also be a marriage that was never recorded by the state."

Laura waited for Detective Martinez to praise her investigative skills. She had it—this was Jane Doe. Laura knew it. The problem was Laura had no idea what the other woman was thinking. The entire time she spoke, aside from her reaction to the isotope report, her face had remained neutral.

"You clearly put in a lot of time on this," the detective said, glancing at her phone. Her face didn't move a muscle. "Do you mind if I keep these copies?"

Laura wasn't sure what her own face was doing, but she managed to nod.

"Thanks. I'll get your contact information from up front when you signed in. It was Laura, right?"

"Yes."

"Laura—thank you for coming in."

Before Laura understood what was happening, the detective was leading her out the front door, back to the lot and her rental car. She sat in the white Sonata, both hands on the steering wheel, and for the first time in months, felt immeasurably stupid. What had she expected? A medal? Tears welled in her eyes. She typed the address to her motel on her phone. Time to drink herself stupid in a roadside motel with a river view. That was about all she deserved, apparently.

Laura headed to the River's Edge Motel in Truth or Consequences. The main lobby doubled as a gift shop filled with shelves of crystals, bottled mineral spring water, and health tonics. The motel, like every other one in the area, boasted hot springs online. Though when she'd scrolled through online pictures, most "hot springs" seemed to be fenced-off claustrophobic Jacuzzis. For an extra forty dollars a night, Laura had found a place on the Rio Grande with an outdoor pool that ran up to the river's edge—hence the name. She would have paid an extra hundred.

The hotel room key was an actual metal key with the number 58 etched on its head. Once inside, she discovered that the beige travertine from the hall continued into the bedroom. Tile in bedrooms felt cold. She hauled her suitcase onto the bed and found her bathing suit and a cotton dress. Pulling her shirt over her head, she paused at her flimsy cotton bra. She went to the bathroom, flicking on the light, before pulling this layer off too. Sticky surgical tape remained over each breast, bisecting them straight across the middle. She counted the days on her fingers, figuring it had been more than two weeks since her last surgery. It was safe to take it off. Whether she wanted to was another question.

The thin white tape had curled up at the edges and had been catching on clothes whenever she changed. She pulled a little on one edge, waiting for the feeling of her skin tearing. Laura feared her paper-thin skin or surgical scar would open again if she removed the tape. But slowly, millimeter by millimeter, using the opposite hand to reach under the tape and hold her skin down, Laura pulled off each strip. She hadn't seen herself without any bandages across her chest yet—she had never looked in between the two surgeries. Now, she faced her reflection in the mirror.

What were supposed to be breasts were a poor facsimile. The architecture was wrong. Square what should be round. Flat what should be curved. There was none of the gradual ascending or descending of a natural breast. The last traces of her areolae left two long, slender almonds, stretched impossibly thin, along the middle of the surgical scars. Before, when she had asked Dr. Choudhry if she would be able to have something called a "nipple-sparing surgery," her doctor explained: if the pipes of your house become infected, it only stands to reason, the faucet would be too. Laura had no rebuttal to this metaphor.

Laura took a breath. It wasn't as bad as she thought. But they also weren't real. Nothing about it was. She'd had her breasts for fifteen years, give or take a couple with the confusing boundary of puberty. If her cancer didn't come back—if she survived—she'd live longer without breasts than the years she had with them. Did this make her less of a woman, literally?

She stepped into her bathing suit, carefully pulling it up and over each arm. Even she couldn't tell they were fake under a layer of stretchy nylon. Maybe they would look better after nipple surgery. Dr. Fusaro had already explained how it worked.

He would cut two thin triangle flaps at the center and fold them in around themselves, stitching them in place, to make nipples. Once that healed, she could have areola tattooing done. But after her last surgery, the idea of another surgery, even a minor one, seemed impossible. She didn't know why, but she felt like these fake breasts were all that she deserved. She hadn't died. That should be enough.

Laura remembered the last time she had used her breasts. For the first time in a long time, she thought of Tim.

TIM'S PARENTS LIVED IN Westville, the neighborhood of New Haven reserved for aging hippies and Brooklyn expats. They had raised their children there, sending them to the neighborhood public school where Tim's mother, Milly, worked. Laura preferred to fly from apartment to apartment every six months, but Ted and Milly Blackman-Kent—they had both changed their names to this combined version—had lived in the same arts and crafts bungalow on a tree-lined street for over thirty years. Laura loved Westville for its trees. When she and Tim lived there, she could walk from her apartment all the way across Alston to Edgewood, past the one coffee shop and the elementary school, past the park, all without leaving the shade.

Milly—"'Mildred' is some old lady with eight hundred cats"—taught kindergarten, and Ted ran the local nonprofit theater, as though there were any other kind. Their house on Marvel Road didn't feel like a house at all but an extension of all their interests. It was the difference between a house and a home. West African masks hung in the living room, and copper pots hung above the table they used as a small island in the kitchen. Original oak floors ran throughout, having lost their varnish in the late '90s. Iron-rimmed glass panels on the dining room built-ins were irreligiously covered by strings of Tibetan peace flags.

Laura wanted to be left alone so she could walk around and study each of the travel posters. The only trace of their children was the kids' artwork, which had been framed and lined the stairs up to the second floor. When Laura met Milly and Ted for the first time, she panicked. Now she could never break up with Tim because doing so would mean losing Ted and Milly, and at the moment, Laura couldn't figure out who she loved more: her boyfriend or her boyfriend's parents.

Milly and Ted held an annual Halloween party for, it seemed, the whole neighborhood. Halloween in Westville was something of an event. People from all over New Haven and the towns north descended on the neighborhood with its safe streets and large houses on easy-to-traverse small lots. Most people sat on their porches to distribute candy to the phalanxes of children.

The streets were jammed with cars. Laura could hear music as they passed other young people and older people and that guy from the bodega Laura ran into every time she went out for cereal. Tim's parents' house now had giant spiderwebs covering the porch. It didn't stop there. Halloween decorations spilled over every inch of their house and yard. Cats and ghosts made from cut-up sheets and plastic skeleton bones. Their front porch held a hundred jack-o'-lanterns with rows and rows of orange-carved faces flickering yellow candlelight into the night.

Long foldout tables lined the house. There, a small troop stood grilling in the October chill and replenishing fleets of Italian sausages and turkey hot dogs. People came by and dropped off plastic-covered bowls of pasta and nut-free salad and quiche. The entire one-car garage out in the back had been turned into a dessert bar, and in the yard, Laura counted no fewer than twelve round tables with color-coordinated tablecloths and centerpieces. Someone had set up a small stage in the back. All through the night, the music grew in relation to the dark: an all-neighborhood lineup that started with children's choruses, moved on to well-intentioned teens, and ended with a jam fest of Ted on trumpet, two trombones, two guitars, and one drummer.

Laura wanted more than anything to float through the evening, slightly drunk, feeling the night's magic on her skin. Her only problem was the day before, when she had gotten a phone call from a radiologist. The same radiologist who had biopsied a lump Laura had found two weeks ago in the shower. She hadn't told Tim yet about any of it, but ever since she heard the radiologist say the words "breast cancer" over the phone, it was all Laura could do to keep from screaming the words to every person she passed on the street, at work—at this beautiful party.

When someone handed her a beer, she wanted to say, *Thank you, I have breast cancer.*

When someone remarked that the high school band nerds weren't all that bad, she wanted to say, *I know, I have breast cancer.*

When someone asked if the quiche was good, she wanted to say, *They must have used a ton of cream, and I have breast cancer.* By the end of the night she couldn't hold the words in her mouth any longer.

Laura saw Milly sitting by herself by the side of the stage. It must have been the first time all night she wasn't surrounded by a cluster of friends. Laura took her beer and went over. She hoped this woman whom she had come to regard as a stand-in mother would know the right thing to say to her.

"I need to tell you something," Laura said, sitting down at Milly's side. Milly smiled the unknowing smile of someone who doesn't know you're about to tell them a bad thing. She looked like an idiot. Laura watched her face and braced herself for how it was about to change. "I found out yesterday that I have breast cancer."

Milly's face crumpled like a delicate flower under a hard hose. Then she did the one thing Laura wasn't prepared for: she started to sob. Laura had to pivot from the position she thought she would be in—the one being reassured—to the one doing the reassuring. Once she got Milly put back together again, she pulled out her phone, walked out to the street, and under the dappled orange light of streetlamps, called the person she should have told from the start: Kate. Within fifteen minutes they had come up with a plan of attack. She needed someone to count on for the times she would be sick. Laura couldn't bring herself to tell Tim that night. She needed one last thing from him.

The next morning, she ran her hands across his middle and pulled him over to her. It was the last time she had sex while she still had her breasts. It was the last time she had sex, period. She hid her face in her pillow after, trying to remember each moment, each sensation, because she knew—in their bed, she was attending a funeral. When he asked why she was crying, she had no choice but to tell him. He only said, "I'm sorry." Neutral, as though the dry cleaner had lost her favorite dress. "My cousin had it, and she's fine. You know, I read that there's all sorts of studies showing breast cancer could be linked to birth control pills."

She packed up her things and bought a used Ford Focus with her only savings, and she and Bella moved out by the end of the week. She knew he wouldn't step into the dark with her, not for a moment. It would be a small circle she would let inside. Maybe only Kate, and even then, there would be parts her sister could never understand. Unless it happened to you, no one could.

❉

LAURA REGARDED HER CHEST in the mirror one more time before pulling on a cotton sundress. She adjusted the straps to cover her chemo port, a reminder her cancer could come back. She imagined Tim would have suggested staying flat and covering her chest in tattoos. Maybe a spray of flowers. She knew some women, mostly young, went this route, proudly posting their bare, printed chests-as-canvases online. Laura wanted the illusion of normalcy. So she could fool others and herself—as long as they never got inside. Laura tucked her room key and credit card into the top of her suit and went out to find the bar and pool.

Three tiers of deck housed a wider view of the river. A pergola covered the bar on the highest level, the second held lounge chairs, and the lowest, a large bean-shaped pool of rough-edged natural rock. Patches of tall feathered grass gave the illusion the pool sank directly into the river. On the other side of the Rio Grande, mountain ridges blocked the diaphanous sunset. Everything had a pink hue to it, with ceramic pots punctuating the deck. Laura ordered a diablo margarita from the bar and sat enjoying the cold drink in her hand and the still-warm air on her skin.

She ordered tacos from the bartender and, while she waited, she noticed the couple leaving the pool. This was her chance. Taking her drink, Laura waited until she reached the third deck to slip off her dress and step in. The water was warm and smelled of salt. Laura couldn't remember the last time she had gone swimming. Another thing she hadn't been allowed to do during chemo. She floated in between the mountains and the river and the trembling pink sky. Laura lowered herself in, letting the water lap her chin. Then she slipped her hand underneath her suit, feeling her implants. They were warm, as warm as her body—for the first time. A little wooden sign at the pool's edge urged her to "Whisper Please." Smiling, she approved of the sentiment. Though not in the way they meant.

With her mouth hovering above the water's edge, she complied: "I'm coming, Margaret."

JEAN

THE LIBRARIAN HAD GOOD INFORMATION, BUT JEAN couldn't understand how she had gotten access to lab work that Jean herself never had access to. Was this like the directories, mysteriously relocated to the basement? Was someone interfering with the investigation? She mentally logged a note to ask Paul Henderson—the cold case detective who had taken over the case in the early aughts. She had promised Moreno she'd visit him.

Jean would have to verify everything that Laura had given her before she could determine whether it was worth moving forward. Testing the remains' DNA against the possible half sister wouldn't show anything. They shared a father, not a mother. The only DNA left from Jane Doe was mitochondrial—it showed maternal lineage. But Jean had more pressing problems.

She pulled up to the west side central command division of the El Paso police. She showed her badge at the front desk and waited for Parker's basketball buddy to meet her. A few minutes later, the detective emerged, apologizing for the wait. They didn't have enough to hold the girl. She had been given a court date and a phone call, but Ally declined. Jean asked if they saw if anyone picked her up. She'd left on foot.

"I only just saw her name on our logs. If I had seen it sooner, I would have made sure you all got down here before we let her go," he said, hands in pockets.

"It's all right," Jean said.

She went back out front and scanned the street. Chest-high feathered grass lined the walkway. A Cracker Barrel and a Red Roof Inn completed the intersection. A McDonald's and a couple of gas stations finished the stretch. Sunset Road could have been any street in America—any street lined with palm trees, that is. When Ally didn't turn up in any of these spots, Jean got back in her car and drove under the highway overpass to Walmart.

Right up front, at the Subway, Ally sat sucking down a Mountain Dew with a half-eaten foot-long in front of her. When she saw Jean, she didn't miss a beat, taking another bite of her sandwich. Ally looked okay—Jean had been prepared for worse. Her blond highlights were growing out. She was too skinny. Her black hoodie was zipped all the way up, and a small tattoo of a bird peeked out behind her ear.

"You didn't need to drive all the way down here," Ally said.

"I know," said Jean, sitting across from her. She watched as a woman paid for six subs, stacking them in her cart and unwrapping the first as she began her Walmart sojourn. America, land of plenty.

"Eli sent you?"

"He's worried."

"He doesn't need to be," Ally said, finishing her sandwich.

"You want me to try and get you a bed?"

"You know what the waiting list is like?"

"It's worth a shot."

Ally bunched up her napkin into a ball and shoved it into the long Subway bag. "You didn't need to come down here."

"You said that already."

"Don't you have, like, any real cases you should be working? Any other little girls need rescuing?" She wasn't normally angry. But Jean let it slide. Ally had had a day. Jean counted herself lucky that she had sought out something to eat before finding a fix.

"I'm working cold cases now," Jean said.

Ally's expression softened. "What's that like?"

"It's all right. Actually—I like it. I really like it. But they're going to cut down the position. Budget problems."

"Of course," Ally said.

"Can I drive you back north somewhere?"

Ally peered out the window to the parking lot. "What's the point? This is as good a place as any. There's a country club nearby. Maybe I can get a job there."

They both knew that wasn't going to happen. A man pushing a cart with his forearms sorted his wallet as he made his way to the door. An older woman had stopped in front of him, searching for something in her purse. Jean watched as the man paused next to the woman and asked her a question. She smiled and laughed before pulling out a tangled mess of key chains and keys the size of a small cat.

"You have friends down here?" Jean asked.

"No."

Jean scanned the aisles behind them. "Well—you need anything from here?"

"What do you mean?" Ally asked, finishing her soda.

"Clothes, shampoo, lawn mower."

"Funny."

"It's on me. Come on." Jean pushed her chair back while Ally tossed her trash.

They started in clothing, walking the scattered clusters of flimsy metal racks. Ally pulled out a pair of dark jeans, hopefully to replace the ones she was wearing. Jean held up a sweatshirt that Ally made a gross face at, and Jean smiled, returning it to its shelf. The clothes gave them something to talk about that wasn't their past and wasn't exactly their present either, but a safe in-between. Here, anything was possible. A top could be for a night out with friends, another for a prospective job interview. Ally picked out a few things without trying them on, but Jean wondered if she had fresh needle marks she was trying to hide. They found the section with soaps and shampoo, and Ally picked out a few things there, including some hair dye. She passed on the lawn mower, same with a set of kitchen pots and pans, which for some reason, Jean felt compelled to buy for her against her will, as though the literal weight of a set of stainless steel could anchor her to one spot, one apartment. They went to the front, and Jean paid for her things.

"Thank you," Ally said, twisting the beige plastic bag handles around her fingers.

"Anytime," Jean said.

Ally followed Jean out to her car. Jean texted Parker that she had Ally and texted RJ that she'd be home late before starting the car. The sun had begun to set, casting the cement parking lot in a rose-colored haze.

Ally changed the radio station and rolled down her window. On the southern side of Albuquerque, not far from the airport, Jean pulled up to an apartment complex of squat stucco buildings, waiting in the dark.

"When's your court date?"

"Month from now," Ally said, retrieving the Walmart bags from her feet.

"Text me. I'll drive you down."

"Don't worry about it."

"You sure you're good here?"

"I'll be fine," she said. Jean wondered if she believed it herself. "Thanks for the stuff."

"Take care of yourself."

Ally smiled thinly, closing the door behind her. She disappeared into the space between two buildings. Jean waited to see if the outdoor light would flood the walkway once Ally passed through, but it stayed dark.

✳

JEAN COULD SMELL ONIONS and garlic cooking as soon as she walked in the door. She locked up her service revolver before going through the mail.

"Dinner in twenty," RJ called from the kitchen.

"Thanks for waiting for me," she called back.

Sorting the mail, she was surprised to see a lingerie catalogue mixed in. How had she gotten on *that* mailing list? She hadn't purchased anything little, black, or lacy in years. She didn't have much need for it: a frequent point of tension in their marriage. For a period of about four years when the kids were in high school, she had tried everything she could think of. Which led her to buying an obscene amount of lingerie. Mostly she felt stupid playing dress-up for a man who had either lost interest or failed to notice that she had replaced all of her cotton bikinis with lace thongs.

RJ already had a bottle of white open on the counter. Jean poured herself a glass from the sweaty bottle. She kissed her husband on the cheek.

"Colleen called," he said. "She's coming over tomorrow night."

"I should make lasagna," she said.

"What?"

"Before the baby comes, I should make some lasagna to keep in her freezer."

"You're aware that you've never made a lasagna before in your life?"

"Slightly."

"Whatever you want."

If only you knew, she thought.

Jean saw that RJ had a cruise line site open on the tablet.

"You trying to get me on"—what had Moreno called it?—"a floating coffin?" A ship in the middle of nowhere where she'd be trapped with four hundred of her closest friends was about the last place in the world where she'd want to go on vacation. Stomach bugs and going overboard were two unadvertised amenities.

"That one goes to Alaska."

Add freezing to death to the list.

"And there's a casino and a theater."

She tried to imagine what kind of shows played on a cruise ship. Nothing worth sitting through on board Princess Death Lines.

Once dinner was ready, they made plates and moved to the table. When RJ started talking about resodding the front yard, he was picturing a For Sale sign sitting on all that green, thinking curb appeal, or something like that.

After dinner, she cleaned up, and RJ moved to his laptop for the night. Jean showered and opened the drawer hiding all the old lingerie. She tried on a few, more for herself, and checked herself in the mirror. Not too bad. She slipped one on that she didn't feel ridiculous in and got in bed to read. She fell asleep before RJ came upstairs. When the phone rang in the middle of the night, she felt the untouched lace against her skin as she answered.

"Colleen?" she said.

"What?" said a raspy baritone.

Not her daughter's voice.

"What's wrong with Colleen?" Parker asked.

Jean checked RJ, who hadn't moved, and slipped out of bed, whispering, "Hold on." She went into her closet and pulled on a sweatshirt and sweatpants in the dark. Once she was down the hall, she spoke again.

"What's wrong?" she asked.

"Were you up?"

"Parker, it's two in the morning. No, I wasn't up." She listened for alcohol between his words.

"Come outside."

"What?" She walked to her front window, pulling the curtain aside.

"See. You are up."

"Goddamn it." She hung up and closed the door behind her as quietly as she could.

Once she was outside, Parker slipped out of his car, closing his door as softly as Jean had closed hers.

"The fuck you doing?" she asked. She couldn't hear the alcohol over the phone—he was too practiced—but she could see it in the way he leaned against his car. "You drunk?"

"A taste," he said, planting his feet shoulder distance apart.

"Look," she said. "Ally's fine. I dropped her at a friend's apartment. She has a court case in a month, but she seemed okay to me."

"That's not what this is."

"Then what is it?"

"They found that girl I asked you about."

It took Jean a minute to remember which girl he meant. Then—in a flash—she remembered the little girl whose face she hadn't wanted to see. Her knobby knees pressed together as she sat on the edge of the bed, her long hair falling around her face. The bedroom with the cheap furniture and the black-and-white zigzag rug and the octopus-ottoman.

"I thought you found her." As soon as Jean said it, she knew she was wrong. Parker had never mentioned finding the girl. Jean had filled in an ending, a happy one, because she didn't want to face the alternative.

"Nope. Off 25. By that pistachio farm. Thrown away."

Jean knew he had been through this before with other cases; they both had. But he hadn't gotten this way in a while.

"Any forensics yet?" Get him focused, thinking of the investigation, not the image of a dead kid.

"I'll know more in a few days." Parker peered into the night, searching. "Let me ask you something."

"Shoot."

"Would you rather be good or lucky?"

"You getting philosophical on me?"

"Answer the question."

"Lucky."

"Why?" he asked.

"Because I'm smart enough to know I have no control. This shit isn't about me."

"That's exactly right," he said, stargazing.

She felt a tenderness toward him that she hadn't felt in a long time.

"Also, Rayna moved out," he added.

"So you're having a night."

"She said I wasn't in love with her. Do people talk like that?" He shifted his stance. "I guess they do. Said I was in love with someone else."

"The job?"

"Someone. Not something."

Jean stared at him. For a moment, when he turned to her, it was as though no years had passed. She saw an alternative to her life play out in flashes. A house, not here on a cul-de-sac but on one of those roads that twist and wind their way into the mountains. The yard filled with wild things, wild things ready to light with the next wildfire.

"Billy." It was all she could say. It was everything she could say. The rest wouldn't make sense out loud.

"Never mind," he said. "I don't know why I called."

"It's okay," she said, though she knew why. She nodded to the yard. "I was thinking about putting in some wildflowers and see what happens. What do you think?"

"Why not, but I don't know," he said. "Around here, everything dies."

Before she could say anything, he cut her off. "Anyway, sorry if I woke RJ up."

"Not sorry that you woke me up?" she asked.

He looked her dead in the eye, and she knew everything he was thinking: "No."

She became aware of her skin—felt the hidden black lace underneath her sweats. Parker got back into his car without another word, and Jean watched, waiting until his red taillights turned at the corner. Finally, his car disappeared. She had been waiting for him to turn around, waiting for those lights to return. Before she got back into bed, she changed out of the lingerie.

I hear it at the same time he does. Music—a radio.

He steps through me toward the sound, and I fly ahead of him. The sun has begun to set behind the western peaks and darkness brushes us, but neither of us needs light to find our way in these woods. A hundred yards off or so, on the other side of a small ridge, sits another tent. This one olive-colored, bigger, newer. The end of a small campfire is safely nestled behind a circle of rocks. I have never seen people camp here before. Two voices drift out from the tent. A man and a woman. I can hear them talking. The woman laughs. I forget when I am and think it's the same hikers who found our barrels. Haven't I played out a scene between Andy and Elise like this? Could this be Andy and Elise?

A moment later, he enters the campsite. A switchblade, its blade already open to a grin, quivers in his hand. He's angry these people are trespassing—trespassing on his land. His entire life has been about control. He considers all this land his domain. But it's broader than only the land. He controls people too. First, himself—changing his personality to fit his audience, allowing himself the space to get away with whatever he wants. Second, controlling others. It feeds him.

I turn to the fire, remembering Jo and her rock pyramid.

There's no wind here, nothing natural to help. So I close my eyes and imagine fire, monolithic and wild, like something bursting from the base of a great beast's throat, exploding from the circle. I smell ash and carbon and smoke. Its heat radiates around me. When I open my eyes, a single large ember, the size of a thumb, lifts from behind the stone, floating in midair.

He sees it too.

The ember drifts on the air beyond the stones, settling into a small nest of pine needles. Like magic, they light.

He stares at the tent, then the small flame, then back to the tent again. In that second of indecision, the fire turns, grows to the size of a fist—my fist.

Age has slowed his instincts. But I have made the decision for him. Stepping toward the tent, he pauses and turns to the fire, stomping it out. At the sound, a man from inside the olive tent swears, the tent unzips from within, and a man's head emerges.

"What the—?"

A young man steps out from the tent, shirtless. The hunter realizes he has lost the element of surprise. The younger man is broad, fit—not Andy. The real Andy would be old by now.

"Heard your music," he says, flipping the switchblade closed behind his back. "Ember caught. It was lucky I was passing by. You should be more careful."

"Thanks," the younger man says. "I thought it had died out." When he doesn't make a move to leave, the younger man asks, "You need anything?"

He has his lie ready. "I forgot matches, pretty stupid."

By now, the woman has emerged from the tent. She studies the back-and-forth like dialogue in a play, trying to figure out who the players are and how it will end.

"We have some extra, let me grab you a few," the younger man says, ducking back into the tent. When her partner disappears, the woman studies the old man. I whisper in her ear. I curl my hands into fists and shove them into her stomach, pushing them up through her middle. Her eyebrows crease, then smooth, the whites of her eyes flashing.

"Here you go," the younger man says. He has thrown on a T-shirt, pulling it flat as he offers a pack of matches to the stranger.

"Thanks," he says, pretending to smile. "Enjoy yourselves. And watch that fire. You can't ever be too careful."

Then he retreats to the dark.

Once she's sure he has gone for good, the woman pulls her hair up into a knot and tugs on her partner's arm.

"We're going," she says, already grabbing items on the ground: a mug, a boot, a hat.

"What? It's dark. He was some weird old guy."

"We're leaving," she says again. This time, he listens. Smart girl. Smarter than me.

They pack camp in under five minutes and take off in the opposite direction.

Sylvia couldn't be more wrong.

There's always time for the worst.

If I had the chance, I would have died for my girls. He never gave me the option. He took everything from me—every choice I made, even the ones I thought were my own, was tethered to marionette strings he held above my head. He controlled what I ate, what I did. Who I loved. He dealt out impossible choices.

Like who I saved.

LAURA

LAURA PARKED OUTSIDE THE MAIN BRANCH OF THE Albuquerque Public Library. The building took up an entire city block. It had the shape of other late '80s poured-cement monstrosities but was painted orange like an oversized terra-cotta square pot. Architectural no-man's-land. She entered through a black glass atrium at the front. Taking the elevator to the second floor, Laura found the Genealogy Center. Tables spread out across the room with people hunched over books and laptops. More books lined the walls. Center islands with rows of shallow and wide drawers holding maps filled the room's center. Their collection of Sanborn Fire Insurance Maps was spread atop one island. New Haven didn't have a genealogy section. This library had dedicated half a floor. She signed in at the front desk and waited.

A white-haired woman came out from a back office and approached Laura. "Ms. MacDonald?"

Tami Wheaton-Pemberley, the staff genealogist, appeared to be playing the role of kindly grandma, complete with a turquoise necklace holding her glasses around her neck. Wearing a light pink cardigan and unironic '90s mom jeans, Tami erased any lingering tension when she put out her sunspotted hand to greet Laura. "Tami. So great to meet you. I'm excited to work with someone else in the field. Follow me this way and we'll get started."

Laura followed the woman to her office, saying a little thank-you for kind librarians with even kinder faces.

"Any direction on where to start next would be extremely helpful," Laura said.

The thing about genealogists, Laura found, was that nothing surprised them. For the first time since she had started working this case, Laura felt no hesitancy about laying out every detail about the Sierra County Jane Doe and Margaret Ann Washington. Tami agreed that Washington was an uncommon enough name for the Southwest that the two women, Margaret Ann Washington and Margaret Washington Crown, could be one and the same. Tami thought for a minute, and as she did, she tapped each finger in turn to her thumb, repeating the silent drumbeat over and over.

"The way I see it, you have two options," she said, still tapping.

Laura leaned forward in her chair.

"First there's the oldest girl. If you found a record of baptism from a Catholic church in California, there's a chance she received First Communion at a Catholic church here. The problem is, not all those records have been digitized, especially if it was held in a rural church. The second is the woman. If she died here, there should be a death certificate, and all those documents, regardless of whether the county is rural or urban, have been digitized. Of course, you're looking for the absence of proof. Not finding her death certificate doesn't automatically mean she is the Jane Doe. Absence of proof isn't proof."

"I know."

"Then I'd start with the communion records."

"I agree."

"Let's make a list of places to start," Tami said, pulling out a pen and paper.

�֎

LAURA PUT THE ADDRESS for San Miguel in Serrucho in her phone. It wasn't the largest church, and no one had answered the number she tried first, but it was the closest to the barrel site. An hour later, when she pulled off the highway and onto the one street that made up the town, she had to work to keep her jaw closed. She had never seen a place so empty.

It was like someone had come through with an old straw broom and swept out what little town there had been in the first place. Dirt lots lined the road. One white trailer sat way off the road, backed up against a low ridge. A fence made of crooked branches stuck out of the ground every few feet, thin wires running between them. One lone election sign stuck into the dirt. When the white steeple of San Miguel arose between the baked brown earth and the blue sky, Laura held her breath, waiting for a crowd of zombies to appear from behind one of the neglected buildings.

Laura couldn't believe how narrow the church was. She parked in the dirt lot. Rocks crunched under her feet as she walked around to the front. Checking up and down the street for any cars, she went up the cracked steps, framed by dirt-filled planter boxes. Two black crosses baked gray in the sun were affixed to either side of the entrance. A pair of flimsy glass doors with thin wooden frames separated the church from the outside. Behind them, white lace obstructed the view inside. Jiggling one of the doors, Laura thought it was catching at the handle. She pulled out a credit card she didn't care about and slid it between the handles and, after a couple of tries, found the latch. The door opened without any fanfare.

There were no stained-glass stations of the cross lining the wall—only three plain windows running on either side of the nave. She had stepped directly into the sanctuary. The pews belonged in a doll's house. Laura debated closing the doors behind her. Leaving them open would announce her presence to anyone driving by, but she was less worried about that than not being able to make a run for it.

It took about ten steps to get to the altar. A stone table stood atop a ragged crimson carpet, with a tall wooden chair and a dirty gold crucifix. A wall tapestry hung behind the chair. She'd had studio apartments bigger than this church. She studied the nave again. Something wasn't right. There was small and then there was too small. Something was missing.

She went back outside to the parking lot, thankful for the fresh air. There were four windows on the outside wall. Jogging back inside, she counted three. She crossed herself for security and took the two steps onto the altar. There were no visible side doors. She pulled the tapestry to the side and found a narrow wooden door.

The door was unlocked. An office no bigger than a closet faced her. The missing fourth windows filled the walls on both sides of the room. Along the back wall ran horizontal rows of low shelves. The air sat in the room. Could she hear a ticking watch, forgotten in a drawer somewhere, or was she imagining it? Aware of the sweat coating her skin like a too-thick layer of sunscreen, she stripped off her outer shirt. It helped, but not much. She opened both windows as far as they would go.

Laura scanned the rows of books on the shelves. Sets of theological treatises, leather-bound: Aquinas, de Lubac, Latourelle. Nothing like church records. There were no telltale filing cabinets. In fact, nothing about the books looked particularly old. The bindings cracked and creaked with newness when she opened them. At the spartan wooden desk she found a Bible, a receipt for some roof repairs, not much else.

She didn't know why, but something told her to freeze. The imagined clock had been replaced with the distinct sound of footsteps. Laura pulled her phone from her pocket. She didn't have a signal to call the police. Given the situation, someone could rightly be calling the police on her. Searching the room, she thought briefly about grabbing a large golden cross on a staff. She considered the window. She could fit—she could push the dirty screen out and jump. Instead, she grabbed the Bible sitting on the desk and sat. It seemed like the least criminal thing she could do.

Even though she knew someone was coming, she heard herself scream when the underside of the tapestry undulated and moved to reveal a hand, followed by a face. It was only when the stranger's face came into focus that she stopped, as abruptly as she had started. She recognized that face.

"So we meet again," Laura heard the detective say. "I'll say this about you. You're persistent."

Laura stood, Bible still in hand. She felt the cover. It bent and moved like a living thing, soft and supple in her hands. "I'm sorry, I tried knocking." *A small lie.* "I was only looking for records."

"You know you're breaking and entering here."

"I mean, if you're Catholic"—*lapsed Catholic*—"I don't think you can be charged for going inside a Catholic church." She slipped her finger into the cover of the Bible, pulling open the last few pages in front of her.

"I'm not sure that's how it works."

"No, but—okay. Let me start again. I know. Now, I know. Margaret Ann Washington *is* your Jane Doe. She had another baby. Her name was Amy."

JEAN

"START AT THE BEGINNING, ONE MORE TIME."

It was lucky for the librarian that Susan Waddell had called Jean and not 911 when she saw a person lurking around the church. Now, Jean sat in a chair opposite Laura, who had followed her back to the station. Jean, who hadn't said anything when Laura left the church with the Bible clearly not her own, now listened to Laura's story a second time. It was clear to her that this young woman wasn't going anywhere. Better to have her on her team than, you know, breaking into churches across the state unaccompanied.

"Originally, I was looking for communion records for Daisy. If she was baptized, there is a strong possibility that she received First Communion. San Miguel is the closest church to the site. I didn't find any records for Daisy—I didn't find any records at all, which makes me think the church could have flooded at some point. Though I'm not sure how a church floods in a desert."

"A flash flood. Keep going."

"There were informal records of baptism." Laura opened the back of the Bible, scanning for the name. "In this Bible, I believe the priest, a—" She glanced at the name again. "Father Gregory. He kept a personal record of the babies he baptized. I think

Margaret had another daughter. One that wasn't in the barrels." She pointed to the list of names, dates, and parents' names scrawled in cursive. "Amy Gloria Crown was baptized on July 12, 1967. People often repeat prior generations' names in their children's names. Gloria was the name of Margaret Ann Washington's mother."

Jean leaned back. "You think there was another daughter who survived."

"Yes."

Jean opened her computer and logged into several of the databases she had to search.

"I have no records for an Amy Gloria Crown in the state of New Mexico."

"What software do you use?"

"Does that matter?"

"No, but that was fast."

"This is literally my job." Jean wavered between amusement and exasperation.

The librarian was about to say something, then decided against it. Jean thought for a moment. "Most of this—no, all of this—is circumstantial," she said.

The young woman nodded. Jean couldn't tell how fluent she was in cop talk. "It's not like it needs to hold up in court," Jean said, trying to help. This translated. Jean asked, posing the question as much to herself as to Laura, "If Jane Doe is Margaret and Margaret had another daughter—what happened to her?"

Laura shrugged, but Jean watched as her face changed from genuine befuddlement to something else—something Jean recognized. Laura's brain had shifted gears. She might not have a person in her sights, but she had an idea. If only in her head, she was on the hunt.

"Where would you start?" Jean asked, leading her on.

"Crown isn't common for the area. I'm not positive it's a proper surname at all."

Jean spun her chair to the pile of directories. She didn't need to explain before Laura began organizing them by date.

"Is there a computer I can use?" she asked first.

"Is there any coffee around here?" she asked second.

"As a matter of fact," Jean said, sliding open her desk drawer, "we have both."

With Jean's dark roast brewed, directories sorted, and their mission established, Jean felt herself warming up to the citizen sleuth. It wasn't only having someone to talk to—asking Parker for another favor was now firmly out of the question—it was that Laura changed the room. Jean didn't want to admit it to herself, but the room felt—well, warmer. The light stayed lit, the room stayed climate-controlled, and Jean had someone to bounce ideas off. She had missed having a partner. So what if this one broke into churches in her free time?

"What did you mean before, when you said you weren't sure Crown was a surname at all?" she asked.

Laura had ruled out using the station's old desktop computers, comparing them to molasses rolling down a gradual incline, and had switched over to yellow legal pads materializing from her bag.

"Crown could be German—Kron. Or Polish. Or English, or Irish," she said, pausing her writing. "Or it could be something else. It's something you see in genealogy. Sometimes, usually in parts of Germany, actually, people's last names derived from their farm name. In other parts, though, the last name changed with people's lineage. People have a hard time tracing German lineage because there are so many regional peculiarities around naming. In northern Germany, people took their surnames from their father's first name. Peter Christensen's son Friedrich would have the last name Petersen, as in 'son of Peter.' Then *his* son would have the last name Friedrichsen. Following lineage is like pulling a braid apart."

In all her years working, with all the people she came across, Jean had never worked with a librarian or a genealogist. "So you learn the different ways to track people by their last names?"

"It depends. Usually, yes. But middle names can tell you almost as much as last names sometimes. People like to show where they come from in their middle names."

"What about the Irish?" Jean asked, thinking of her own family. "Are they hard to trace?"

"Irish ancestry is notoriously full of brick walls. Dead ends with no work-arounds, mostly because a lot of the records people need don't exist. There was a fire in 1922 in Dublin's Public Records Office that destroyed a lot. Then there was a law passed in 1938. Britain divided Ireland into geographical areas called 'poor law unions' to distribute aid. Local registrars kept their own records of birth, marriage, and death, but before 1864, only non-Catholic marriages were recorded. There's a real lack of records for many people. In general, the hardest brick walls are from slavery and immigration."

Maybe when all this was over, Jean would try to trace her own family tree. They gave the directories a second pass, but neither found any Crowns. Jean searched the private databases she had available. There were a few Crowns in Albuquerque, but nothing closer to the barrel site.

While they had been working, a semi-insane idea had been percolating in Jean's head. She wanted to bring Laura into the investigation—in a real, substantive way. She wasn't sure how long the woman planned to be here, but for as long as she had her, Jean wanted to put her to good use. "Hold on," she said. "Be back in a minute." She returned with a form that she placed in front of Laura. "I need to see some identification."

"Am I under arrest?" Laura asked, her eyes doing the cue ball imitation again.

Jean fought the urge to smirk. "No, I'm deputizing you. Sign here."

Something close to suppressed exhilaration painted Laura's face, and once she had signed a form swearing she wouldn't divulge any details of the investigation, Jean brought her into her thinking.

"Before you introduced Margaret into the equation, I had been investigating the Tellefsen family. Let's pause on the Crown idea—hear me out. The Tellefsens own and manage a mining operation next to the barrel site. The current owner is the grandson, Reed Yates. At the time when the barrels were placed there, the land was still technically their property." Jean walked Laura through what she knew. Bjorn, his two children, Gerry and Nancy. Bjorn's noted anger, Nancy's disappearance.

"Do you think Nancy is Jane Doe?" Laura asked, turning the possibility in her head.

"No. It doesn't account for the girls. And the ages are wrong. Nancy disappeared well after the time we think the bodies were originally placed."

"So it's—what? A strange coincidence?"

"Maybe. I've seen it more than a few times. I think we should focus on Gerry Tellefsen. He's retired now—lives in Colorado. I had a deputy out there do a drive-by, make sure he's still around. He is. Gerry was the right age, and never had children of his own. Maybe one of those girls is his daughter. The remains only have mitochondrial DNA intact. Even if he volunteered a sample, it wouldn't tell me if he was their father."

"Wait—does this mean we're trying to figure out Margaret's killer?" Laura asked.

"Possibly."

"I thought we were only trying to confirm her identity."

"There's nothing that says you can't do both at the same time."

"Does the paper I signed give me access to your databases?"

"Are you going to run a background check on either old boy-friends or prospective boyfriends while you're at it?"

"Highly doubtful."

"Then yes, you can use those databases." Jean checked her watch. "But I need to head home. I have company headed my way. Can we pick this up tomorrow?" she asked.

"Absolutely."

Jean could tell the librarian was crestfallen and with all that coffee could have kept going for hours on end, but Jean had a dinner date. "We'll pick it up tomorrow, right where we left off."

❧

JEAN COULDN'T REMEMBER THE last time she had made dinner herself, but she was looking forward to having her daughter home for the night. The recipe, printed from the internet, was barely legible by this point, having been splattered with tomato sauce and smeared by oily fingers. Jean pulled the lasagna sheets from the boiling pot and placed them on a sheet pan. She should do more of this. Fill her daughter's freezer with meals. Help her wash all the new baby clothes. But thinking of newly washed baby clothes made her mind travel to a desert church, a newly baptized baby held over a basin of holy water. Guilt crept in, right behind a mental note to stop thinking about work and to buy hypoallergenic laundry detergent. Jean had to admit, in terms of being a first-time grandmother, she was ranking low on the scales. She thought of Parker. Maybe she was ranking low on the wife scales too.

RJ came in with a bottle of wine and a case of beer, leaving one on the counter and putting the other in the fridge. "How's it going in here?" he asked, coming up behind her.

Jean was trying to pull one of the noodles from the sheet pan, but it was tearing into long strips. "Great!" she said. She never spoke with exclamation marks.

"How about a glass of wine?" he asked, surveying the shredded lasagna, intent on turning itself into spaghetti.

"Yes, please. And could you grab the pasta sauce?" Jean asked, rinsing her hands at the sink.

He placed two jars on the counter along with her wine. "Anything else?"

"No—thank you."

Jean tried her best to layer sauce and pasta and cheese and meat as neatly as possible, but she lost track of which layer she was on and ended up with extra sauce and not enough cheese. Whatever. Lasagna was lasagna, right? After sliding it into the oven to bake, Jean turned to survey her kitchen. It looked as though an improvised explosive device, set with marinara and cheese, had gone off in her kitchen.

The front door opened and Colleen made a dash as fast as she could waddle. "Hi," she yelled en route. "Bathroom!"

While Jean finished cleaning, RJ and Colleen planted themselves in the living room, talking about what, Jean didn't care—her daughter was home. When her cell phone rang, it took Jean an extra second to register the sound. She pushed herself up from the couch, praying it was a telemarketer.

"Jean, I'm sorry about this," Moreno said on the other end. "I know it's late. But Paul's asking for you."

"Colleen came over for dinner," she said. She had been meaning to ask Paul about the isotope testing and if he had ever seen it but had gotten side-tracked. "Can't this wait?"

"Not to be life-and-death about it, but this is the death part."

Jean sighed, wrote down a room number, then wrote out a second note for when to take the lasagna out of the oven. One note went in her pocket and the other to Colleen, and for the first time in a long time, she hated her job.

If she could divide herself into three people, maybe she could make her life work. Give one to her husband: a partner eager to retire and—well—she wouldn't know what to do with that much free time, but they could think of something. Give one to her daughter: a caretaker for her granddaughter when Colleen had to go back to work full-time. The third she'd keep for herself.

✤

PAUL HENDERSON HAD ALWAYS been something of a ghost around the squad. He spent most of his career investigating white-collar crimes before sliding into cold cases. He kept to himself, emerging once or twice a month to pepper someone with questions about what they remembered about that homicide from '02 ("The guy wore gloves, a mask, and the surveillance tape was out. What else is new?") or what the drug of choice was by the late '80s ("One word: blow"). Then he'd return to his office, muttering to himself, and close the door. Which was fine by everyone else. They were station-sludge-coffee people.

But he had cleared a particularly vexing B and E from '92 that had left everyone feeling like millipedes were marching on their skin. Paul earned the squad's respect, and then got a lung cancer diagnosis the following month. He worked until the headaches started, then slipped out the back door before anyone could buy a sheet cake with the cheap, too-sweet frosting.

But tonight, of all nights, Paul wanted to see Jean. She guessed he had earned the right to summon her. She had taken his job. Though she hadn't expected the call to come at dinnertime. She made the drive down to Memorial in Las Cruces.

A nurse wearing purple Crocs and walking with a stiff back led Jean to Paul's room. The nurse's rubber shoes caught on the linoleum tile twice down the long hall of closed doors and half-light.

"Now, when you go in there, watch out for his right arm. It's in a sling, hard to miss," she said. Her ID badge read *Denise* above a picture taken a good thirty pounds and ten years prior. Jean half listened, distracted by a bright pink piece of paper

179

taped above his door. By her best guess, it signaled that the patient inside was DNR and terminal.

"You got that?" Denise asked.

"Did he fall?"

"What?"

"His arm in a sling, did he fall and break it?"

"No. Tumor fractured it. Can't set it, so it's an open break."

Oh, Jean thought. Her question about isotopic testing suddenly felt a lot less important.

"He's been asking for you. I'm glad you got down here in time," Denise said, checking her watch. "You should have a good ten minutes."

"What happens in ten minutes?"

"He'll be able to self-administer his next dose of morphine."

As soon as she ducked under the bright pink paper and into Paul Henderson's room, she wanted to leave. She wished she had made Parker come with her. He could distract from the hum of monitors and the quiet constant whoosh of the oxygen line running into Paul's nose. Two IV stands flanked his bed next to a monitor. Jean remembered, vaguely, a story about his child dying young and another about his wife passing in her fifties of a sudden stroke. He had a bunch of nephews he looked after like they were his own. Pretty sure one of them had joined the force.

"Martinez," Paul said, barely audible over the oxygen. The shock of him speaking nearly drove her out of the room. She had thought he was asleep. His eyes opened to thin slits.

"Hey, Paul," she said, trying to remember why he was Paul and not Henderson. Some people are first-name people, some last. Paul was Paul, always had been.

"Sorry about the setting," he said, trying to sit upright in his bed and grimacing when he moved his arm. Finding the remote with his good hand, he raised his bed.

should be obvious he's a bad man. He hunts people with knives.
wish he had hunted me with a knife—because then I would have
nown to run away. His weapon of choice with me was far more
ffective, more deadly, more calculating. He hunted me with words.

A word will always be more cunning than a knife. A knife is one
ing. A knife has one purpose. A knife cuts. But words blur, bend,
fuscate. They paint a picture, draw you in, and you don't feel the cut
til you look down at your palms cupping burgundy pools.

I wait by the night flowers, making sure he won't go back for the
ple. Their white faces have opened beneath the moonlight. Each
l the shape of a heart, one connected to the next, drawn together in
umpeted bell. I press my face to them, remembering the perfumed
ning primrose at my mother's house. But I can't smell anything
in the clearing. It's not the flowers' fault—it's mine.

He took so many choices from me over the years we were together,
ng me, at the end, with an impossible one. I won't let it happen
. He won't hurt my girls anymore. I'll make sure of it. As long
s alive, I'll watch him. I'll take from him what he took from me.
go to the creek, where I can keep an eye on his tent.

re you there?" a voice calls from behind me.

roll over, facing the water.

re you there?" a voice calls again. In the night, the woman's face
harder to see.

m here. I'm waiting for him to leave. I'm going to follow him."

hy?"

at if she doesn't approve? "Just to see where he lives."

nothing to get excited about," she says.

about to ask how she knows, but I stop myself, swallowing

"Don't worry about it. I'm sorry I haven't made it in sooner," she said. She had a joke about a late-night rendezvous, but kept it tucked in her pocket. She didn't know him that well.

"Your Doe," he said, cutting to his point. "Where are you?"

Jean glanced at the clock over the door. *Speak quickly and clearly*, she thought.

"I retested for autosomal DNA—they can do all sorts of new genealogy work with it now—but it didn't show anything. Right now, I'm looking at the Tellefsen family."

"You looking at Gerry or his old man?"

"Gerry, for now," Jean said, not having expected Paul to have the name right off the top. She didn't know he had been looking at the Tellefsen family himself. There wasn't anything in the file on them.

"I always thought," Paul said, pausing for breath, "that the case picks the cop, not the other way round." Jean supposed this was technically correct, though she thought he meant something more.

His parchment skin pulled tight around his eyes as he grimaced again. Black creases fanned out at the corners of his eyes like spider legs. Jean checked the clock again. He needed that morphine.

"You okay?" she asked.

"I'm fine. Two questions," he continued, scrunching his eyes. "Why did you take my job?"

If she lied to him now, there was a good chance he could tell on her within the next few days. Maybe hours.

"I couldn't do pedophiles anymore. I wanted to kill everyone. I got too angry." There, for the first time, she had said it out loud.

He opened his slit eyes to study her. She hadn't seen them until now. The irises had faded into a gray that sank into the dull ring of brown around them. Jean remembered that he had deep, dark brown eyes before, flecked with gold. She wondered where the gold had gone.

"I can see that," he said. "Second question. What makes you think you can solve this case?"

She kept her face neutral.

"I've done it before—"

His groan cut her short. He sounded like he was tied to a rack and some invisible executioner was pulling the lever. Jean checked the clock again. Her ten minutes were up. "It's seven thirty," she said.

Paul drummed the button with his good thumb like a signalman punching out an SOS. One of his IVs clicked four times and she heard the little box attached to the pole begin to whirl. She watched him, watched the IV, watched the clock on the wall. The creases around his eyes smoothed out. He was riding a first-class ticket to Candy Land.

"Paul, I should go. But I'm going to find her. I promise."

His eyes opened, but rather than look at Jean, Paul stared at something above her, like the ceiling tiles had turned into an open night way out in the desert, where if you drove far enough, the city lights would disappear and all you'd be left with were the stars, reminding you of how insignificant you were.

"Paul, you take care," she said, his name catching in her throat.

"Keep an eye out for Josh."

"I'm sorry, Paul—who?" She had no idea who he meant. But as soon as she said it, she saw there was no point. He had hit cruising altitude.

"Followed the father," he said.

"What?" she asked, turning on her heel. "Paul, what did you say?"

His neck relaxed, and his head sank into his shoulders. His eyes closed, and his chest rose and fell in a steady wave.

On her way home, she bought a full-sized bag of salt and vinegar chips that she ate sitting in her driveway, thinking through what Paul had told her. He must have meant *follow the*

father, right? The father of the children, that woul[d] choice. Had Gerry gotten Jane Doe pregnant an[d] reason, not wanted to deal with the mother and if he meant the father of Ironside, figuratively? [...] of Gerry and Nancy. And who the hell was Josh[...]

Jean finished the bag, pickling her fingers i[n] taking the evidence directly out to the trash before entering her darkened house. There sh[e] over lasagna somewhere.

the question. Maybe I don't want to know who she really is. Maybe it would open up another wound I'd have to mend. "Do you still want to know what happened to me?" I ask.

"What made you change your mind?"

If I'm going to fix the broken parts, I better examine the pieces, I don't say. Instead: "Maybe you're right. Maybe it'll help."

I nestle myself into the ground, like I'm snuggling in to tell myself a bedtime story. The moon makes ripples of light dance across the water's surface. I remember the first night I met him. "I went with my friend Marisol to this club on Santa Monica."

"How did he make you feel?"

I think back to what it was that drew me in. "Like I was a celebrity. Famous. Worthy," I begin.

"Yes—like you were seen," my reflection echoes.

"Yes." I pause, remembering who I had been when I first met him.

Sad stories can often begin with love—and, for the first time, I tell my story.

PEGGY

I GOT PREGNANT IN COLLEGE. WHEN I COULDN'T HIDE my stomach anymore, my father sent me to live with my mother in California. He didn't want my younger half sisters to get the impression this kind of behavior was permissible. An example must be made. And I was it. I got shipped back to my mother—my mother who had left me those years before. I was raising a newborn in a city I hadn't lived in since I was in kindergarten. I should have been in college. I should have been a lot of different things.

We met randomly, at a dance and dinner club, one night when my mother offered to watch the baby so I could go out with a neighbor girl, feel and act my age. I didn't want to dance. Compared to the other girls who, I imagined, didn't have babies at home, I felt fat, stupid. After he found me, asked me questions all night long, I felt seen. I felt important. I had never had a real relationship before. Frank, Daisy's dad, didn't count. I had nothing to compare it to. I thought it was love. After the first night, we didn't go a day without seeing each other.

Daisy had been born in the spring. By that Christmas, my father made plans, along with my stepmother and half sisters, Cynthia and Patricia, to visit me and the baby in California.

To acknowledge my existence. I invited him over for the holiday, knowing my father would be there. Knowing he wouldn't approve of his daughter dating a man so soon after having given birth to another man's child. I wanted to rub it in his face.

At the time, my mother lived in a little bungalow in Woodland Hills where she planted evening primrose in the front garden. They only bloomed at night, filling the yard with perfume. That Christmas morning—all day in fact—my mother was a nervous wreck. She sliced her finger chopping onions. Burned herself on the oven door checking the ham for the hundredth time. My younger sisters hadn't seen our father in years and didn't know what to do with themselves. They kept sneaking off to their rooms. Cynthia and Patricia didn't understand the silent film playing out in front of us and sat on the couch, watching TV instead. I wanted to scream.

When he came over, my father hadn't yet arrived. He hadn't shaved and there was still black oil in the creases of his nails. When my father walked in the door, I pulled his hand around my shoulder with one hand and held Daisy with the other. *Look*, I said with my smile. *Look what I've done. See how happy I am here without you?*

He introduced himself to everyone, then gave me my Christmas present. He had made me jewelry: silver bracelets. He was always so handy. He etched my name into one of the bands. I slipped them on, and then he went to help my mother in the kitchen. He was smiling, holding a bowl for her, then she must have said something amiss. I could tell from across the room. His face changed, fast, like flicking a light switch; he went dark, said something to her, quiet, and then went back to normal.

After, he came to my side, whispering in my ear, "I think I should leave."

"Why?" I said, panicking.

"Your mother doesn't approve, I can tell. She thinks I'm no good for you. I'll go."

I remember my face feeling hot. "Don't leave. She doesn't know what she's talking about."

I made a big show of handing him Daisy and her bottle. Had him check the bottle on his inside wrist, then shooed him into the bedroom. I found my mother in the kitchen.

"So," I said, my face still hot, sliding into the question. "What do you think?"

Her hands fluttered above a pot. "I don't know," she said. "He doesn't seem to say much about himself." She started to scrape the bottom of a pan that had burned. The sound of her metal spatula against the metal pot made my teeth ache. "He must have said something to your father's wife. She ran back to his side so fast, you would have thought she saw a mouse."

"Maybe he can tell everyone is judging him."

"I don't think that's what I was doing," she said, not looking at me.

"Maybe you don't like him," I said.

"I don't know him well enough to not like him. Do you?"

I could have set my hand on the front burner and not felt a thing, I was so angry. I went to find him in the bedroom to see how he was doing. He was putting the baby to sleep. I remember walking in after he had put the baby down. His quick-fire questions came next.

"What did you say to her? Did you stand up for yourself?"

"Yes," I lied.

"Good girl," he cooed in my ear. Then his hands were under my shirt. He squeezed my breast hard. This was what I had wanted since I met him, but not here, not now. It was the first hint at what would be our new pattern. I would do what he wanted and be rewarded with attention, touch, affection after.

When I didn't do what he wanted, he'd pull his love out from under my feet, leaving me in a heap on the floor.

"The baby," I said, but also, my sisters, my parents. Everyone.

His face turned again, fast. "I'm an idiot," he said. "I'm disgusting. I should go."

"No," I said, pulling him toward me. "I'll be quiet."

Then he pivoted, changing the subject so fast I couldn't follow his train of thought. That's what he did—start a conversation in one direction, then change so fast you forgot what you were supposed to be talking about: "I don't think you're ready to come to New Mexico with us."

My chest caved. You see, it was something we—he and his friends and, lately, I—had been talking about. California was dead, they said. They had plans to go back to where they grew up. They were going to all go in on a ranch together. They had it all worked out. I could go with them. I had nothing if they left, no other friends, nowhere else to go. Ever since Daisy, my life felt like a motorcycle slipping on quicksand. I thought life was the choices you made, and lately, it felt like all my choices were made for me. Going to New Mexico made me feel like I could be in charge again.

"I want to come," I told him. "I need you."

"Then don't tell them where we're going." His hand slid up my skirt, and I moaned, softly.

"What?" I said, unable to concentrate, his fingers running in small circles beneath my underwear.

"If they know where you are, you'll go running back to them. Or they'll come running after you and you won't be able to say no to them," he said. His other hand slid around behind my neck. "I want you, but I can't tell if you're ready."

"I am, I promise. I won't tell anyone," I said, between panting breaths.

He only used his hands—except for one time, later—he only ever used his hands. By the time I figured out why, it was too late. I didn't think anything of it at the time—he said he wanted to wait until we were married. He told the most delicious lies.

After, we left the room, and I was certain my cheeks were fluorescent. I kept adjusting my skirt. Then I watched my sisters set the table—knife blades facing in—as though they were characters in a TV show. But this time, I knew how the ending went.

Around the table, my father said something stupid about privileged blessings. I heard him cough by my side. It was my time to prove myself. I told them all that I was leaving. My father let go of his careful and cool act, accusing me of naivete and negligence. I told him that he was the one who had been negligent. I told them we were moving to Canada. I made up a town. I heard myself lie, fed them a story about a little fishing village off the coast. I don't know where it came from. He slid his hand under the table, finding my thigh.

"*Do you feel better?*" my echo asks.

I push my fingers into the soft grass growing by the creek's edge. I want to tear it all out. The moon hasn't left us, and I wish it would. I deserve the dark. "We moved to the desert a few weeks later. Up to a ranch in Socorro County. I never saw my family again."

"*I know.*"

"They never looked for me."

"*I know.*"

"They never looked for Daisy."

"*I know.*"

"That's the worst part."

"*I know, I know.*"

Sunrise renders the mountains and sky purple, both rich enough for priests' robes. The two planes of sky and mountain sandwich a marmalade-orange sun spread out over the horizon. Before you know it, the sky lightens. The flowers, sensing the change, quiver at their heart-shaped petals' tips, ready to close. As long as I stay next to them, they'll remain open—even during the day. It isn't night alone that causes their bloom. An overcast sky can trick them, a storm. Or me.

"*The two women who are looking for us—they're on their way here,*" my echo says.

"Two?" I ask. She nods beneath the surface again.

The sun will rise any minute. There hasn't been any movement from inside his tent—not yet. He's an early riser—always was, always has been. If they hurry, they'll find him. They could catch him here, in the clearing. He could be gone, and I could go back to the girls. It could all be over.

I go to the night flowers next to his tent. The magpies, ever curious, leave their perch from branches above and settle into the flowery shrub, finding new homes for the day.

"Where are you going?" the woman in the creek asks. Rather than being muted by the water's depth, her voice is deep and resonant. "Come back."

I ignore her, picturing the detective who knelt here before.

"Come and find me," I say. "He's here, waiting."

Sensing morning, the flowers close, coiling their heart-shaped petals. I pass my hand over the branches and a flower uncurls, opening. Another follows. Then another. The closed petals, long white coils, unspool amid the magpies' black bills and white bellies. In the daybreak, there are hints of iridescent midnight-blue along the birds' sides.

The night flowers shine.

"Hurry."

LAURA

LAURA FELT HIGH WHEN SHE GOT BACK TO HER MOTEL room that night—she couldn't distinguish where the coffee buzz ended and her disbelief about working with Detective Martinez began. She went down to the front lobby and bought a bottle of cheap Australian white wine. Bonus points for a screw top. When it occurred to her that she didn't want to drink directly from the bottle, she also bought a Truth or Consequences mug listing haunted places in town.

Back in her room, Laura winced, unable to grip the screw top tightly enough to twist. Her hands felt like rubber. She took the bottle into the bathroom. Would running water under the lid loosen it, like a jar of spaghetti sauce? Laura tried again, but now, in front of the mirror, saw her skin pucker and pull in long waves across her chest. She was wearing a scoop-neck shirt, one she'd never wear again, favoring crewnecks from now on because they better hid her chest. Her pectoral muscles, directly under her paper-thin skin, striated with the effort of twisting open the cap. Her chest like that of a male bodybuilder, the sinews running in horizontal highways. She turned away from her reflection, swearing when the cap finally gave, and returned to her bed with her mug of wine.

Laura ran through the messages she had missed that day. Kate: "Kids are fine, they miss you. Bella misses you. She chewed one of my shoes."

A voicemail from Cynthia: "I don't even know if this matters. I thought of it after you left. Deb called Margaret by a nickname—Peggy. But never in front of my parents, only if they were alone. Just a thought."

Two cups of wine and two episodes of *Law and Order* later, Laura moved to pick up the mug, holding the rim with her fingertips like the arcade claw game, and as soon as she did, knew it was a mistake. The mug dropped from her hand, shattering on the tile floor. The shattered cup would have been enough. But when she leaned over to pick up the biggest broken piece, she paused midway, realizing—her breasts didn't move. They should have followed gravity, sliding against the underside of her shirt as she tipped over to reach the mug. But like rocks, they stayed in place against her chest. The smallest sensation that she remembered. She sat back up in the bed, leaving the broken mug on the floor, and opened her laptop.

LAURA BROUGHT EVERYTHING WITH her when she returned to the station the next morning. The material from Tami, her laptop, two giant bottles of water from a second trip to the gift shop, and her notepads. She hadn't thought to pack a smaller bag within her bag for such a purpose, which meant she had to use her small carry-on. Pulling it behind her into the station and down the hall to Jean's office made her feel a bit like a sixth grader with too many binders and a helicopter mom worried about scoliosis. At first, she thought the feeling winding up through her middle was chemo nausea—would every flutter, every stomach turn, always remind her of chemo?—but realized this feeling was something else entirely. She had something.

Laura found Jean in her office, ready with a cup of coffee.

"I found the Tellefsen family," she said, before Jean could say anything. "You said Bjorn Tellefsen had two children, Gerry and Nancy. He also had another son—Dale. He was born to Bjorn and Anete Tellefsen." Laura slid her laptop in front of Jean. "He's not listed in any of the directories. But he's real. I have his birth certificate, a driver's license—one in New Mexico and another in California." She slid her laptop over to Jean to show her the records. "But here's where it gets interesting. Dale Tellefsen was declared dead in absentia by a New Mexican judge in 1975. The court order references a missing-person report filed seven years prior. In New Mexico, seven years is the exact amount of time you have to wait between filing a missing-person report and petitioning for a court to declare you dead. That missing-person report from 1968, that matches the time frame when Jane Doe was killed." Laura clicked over to the missing-person report, showing Jean.

The detective hadn't touched her coffee yet, hadn't said a word. Laura kept going. "Whichever family member applied for the death certificate had to put down his last known address. Look."

Laura opened the Google map with the pinned address.

"That doesn't make any sense."

"I didn't think so either."

Jean chewed her lower lip for a moment.

"Get your things. Field trip. That address is in the next county over. There's someone I want to talk to on the way."

JEAN DIDN'T TALK MUCH on the drive, and Laura fought the urge to fill the silence with her own running commentary. When she had driven to the church, she hadn't been able to study the landscape, too afraid she'd miss a turn and end up lost in the middle of the desert with no signal. Laura had grown up in the Northeast, gone to school in the Northeast, lived her adult life in the Northeast, and, as one does, developed a working ethos that it was the only and best place she could live. Schools, the ocean, lobster rolls—why would one live anywhere else? But as she gazed out the window, she saw a counterclaim: space. Wide-open space felt like magic.

The plains with scattered brush dotting the desert were as alien to Laura as the moon. She had never lived more than an hour's drive from the coast, but she thought for a moment, watching the desert to her right and the forest on the left as the Gila came into view, that for all this space, maybe, maybe she could. Jean had kept her own window down, and Laura rolled hers down all the way too, letting her arm rest on the door. Even in the wind, she felt the sun sink into her skin. She imagined herself living here. Could she? She'd miss the ocean, but it's not like she went every day. She could leave the Atlantic, but she couldn't leave her sister. Move out, yes. Move more than halfway across the country, probably not.

When they pulled into the parking lot of Ironside Mining, Laura went to open the door before Jean stopped her.

"It's probably best if you wait out here. I'll only be a couple minutes," Jean said and handed her the keys. "I want to see what Reed has to say about the missing uncle he failed to mention the first time around." But something in Jean's face told her that Jean didn't want to go inside.

Laura decided not to be upset about being left in the car, considering she had no idea what she could contribute. Though it left her with distinct memories of being left in the car with her sister while her mother ran an errand at the bank.

True to her word, Jean returned ten minutes later, opening the door and swearing in combinations of words Laura had never considered before.

"Apparently the uncle went missing in 1968. No one's heard from him since. His brother Gerry had him declared dead so there wouldn't be confusion about the company. If he were alive, the company was supposed to be split between the two brothers."

"What about the daughter, Nancy?"

"Guess she didn't count."

"Sounds sexist," Laura said.

"Sounds bullshit," Jean said, drumming her fingers on the steering wheel. "Makes me think about the father differently."

"How much of this applies to Jane Doe?"

"Could be nothing. Could be something. Reed didn't mention any of this the first time I stopped by because he said he didn't think it mattered."

"A missing uncle who was declared dead didn't matter?"

"He said he never met him. No one talked about him much, kind of a taboo subject. When he was younger, he ran off to California with some girl." Jean turned to Laura, whose eyes had grown two inches wider.

"To California?" Laura asked. "No clue about whether he came back?"

"Not that his family knows," Jean said. "Could be a story, could be real."

"Then what's next?" Laura asked.

"Let's go find that house."

"Wait—" Laura said, putting her hand on the detective's arm. "Aren't we close to where they were found?"

When Jean didn't answer, Laura needed a moment to recognize the expression on the detective's usually stony face. The woman sitting across from her was scared.

"Unless—" Laura said, trying to give her an out.

"No, we can go. It's right down the street."

※

THE DETECTIVE DIDN'T TALK the length of the short trip. Didn't talk in the parking lot or down the trail. Laura wasn't expecting tour guide Barbie, but she wouldn't have minded a couple of words of direction. She filled in her own assumptions against Jean's lip-sealed march into the woods. This was the way he had come, maybe. This was the path he had found at night, a path he had known from many trips into the wilderness during the day. Could be.

They pushed through branches with pointed pine needles, unlike any pine she recognized from home. Shorter and rounder. A local species, perhaps. Denser bush farther in. Birds scattered in alarm above them. She was following the detective's feet, watching for rocks and roots and tripping hazards. They had turned off the trail and were making their own way through the woods for longer than Laura had expected.

When Jean stopped, Laura stopped herself an inch before she plowed into the woman's back.

"They're open," Jean said, ahead of her.

Laura poked her head around the taller woman's shoulder. What was open?

Jean stepped to the side, allowing Laura a view of the clearing. A mass of leaves, like a bush, but growing without rhyme or reason, like the overgrown rosebush in her grandmother's backyard. Huge white blooms covered the small mountain of green. Their scent almost hypnotic in power—it made her picture Marilyn Monroe's vanity table, a row of vintage perfume bottles, some with crystal stoppers, some with silk-woven pumps.

"The last time I was here—same time of day—the flowers were closed. I thought they were the kind that only opened at night," Jean said, shaking her head. "Guess I was wrong."

"This is it then? This is where—" Laura didn't want to say the word *barrel* anymore. It felt cruel.

Jean filled in. "This is where they were found."

"They had been here for, what—how long do you think?"

"Fifteen, maybe twenty years."

They stood, shoulder to shoulder, in silent communion.

The detective broke the spell.

"Holy shit," she said. She had turned, her attention focused on the ground.

About ten feet from the flower patch, the grass lay flattened in a long oval. Like something had been lying on it, very recently. In one motion, Jean pulled gloves from a pocket and bent down, examining something on the ground. She took a picture with her phone, then picked up whatever had her attention. Turning, she held out what looked like a small square piece of litter.

"Gum wrapper," she said, spreading out the tiny square. One side was shiny, the other smudged with dirt. "Wrigley's. Someone was here. Someone was camping here. Who—"

"It was him. It had to be," Laura said.

Jean took another pair of gloves out, giving them to Laura. "Or it's a couple kids with a Ouija board and a true crime obsession. Carefully, search the ground. Maybe they spit out the gum."

They crawled on hands and knees, dividing the clearing into a grid. It took an hour to comb the entire area, but they couldn't find any other trace of him. When they were finished, Jean held the gum wrapper in her hands. "I miss the days when everyone smoked," she said. "All that carcinogenic death and trace DNA." She shrugged. "Probably nothing. Let's go find that house."

JEAN

ACCORDING TO THE SATELLITE IMAGES OF DALE TELL-efsen's last known address, there was a lake over the border into Catron County. Google Earth showed a dilapidated house nearby. How that address had ended up on his death certificate was anyone's guess. The lake wasn't a lake but a maar—a shallow volcanic crater filled with water, said Google. On the drive, Laura read that people traveled to the lake for the same reason people trekked to Truth or Consequences—the water's supposed medicinal qualities.

The road evened out and Jean could see a broad mound of sand up ahead and the shell of a building, empty squares where glass should be. No one had lived here in a long time. Once she opened the car door, Jean could taste salt in her mouth.

"I know the sheriff over here," she said, closing the door behind her. "He's way up in the mountains. I can call him if we find anything. No need to waste his time if this is all nothing."

A footpath cut up to the maar—similar to a meteor site with a hard-edged rim of sand, the top as sharp as a knife's blade. Jean went to the water. A brown line ran across the middle where the water reflected the opposite shore. Jean wondered how far down the crater went. She dipped her fingers into the water—it was as warm as a bath. It smelled of salt, almost like the ocean if she closed her eyes, but with a cloying metallic undertone that slicked her tongue.

Laura called from behind, "Come look at this."

Laura was standing in the old house. Stepping through the doorless doorway, Jean had a hard time imagining this structure as a house. The wide floorboards were missing nails in places and ran unevenly under her feet. What was left of the walls had fissures and cracks running across their face. Jean followed Laura's eyes to what had caught her attention.

"Can you read that?" Laura asked.

A picture of a seated person had been painted on the wall years ago, judging by its wear. Next to each part of the body, a thin, faint line fanned out to a symbol and a few words in, by Jean's estimation, Hindi. Laura pulled out her phone and took a picture, then peered at the weathered image.

"Look at this top one," Laura said, pointing to the writing above the figure's head, which appeared to be in English. "What do you think that says?"

Jean squinted, trying to make out the faded letters. "Connect— no, connection to the divine by the—the crown."

"Margaret Washington Crown," Laura said. "It's not a common name. It's not a name at all."

They both studied the wall.

"You got a change of clothes in that bag of yours?" Jean asked.

FOR MOST OF THE ride through the switchbacks into the mountains, Jean was certain Laura was going to puke. She had called Sheriff Harmon and made an appointment to come talk with him the following morning. Then, in the same ten-minute window while they had signal, she had Laura find a couple of rooms at the only motel in Reserve. The task seemed to take her mind off the ninety-degree drops outside her window.

Jean kept Laura talking when her face went chartreuse at one bend.

"So Dale meets Margaret in California. He's some sort of black-sheep middle child. Why do they move back here?" Jean asked.

"But Reed said Dale went to California *with* a girl—as in, she was from around here."

"True," Jean said. "Maybe he ditched her for Margaret. Or maybe Reed got the story wrong. Family gossip got twisted in the retelling."

"Could be. The second daughter I found in the Bible— Amy—maybe she's their daughter. Dale and Margaret's."

"Could be."

"Maybe that's why Amy wasn't in the barrels. Her father couldn't bring himself to kill her?" Laura asked.

"We're jumping a few steps ahead of ourselves, but it's not an unreasonable claim."

"But that leaves the third victim. The girl unrelated to Jane Doe. Where did she come from?" Laura asked.

"I don't know," Jean said. "I think Margaret adopted her."

"I can't think of many single mothers with two small children of their own who are willing to take on a third."

"Maybe that's just who she was."

"Maybe," Laura said.

"They get in a fight, he kills Margaret, Daisy, and the adopted girl, then takes off with the baby. But he tries to hide them on his family's land. Why incriminate your family?"

"Because you're estranged from them? You want them to take the blame?"

"Which will eventually draw attention back to yourself," Jean said. She paused, thinking. "Or—he knows the land, simple as that. It's the area he knew best. But it raises the question: Did he have help? From his brother, or I suppose his father too."

They pulled up to High Country Lodge before Laura could answer. Playing up the Southwestern theme, the hotel had a covered wagon parked out front—decoration, not viable transportation. The whole place had desert suns hanging from rafters and over doors. They checked in, got their separate keys, and parted ways with plans to meet across the street for dinner.

The floor in Jean's room had a tile mosaic of turquoise and orange where she entered. The plain white walls accentuated the wooden furniture, and each ornamental groove carved into the headboard and the chair back stood out against the walls' blank canvas.

After dumping her bag and washing her face and checking in with RJ—"I'm fine, Shay called to say he'll be home for Christmas, Colleen sounds pissed at you for some reason"—Jean headed over to Ella's Bistro.

Jean saw Laura sitting at a far table in the restaurant. There were only a handful of people in the place, and the librarian stuck out with her pale skin and short hair. And a bright turquoise T-shirt with a picture of a sunset-flanked mesa. A waitress came to their table right away.

"Y'all know what you'd like to order?"

"I'll have the tortilla burger and a beer. Whatever you have in a bottle."

Laura read from the menu, twisting her lips before making a final choice. "I'll have the chicken enchilada with green chili sauce."

Jean sucked down her water, and as the waitress was about to leave, Laura piped in, "And a beer too, please."

Jean couldn't help herself. "New shirt?"

Laura pulled at the bottom edge, reviewing the upside-down picture. "There was an issue involving an errant stick of mascara I may or may not have dropped, and it turns out I did not have a change of clothes in my bag."

"I see. At least you got a souvenir."

"The gift shop back in my hotel in Truth or Consequences has an extensive collection of crystals. I may have to buy one for my sister. She'll hate it."

"You can call it T or C."

"What?"

"T or C—it's what locals call it."

"Oh. Makes sense."

Jean could tell Laura was nervous from the way she kept adjusting her fork and knife. Their drinks and food came out fast. The burger tasted like it had at least half a stick of butter running through it.

"I read somewhere that you worked major crimes most of your career," Laura said in between bites.

"That's right."

"Why'd you move to cold cases?"

"The simple answer is there was an opening in cold cases. The longer answer is harder. 'Major crimes' is a poor euphemism for child abuse. Major makes you think of vast criminal networks that cross oceans or bank heists like in the movies. Not kids." She sighed and took a drink of her beer. "It's important work, and there aren't a lot of people who can do the job. I did it and I did it well, but it takes a toll on a person. I feel bad about it sometimes, but I couldn't do it anymore. I was done." Jean took another sip. "But that doesn't mean I'm done being a cop. I have things to contribute." Jean considered whether to say more. Laura had a kind face. She decided to go on.

"When I worked major crimes, same as working a homicide, there are big stakes. You're hunting a bad guy, usually a guy, though not always. But in child sexual abuse, you're also working to save a child. Those are really high stakes. It may sound bad, but there's a degree to which cold cases—" She tried to think of a way to put it that didn't make her seem insensitive. She tried again. "With cold cases, what's done is done. Not for victims' families, but the crime itself is more removed. You're looking for the truth. A piece that went missing. That's about as much as I think I can handle these days."

"I get it," Laura said.

"Except I won't be doing it for much longer. The county's cutting back cold cases, putting me out of a position at the end of the year. I'll go babysit newbie patrol officers until I can retire. Besides, soon all our cold cases will be solved with a tube of spit—isn't that right? Third or fourth cousins who unwittingly put long-distance relatives behind bars for decades-old rapes and homicides?"

"Maybe," Laura said, giving her plate far too much study.

"It would give you more work—genealogists, I mean. There could be a genealogist on staff at every police station. What about you?" Jean asked, trying a new subject. "Why are you out in the desert?" She watched as the young woman's face changed.

"My hair," Laura said, running her hands across her scalp. "It's not like—" She paused, running a finger over the middle of her forehead like she couldn't remember a word. Jean glanced at her beer, but unless she was a teetotaler, half a beer shouldn't cause this much confusion. Laura picked up her train of thought, saying the next word like it was its own sentence. "Political—or anything. I had breast cancer. I don't like the term 'survivor' because it either sounds like the TV show or the Holocaust, and clearly, those two ideas don't belong together. But it also makes it sound like it's over. I've finished chemo and surgery, and everything looks good—my prognosis, I mean. But you don't know." She shrugged. "I have more drugs I have to take." Jean watched as Laura struggled to put together the next part. Her face changed again—like she had seen a ghost in the corner and instead of turning away, held the apparition's gaze.

"And that was bad—I mean, chemo was really bad. But after my second surgery, I had a complication. An infection they missed. I was in the ICU, and I got worse and worse. I knew I was going to die. I knew there wasn't anything I could do about it." Laura swallowed and tried to make herself laugh. "If I'm being honest, I started working on this case as a distraction more than anything else," she continued. "I wanted to see if I could figure it out. But after the emergency—" Laura paused. "The universe can come for anyone. Once you know, you can't unknow it. You can't do anything to change it, but you can use your time—" She stopped again, weighing. "You can make it matter."

Jean knew she had good reason to trust the young woman across from her. "I understand what you mean." She gave Laura a minute before asking, "When you talked about the ICU, did it feel like you were back there again?"

Laura swallowed. "Yes."

"There's a good chance you have PTSD. It'll get better with time, but there's therapy too. There have to be cancer support groups and things. What happened to you—like what happened to Jane Doe—it could have happened to anyone." She took a sip of beer. Talking to Laura wasn't like talking to Ally or Colleen. She didn't feel the burden of having to have the right answer—she hardly ever did, it seemed. And it wasn't like talking to Parker with all their verbal dancing. It was like talking to a friend.

"There are support groups. I went to one once, but mostly they seem lame. The breast cancer ones are mostly for older women. No offense."

"None taken."

"I went to one for young people, when I was first diagnosed. It was too depressing. There was this real skinny guy talking about how his lung cancer was in his bones—I couldn't." Laura shook her head. "I could try another one, I guess."

"When did you start doing genealogy?" Jean asked, knowing Laura could use a change of subject.

"I had been doing it on the side for a while, usually as a search angel—helping people find their adoptive families. Some bigger cases I'd charge for. Mostly it was pro bono."

"That was generous of you."

"My mother was adopted. I tried finding her biological parents but couldn't. That's how I got started. It messed my mom up, never knowing why. Her adoptive parents, my grandparents, they loved her. But it was hard."

"I can imagine," Jean said, taking another bite.

Laura paused a beat. "That's a lie."

"What?" Jean said, nearly choking and taking a long drink of water to dislodge the chunk of burger in her throat.

Laura picked at the peeling label on her beer. "I told my mom I couldn't find them. But I did. I found them. It wasn't even hard. Her biological parents had her young—they were sixteen. They gave my mom up for adoption, but then they went to college, graduated, got married. They went about their lives and ended up having a family of their own. I told my sister. She thought if we told Mom, it would kill her. I didn't think it was right to keep a secret. It probably wasn't, but I couldn't imagine knowing there was a family out there that could have been yours. Sisters, a brother. I bet they feel guilty. I mean, wouldn't you? Giving up a baby, then making a family later? As soon as I found them, I knew it was them. They all looked related." Laura laughed to herself. "But one day, my mom went out to her car and forgot what she was doing and wandered down the street. Then she forgot who her neighbors were, then her friends. Dementia is awful. I've been trying to think which is worse—going from dementia or cancer. I think dementia." She stopped fidgeting with the fork and knife. "She couldn't be alone. It was too dangerous and she'd get real disoriented. She'd call at two in the morning, thinking my stepfather was dead. He slept in the other bedroom because his CPAP machine kept her up. It got to be more than we could handle. By then, it didn't seem fair to tell her. She started confusing my sister and me with her friends, like she was stuck in a time loop or something, when they were all younger. Once we moved her, she went faster. She stopped remembering our names. And that was it." Laura spun the bottle one more time before finishing it off. "I told myself I was trying to protect her—we both were."

"That's a lot."

"Life's a lot. Also, my boyfriend was a jerk."

"Well, we've all got one of those." Jean decided it was safe to ask, "Have you mapped out your entire family?"

"Only to see if there was a family history of cancer. Otherwise, I was fine not knowing. I ended up cold-calling people, pretending to be someone else doing a hospital survey. My father was never interested in being a father, I never knew him. I would have been fine not knowing."

"Was there a family history?"

"Nope. I'm the only one."

They finished their dinner, paid the bill, and walked out to the street. The air was clean and thin. It reminded Jean of the Colorado base she'd lived on when she was eight, maybe nine. Could be the same air. The land had been divided into lots—parcels, acreage. Private and public. County-controlled and federal. All arbitrary when it came down to it. But as long as there were people, there were going to be fences. People claiming what was theirs and dividing it from the rest. Couldn't do division with the air.

She wanted to try and explain the difference between the land and the air to Laura. Instead, she started a silent prayer as they crossed the road.

Trucks were parked at odd angles alongside the only bar in town. Outside the lodge the covered wagon waited to say good night. The exterior lights turned the pale terra-cotta walls tangerine. Across the street, behind the paned glass of a closed gift shop, glints of turquoise and silver picked up the gibbous moon's heaven-faced half-light.

Jean prayed for the woman beside her and the woman whose body had been kept from the ground and hoped the air would carry them all where they needed to be. While she was at it, she said a prayer for herself.

The women missed him by hours—less. It could have been over. If he were away—locked up, in custody—he wouldn't be able to visit again. We could stay here, in the clearing. We'd never have to run again. I'd figure out a story to tell Daisy and Jo. If he went away, he could never hurt them again.

"That was our chance," I say, pressing my forehead to the ground.

"Not our only chance," my echo says. "You said you were going to follow him, but when he left—you didn't."

"I couldn't—I couldn't stop him," I say, kneeling by the creek. Its water, no longer smooth, babbles.

When he started packing, I couldn't stop him. I thought I was powerful. I tried. I hoped he would spend the day—caught red-handed at the scene—forty-five years later. When I saw him taking up the stakes of his tent, I tried to push the metal nails back into the earth. Grabbed at his arms, his hands. I tore at his shirt, his pants, grabbing on to his pocket to get a hold on him. Anything to slow him down.

I crawled back to the creek side, my arms rooted to the ground. My body pressed into the grass, another fallen tree, waiting for wildfire to take me.

"I wish I had never met him," I say.

"I wish I had never met him," my echo says. "Tell me about the ranch."

"How did you—" I ask. Stopping myself; I don't care how she knows what she knows. I pull myself parallel to the creek, my body in line with its glassy face. One strong wind would push me in, shattering the surface—or not. "I'll have to use names, or it will be too confusing."

She nods, and I continue. For the first time in my story, I say his name.

PEGGY

THE RANCH WAS SIMPLE BUT CLEAN. WHEN WE MOVED
to New Mexico, I had never seen the openness of the air before.
Back East, you only ever catch a small piece of the sky in between
trees or buildings. The sky—it's not something you ever think
about. But in New Mexico, you can see the curve of the earth in
the sky. After the blue came the browns: tawny, amber, oatmeal.
The desert doesn't make you feel alone. The desert brings you
into yourself.

We were living together now—Daisy and me, and Dale and
Alice and Curtis. Alice was Curtis's sister. The three of them
had all grown up together. Dale's family couldn't handle him as
a kid, and Curtis and Alice's family had taken him in.

We moved a little north from the town they grew up in. They
didn't want to be too close to family.

Dale had found this old rancher, Ernesto, who was looking
to rent out his property. There was a cemetery adjacent, but we
weren't responsible for any upkeep. The man stuck around for
a week, until he was satisfied Dale wouldn't run his property
into the ground, then moved to Colorado to be with one of his
daughters. Dale would send him a monthly check.

I remember one morning, Daisy and I were in the kitchen, mixing pancake batter.

He was in the bedroom, packing to leave. His pickup truck sat outside the window. It was brand-new—he saved for years to buy that truck. The only thing he loved more than the truck was being outdoors. He was headed to Texas to go camping with a cousin, he said.

There was a crashing sound from our bedroom. It sounded like the ceiling had caved in.

"Stay here," I told Daisy.

I walked on tiptoes and peered into our bedroom. The door was open a crack. He had pulled out all the dresser drawers and pushed the whole thing over on its side. I stared at the black rectangle gaps left in their place, trying to make sense of it. There were clothes and books everywhere when he swore again, loudly, on the other side of the door.

"Can I help?" I asked.

I felt a hand clamp down on my arm like an animal's jaw as he pulled me into the room and shoved me, hard, onto the bed. I had never seen him like this before. He had wild eyes like a tiger. I could see lines of white above and below his irises. He chest moved rapidly.

"I can't find my license," he said. "Maybe if you kept things neater, I could find things when I needed them. Now look what you've made me do."

I found the license, finally. He had left it in his pants pocket. He snatched it out of my hands—he didn't want me to see it. I read the name, and it wasn't the name I knew. I had heard him go by his first name, and I'd heard him go by his middle name, depending on who he was talking to. But this was another name altogether. I knew I wasn't supposed to see it once I met his gaze.

I had felt many things with him, but this was the first time I felt fear. And he knew it. He was on top of me fast, his belt buckle hitting the one last open space on the wood floor.

"Look what you made me do," he repeated.

Then he held both my hands in one of his own over my head and, with the other, pulled off my underwear. He was hard and fast, and he swore in my ear. I stared at the ceiling, at the small black line where the molding didn't meet the wall.

It was over as quickly as it had begun and after, he lay on top of me. His body started to flutter up and down, his chest spasming. I didn't know what was happening. Then I realized: he was sobbing.

"I can get to thinking such bad things," he said, stroking my hair. "You're the only person who makes me feel good. If you ever left, I'd kill myself."

I was holding him, apologizing, consoling.

Then he was gone.

I went to find Daisy, afraid of what she had heard. She was in the kitchen, standing on her chair at the counter, a large mixing bowl in front of her, a wooden spoon in her hand. When I turned the corner, I saw that her dress was wet and thought she had spilled milk. Until I remembered that milk was white. A yellow pool sat in the center of the chair under her feet.

Later that night, after I put the house back together and got Daisy to bed, I told Alice what had happened.

"He's always had a temper," she said, her eyes glassy. "Growing up, he always—" Then her voice cut out; she was unable to finish the sentence. Her eyes weren't focused on anything but space. "It's best to give him what he wants."

When he came back from Texas, he had Jo with him. His brand-new brown truck was caked with mud. Only the top of her little head appeared above the door in the passenger seat. He explained: His cousin had lost his job. Could we look after her until he got back on his feet again?

"You do so much around here, taking care of us. You have so much on your plate," he said, with none of the anger in his eyes from the last time I saw him. His eyes dripped sugar like melted cotton candy. "If you don't think you can do it, I can take her back."

"No," I said. I wouldn't know where Jo really came from until later. But as soon as I saw her, I knew she needed a mother—I knew she needed protecting. I thought I could be the one to do it. And in the time he was gone, my own needs had changed. I needed something from him—and I saw how this child could be part of my bargain. It's one of the truths I don't like to admit. I wanted to protect her, yes. But I wanted something for myself too.

I lie beside the creek. The love he drowned me in those first years we were together dissolved over time. The tenderness, the affection— gone. Like me. Resting my stomach against the ground, I stretch one finger into the creek, imagining the water licking my skin. My echo lies concealed behind the water's surface. I study all her lovely features, melted.

"You never asked which one," I say.

"Which one?" she repeats.

"Dale or Curtis. I didn't say who it was—I was vague, on purpose. You knew them both, didn't you?"

She doesn't answer.

"How did you know them?"

"I knew them."

"How did you know them," I try again, more firmly this time.

"I knew them before and I knew them after."

"How?" I ask, growing angry. She has asked me to tell my story, but isn't giving any of her own. "How do you know them?"

"Know them," she echoes.

"Stop repeating me," I shout. I press my eyes closed, frustrated. The rippling water sounds like a chorus of women gossiping. Their voices layered, one over the other, as they press powdered brushes to their cheeks. Fix bobby pins to loose strands. In the mirror, they examine their work and steal glances at each other. I open my mouth to ask if my echo is who I suspect she is, but before I have the chance to add my voice to the chorus, something drags me into the water.

LAURA

WHEN SHE AWOKE THE NEXT MORNING, LAURA NEEDED a minute to remember which motel room she was in. Then another minute to process what she had told Jean last night. It was the first time the sentence "I have cancer" had passed through her mouth without causing her to choke. Progress, maybe.

Until she checked her phone. A news item appeared with a link to *People*, with a headline she couldn't avoid: "After Three-Year Remission, Actress Announces Stage 4 Breast Cancer Diagnosis."

An actress semi-famous for her roles in two teen television series that Laura and Kate had obsessively watched had been diagnosed with breast cancer a few years before Laura's own diagnosis. Laura remembered reading about it then, still living under the misconception that those types of tragic, life-altering events happened to *other* people. The actress had taken to social media as a "cancer warrior"—documenting the hair, the bed, the IVs. On her good days, she and her husband took to the mountains for hikes, the Pacific for walks, the Chateau Marmont for dinner.

Cancer fit into a neatly contained narrative. *Battle. Journey. Chapter.* Simple, stupid words meant to contain what was happening to the person and make everyone around them more comfortable. Laura thought it worse when the person reinforced the language herself. The actress's public-facing positive mind-set never wavered: Cancer doesn't control me, and cancer won't change me. Going so far as to say she was *grateful*—not for cancer itself but for what cancer had taught her. She'd finished treatment, been declared cancer-free, let her hair grow. The end.

Until now. The cancer had come back. Laura knew from other reading, knew from stories overheard, knew from other articles, that when breast cancer came back and came back as stage 4, it killed you. It had traveled to your brain or your liver and your bones. It had never left, really; it had hidden among your cells. Chemo wouldn't work a second time because this cancer had learned how to outsmart the drugs. It had evolved, and no language could contain that narrative.

Laura mined the article for clues. How had they found it? Was it in her bones yet? The picture accompanying the text was from a photo shoot promoting the actress's latest prime-time drama. She wore a white suit, three-years' worth of shoulder-length hair. Arms crossed against her chest.

Her eyes blurry, Laura reached for tissues on the nightstand, knocking over her water bottle. Her chest contracted, and her face pulled itself into a knot. She tried to breathe and gave up, clicking a link to a video instead. The actress appeared more honest here, balled tissue in hand. An interviewer sat across from her in a gray suit.

The actress: "I haven't processed it yet. Before, when I was first diagnosed, I was a warrior, you know? I had a good outlook. But this, this is different."

Her language failed her. Not because her body failed her, but because her body demanded honest, truthful language. It was vulnerable. It always had been. Whether anyone wanted to admit it was another question entirely.

Then, four minutes in, the interviewer asked *the* question.

"How did you find out it came back?"

The actress shifted in her chair, no doubt remembering the first odd sensations when she knew something was wrong.

"There were odd aches. I knew, I mean, I didn't want to know, but I knew. And I didn't want to tell people after I got the diagnosis. Stage 4, they look at you, you know, like 'dead man walking.'" She paused, stared into space for a moment. "It's pretty isolating."

It was the interviewer's turn to shift in her chair.

The actress continued: "There are definitely days where I say, Why me? And then I go, Why not me? Who else? Who else besides me deserves this? None of us do."

Laura slid out of bed onto the floor, ignoring the pooled water. On the hard tile, great sobs rocked her body. She was in the SICU again; she was lying on the table, drugged, waiting for the port to go in; she was in the MRI, its banging in her ears and brain; she was crawling along the floor trying to get to the bathroom; she was staring at the ceiling with her phone in hand, hearing her diagnosis for the first time; she was staring at flashing monitors; she was everywhere at once. She had lost control, spinning from one moment to the next.

She scanned her body. Did her pelvis hurt? Her sternum? These were the largest bones. What would be next? Her femurs. She raised one arm above her head and slid her other hand under her shirt, running her fingers down the length of her armpit, searching her nodes. Then switched. And repeated.

Laura had never adopted the chapter-journey-battle language because she had lived in the place where *Why not me?* was gospel. Here was the part she couldn't tell Kate, could never tell Tim. There was no reason she couldn't be the one in ten people who would die from breast cancer. She wasn't special. Even now—perhaps especially now, now that treatment was winding down, now that she was transitioning from actively doing something to fight the cancer to merely waiting—the cancer could come back. Or she could be hit by a car, by some idiot texting. She could get a *different* kind of cancer. Here was the truth she had to live with every day: she could die.

It wound through her middle. She didn't like knowing that this was how her mind worked now, but she saw no way to undo it. A part of her wondered if she was being melodramatic, another part worried she was clinically depressed, but mostly, she was being honest with herself. *I could die.* Closely followed by the memory of the SICU. *I almost died.*

Laura checked the time. She was going to be late.

She got dressed, pulling on the stupid tourist shirt again. Checking her reflection, she saw that her eyes were blotchy, and she was three shades paler than normal. Her hand warbled like a hummingbird when she held it out in front of her. Then, without warning, a shot of neuropathy sliced through her right leg below the knee. She had never had nerve pain in either leg before. Trying to step, she nearly toppled over. The pain was twofold. It hurt, hurt like hell, but the worst part was the daily reminder of what had happened to her. She had almost died. Tears burned their way around her eyes again. She gave herself a minute.

After a minute, she limped out to the lobby to find Jean. Trying to walk normally only caused her leg to buckle underneath her.

When Jean saw her, she asked, "Everything okay?"

"Stubbed my toe on the end of the bed," Laura said, not missing a beat.

"Should we drive?" Jean asked.

Laura knew the station was only two blocks away. The town fit into three blocks.

"No, I'm okay."

They walked the short distance to the Catron County Sheriff's Department, but all the while, Laura couldn't push the actress's face from her head. Her eyes kept welling up, and she'd turn away, pretending to look at something on the ground, so she could wipe her eyes dry.

The police station had a brick exterior painted an orange that blended into the dust from the road, so that the black door appeared to float in midair. Two patrol cars were parked out front next to some pickup trucks. Jean showed her badge at the front desk, and a young officer walked them back to the sheriff's office. A tall, broad-shouldered man with a matching broad smile stood from behind his desk. Laura felt only half-present, listening to Jean make introductions.

"Sheriff Harmon," the man said, putting out his hand. "Detective Martinez, it's been a while." He turned to Laura. "Nice to meet you. Call me Ben."

Laura forced herself to focus as they all sat down. The sheriff had as much gray hair as he did sandy brown. He had one missing tooth on the side of his mouth, suggesting he was either indifferent to or lacking proximity to general dentistry services.

"Laura MacDonald here is a researcher, helping me with one of our cold cases," Jean offered, and Laura silently thanked her for trying to make her feel less like an impostor.

"One of your Does, right?" Harmon asked.

"It's our oldest case. We'd like to clear it. Mother and her two kids out on the edge of the Gila."

Be here, Laura told herself, trying to listen.

"Think I heard about it. Early '80s? Couple of barrels, that right?"

"Around there," Jean said.

"Don't know how I can help, but I'm more than happy to try," the sheriff said, leaning back in his chair.

"We think our Jane Doe and a possible boyfriend or partner, not sure, may have had a connection to that lake down in the valley."

"Detective, I thought you were precise. That's no lake."

"The maar. Excuse me," Jean said, smiling, though Laura had spent enough time with Jean to know she wasn't in the mood for banter.

"The little shack of a house sitting next to it came up as the last known address of a person of interest," Jean continued. "There were some strange drawings on the wall. Sort of like a seated figure. It's a detail that may connect back to our Doe."

"You mean some graffiti?" Sheriff Harmon asked.

Laura couldn't tell if he remembered the image or was poking fun at its insignificance.

"It doesn't look like your typical graffiti to me, sheriff," Jean said, sitting forward. Laura felt her chest tighten and watched Jean out of the corner of her eye, afraid this was going in a direction neither of them wanted.

"Could have been kids hanging out," he said.

"Could have," Jean said.

Maybe Jean was realizing that she had been led down a rabbit hole only to have the obvious pointed out: it was a bunch of kids getting high and skinny-dipping. Laura was about to explain the connection to the name Crown when she felt Jean's hand on her arm.

Sheriff Harmon thought for a moment. "You want to repeat that address for me one more time?"

As Jean did, he typed the address into his computer using only his pointer fingers. Laura winced. "Hold on, let me print it out for you." After two failed attempts to navigate the printer, he had an officer come in who got it to cooperate.

"This damn thing never wants to work," he said by way of an apology. "This is all we have for it." He slid a couple of papers toward Jean. "Sorry I can't be of more help."

Laura watched as Jean read through the pages. As her face began to drop, Laura thought she might throw up on the sheriff's desk. Or under it, maybe. She had led them all on a wild goose chase and was wasting their time.

"I don't want to take any more of your morning," Jean said. "You've been more than helpful. I appreciate your help."

Sheriff Harmon held the door open for them. "You let me know if there's anything else I can do for you."

They thanked him again and found themselves on the street. For the first time since she had started her hunt, Laura felt she didn't know what she was doing. Some name scrawled in the back of a Bible wasn't proof of anything besides shoddy record-keeping on the part of a long-dead priest.

When they were away from the door, Laura decided it was safe to ask: "What did the file say?"

"That it was a stash house for a Mexican cartel."

"Seriously?" Laura asked.

"No. It's a known vacant house where kids smoke up and have sex. Their county patrol hits it every night and kicks kids out every other. It's a dead end. Like he said. Some bored teen-agers with nowhere to go and nothing to do and a hard-on for cosmic mumbo jumbo."

How had this happened? Dale Tellefsen's death certificate had been real. Same as the address. Her leg gave out again, sending Laura pitching into the curb. She caught herself. Then her chest sputtered against her ribs. She was afraid she was going to start crying in the middle of the street. She didn't want to talk herself down. She wanted to crawl into this feeling.

"Ready to head back?"

"Head back?"

Her head spun between images of the actress and images of Margaret, smiling on the front porch. Margaret smiling with Daisy. They were the same. "But we should ask around here. Maybe someone knows something."

"Hoping that someone who lives up here in the mountains remembers an old shack that's now only used by teenagers to get high? It's a dead end," Jean said. For the first time, Laura could tell the detective was beginning to lose her patience. A hard line ran down the middle of her forehead, growing deeper each minute they stood on the sidewalk. Laura decided she didn't care.

"Maybe it was a sex club." Laura palmed her forehead as soon as she said it, searching for the word she meant.

"Excuse me?"

"A sex cult. Cult." Somehow, that didn't sound any better. She tried to explain. "A '60s pseudo-spiritual sex cult thing. California in the '50s and '60s—you couldn't drive a VW Bug to a farmers' market without running into at least two different cults on your way. Maybe Margaret had got caught up in one out here."

"Now we are officially wasting our time."

Laura's heart continued to hammer. "What about the middle brother, Dale, who was declared dead by a judge with no body? The address on his death certificate was out by the—" Laura paused. *What was the word?* Her mind was a blank.

"The maar?" Jean offered.

Laura rubbed her forehead. Her brain felt like it was submerged in a murky pond.

"Maybe they put down that address because they didn't want people snooping around their own property," Jean said. "Maybe the missing brother was a false lead. There's other investigative avenues we can work. There's this other name—Josh. And Josh's father? That could be something."

"Where'd that name come from?"

"Someone else I spoke to."

Laura paced, shaking her head, trying to clear the fog. "No—Josh something with a father is—do you know how many Joshes there are? Fun fact: they all have fathers. But 'Crown' on her license and 'Crown' painted on the wall is something. There's no way it's a coincidence," she said, trying to find logic.

"You do this job long enough and you'll learn there are absolutely such things as coincidences. I think Crown's one of them. Bunch of kids messing around, like the sheriff said. Let's go back to the Tellefsen family—or Josh."

"Why are you so hung up on the Tellefsen family?"

"I think we should take another look at Gerry Tellefsen," Jean said.

"We can't leave," Laura said. The case was spinning out beneath her. The invisible string that had been tying her to Margaret Washington, giving her days a focus and clarity she hadn't had in months, was coming untethered. Her brain wouldn't let her find the right word. The nerve running through her arm wouldn't let up. She could feel herself coming apart. She spoke before she knew what she was saying: "It could come back."

Jean turned, confused. "What—"

Laura grimaced at her mistake. "He—*he* could come back. He could be out there, right now. Hurting someone else. What about the campsite?"

"Maybe. Maybe another bunch of kids goofing around. There's nothing left to do here. We're wasting our time."

Something inside Laura slipped off its track. "You don't care about Jane Doe at all, do you?" she heard herself say.

"Excuse me?" Jean said, turning on her heel. Somehow, the line running through her forehead had grown deeper.

"You can't make it right. What's done is done. And you can't fix it."

"When you're done conducting your sidewalk survey—or whatever it is you think we should do, let me know," Jean called over her shoulder. "But I'm leaving in ten minutes."

Laura crossed the street, limping, and not caring if anyone saw the streaks running down her face.

JEAN

IT WAS AFTERNOON BY THE TIME JEAN PULLED BACK into T or C. Her arms had been shaking while she was driving; she hadn't realized someone she had known less than a week could leave her that incensed. The thing that pissed her off the most was the part that could be true. Jean couldn't be sure that she wasn't giving up easy. She twisted the leather sleeve encasing her steering wheel.

Jean regretted leaving the librarian in Reserve, but she needed a minute without a civilian detouring her on wild theories. Her phone buzzed as she got into town, and she expected another message from RJ. He had left a few voicemails, but Jean didn't need any grief for spending the night in Reserve. She hadn't bothered to answer his calls on the drive back. But when she lifted her phone to see Parker's name, she answered.

"Where?" she asked.

Jean pulled up to the apartment complex an hour and some change later. She had pushed the limit of her speedometer on the drive up to Albuquerque from T or C. A patrol car's swirling lights jumped across the street. Yellow police tape twisted in the wind. Parker joined her at the sidewalk.

"But I was just here," she told him, déjà vu sliding down her throat. This wasn't happening. "I was just here," she repeated.

"I know."

"Have you gone in yet?"

"Waiting for you."

The responding officer came out to meet them. "Someone called in a welfare check. We can't be sure how long they've been here until the ME gets here. Her ID was on the table. We saw your name on her field card."

"You did the right thing," Parker said to her. Jean was numb. She knew what was through that door and didn't want to know all at once.

Jean walked past the uniform, thinking she saw something small crouching in the bushes.

"Last door on your right," a second uniform said, this one guarding the apartment door. He stepped to the side to let Jean and Parker through. They both pulled on latex gloves before they entered.

It was like every apartment they had responded to and different at the same time. Shoes piled by the door, the kitchen sink full of dirty dishes. A chair had been pulled up to the counter, and an empty sleeve of saltines lay on the Formica next to a scraped-clean jar of peanut butter. It didn't take long to find the bedroom. Ally's body was wedged in the small space between the unmade bed and the wall, like a forgotten cardigan. For a moment, Jean told herself it wasn't Ally because her hair was different. But then she remembered about Ally's friend who was good at highlights. Jean looked again. Ally was wearing the shirt Jean had bought for her at Walmart. The small bird tattoo sat lifeless against Ally's neck. Jean knelt at her feet.

"I saw her a few days ago," she said to Parker, who came up behind her.

If haunted houses were real, surely this apartment had to qualify. Was Ally next to her, watching Jean and Parker spin silent eulogies? Jean glanced over her shoulder, but the second-hand bureau with scuff marks and the mismatched mirror had no reply. She waited for the cold block to descend on her, waited for the snaking nausea to writhe through her middle. Waited for Ally's ghost to rise from her contorted body. But the room was empty. So was she.

"I'm sorry," she whispered to Ally.

She pictured Ally's mother. They had never met. Jean knew Lisa A. Fulbright by her gravestone. She whispered, "I thought you were going to watch over her."

If Parker heard her, he didn't say anything.

They checked the deceased male in the bathroom, but everything pointed to a standard overdose, too common to count. When they passed through the front door, Jean heard a sergeant telling the uniform to give it to Guz and Larry. Jean inspected the front room. Two child-sized pink Converses stood out against the pile of adult-sized shoes.

"Do kids live here?" she asked.

The uniform had a face like he was trying to remember trigonometry formulas.

Jean asked again, "Do children live here? Did you check for any kids?"

"But there aren't, like, any toys around. There's not a kid's bedroom," the uniform said, confused and staring back into the apartment, as though a missing room would magically appear if he stared hard enough.

"When you got here, were the lights on or off?" she tried again.

"On."

"You get here this afternoon? During the day?"

"Yes," he said.

She went back into the apartment and checked in every closet, checked under every bed. She opened the bottom-most kitchen cabinets, remembering her own kids who would push pots and pans aside to make hiding spots. The chair against the counter and the empty sleeve of crackers further evidence that yes, at some point, a child had been inside this apartment. Jean marched back out to the officer patrolling the door.

"When you got here, was this door open or closed?" Jean asked, pointing to the entrance.

"Closed," he said.

"Was it locked or unlocked?"

"Unlocked."

Jean walked out into the courtyard. Crossing to a corner where the door was still visible, she crouched down in the bushes. They were empty, like the goddamn world.

Her phone rang again, RJ this time. A cold pit filled her stomach. This time, she answered.

❋

IF JEAN HAD BEEN in T or C when RJ called, the drive south to Las Cruces with her lights on would have taken less than an hour. Much less. But Jean was two hours north in Albuquerque, tripling her drive time. She lit out of the apartment, telling Parker only "Colleen" as she ran past him to her car. Jean told herself that first babies take their time. She wouldn't miss the birth of her first grandchild.

Maternity had its own entrance at Memorial Medical Center. Jean parked and ran inside. Once she signed in and entered the locked doors, she found RJ on the phone in the waiting area.

"What happened?" she said.

"Where have you been?" he said, tucking his phone in his armpit. In all the years of their marriage, he had never looked so angry. "She's fine, they both are. She doesn't have a name yet. I think Coll was waiting for you. Go on back. I'll be right there."

"Has he shown up?" Jean asked.

"No," RJ said. "She texted him a couple times."

If Jean were a different person, she'd call in a favor and have a tail put on his ass. Instead, she left RJ to his phone call and followed the room numbers along the hallway to her daughter's room. The door was slightly ajar. A nurse stood outside, typing on a computer console. Jean knocked quietly, pushing the door open as she did. The small room smelled of flesh and blood and birth. There was enough space for Jean to squeeze by the food tray to get to Colleen's bed. Her daughter sat propped up, her pale face framed by sweaty matted hair. Naked across the chest where a tiny baby slept. A blanket covered them both. Jean had forgotten how small newborns were. The baby had a pink cap on. When Colleen was born, RJ had turned to Jean with a miniature knitted cap in his hand, barely big enough to fit over his three middle fingers. "Look," he had said. "Babies come with hats."

The baby's skinny arms extended across Colleen's chest like the outstretched wings of a bird. Her daughter opened her eyes, smiled, then let the facade drop.

"I'm sorry I wasn't here," Jean said.

"It's fine," Colleen said.

Jean knew she was lying.

"It was like, way harder than people tell you."

"I know. How is she?"

"She won't latch," Coll said. "She's quiet now. I think she wore herself out screaming."

That was when Jean noticed a newborn formula bottle on the table. Newborn bottles, slender and short enough to fit in your palm, looked like tiny one-pound barbells.

"Has the nurse tried to help?" she asked.

"They're sending in a lactation specialist or something. I don't know. One of the nurses said a bunch of women delivered today so they're extra busy. I guess babies come in waves."

Jean glanced around the room. The movable crib sat in the corner. Jean found the drawer filled with diapers and swaddling clothes, then went to the attached bathroom to wash her hands first. She took a new diaper the size of a cocktail napkin and two of the pink-and-blue-striped blankets, laying one down on top of the other and folding down their top corners. "Here," she said, arms out.

"What?" Colleen asked.

"Give me the baby."

As she pulled her granddaughter from her daughter, the suction broke between their sticky bodies. The air woke up the baby, and she began to shadowbox, and a second later, yelped with the small catlike cry newborns have.

"Mom!" Colleen said, sitting up.

To her daughter: "Babies cry. She's okay."

To the baby: "Get it up. Good girl."

Jean laid her down on the blankets. Quickly, as though she had performed this origami only yesterday and not years ago, she changed the diaper, then swaddled the baby twice, nice and tight.

"Baby burrito," Jean said, motioning to Colleen's chest. "Let's see if she can latch."

"Mom."

"Get over it."

Colleen begrudgingly pulled down her blanket and put the baby to her breast. Jean walked her through the motions. Showed her how to hold the baby's chin open with her pinky finger while using the other fingers to push her nipple into the baby's mouth. Stopped her when there were bubbles at the corner of the baby's mouth, showed her how to slip in a finger to break the seal and try again until the baby latched.

"Oh my God." Colleen's head fell back into her pillow, relief sweeping her face. Then she watched the baby feed.

"They like to be tucked away." Jean smiled. "Don't look at her too long, you'll get a neck ache."

Colleen watched another moment, then put her head back and closed her eyes.

Jean wanted to warn Colleen, tell her to hold on to her daughter because the universe would come knocking. There was no controlling what would come for you. For now, Jean sat, watching her daughter and granddaughter and the promises they held, reminding herself to hold this image for keeps and a single day.

When the baby finished, Jean showed Colleen how to hold her to burp. It felt urgent that the baby had a name. She tried to mask her panic.

"Your dad said you hadn't picked a name yet," she said. The baby needed a name. If anything happened—she needed a marker.

"I was thinking of Emma Sofia."

"That's pretty," Jean said, relieved.

"Thank you."

"Has your dad called Shay yet?"

"You think he's going to care? He's probably out drinking with friends. What else do college kids do abroad in New Zealand?"

"Maybe he's mountain biking."

"Sure, Mom." Colleen lifted her head from the pillow and studied her mother. "I don't think I can do this on my own."

"You will," Jean said. But she knew her daughter needed more. "Your dad and I will help. We'll figure it out."

❊

JEAN COULDN'T GO HOME, not yet. She made an excuse to RJ about needing to drop something off at the station and drove to the 7 & 7. She paid for the tequila and the two jumbo bags of potato chips in cash, not making eye contact with the cashier, or anyone else for that matter. If she saw her own reflection, she wouldn't try to catch her eye. She drove out to the edge of town where civilization gave way to the valley and, farther out, to the Gila.

The night was cold and quiet. She drove to the water tower overlooking town, passed the No Trespassing warning sign, and parked. She took a long drink from the bottle and opened the first bag. It popped when she opened it and filled the car with the smell of factory-made barbecue flavor.

Jean had seen this night coming for a long time. She felt stupid for being surprised by it. Her job and her family had been two tracks running side by side through her life, and she couldn't ride both at the same time. Jean took another swig of the tequila. The whole town was surrounded by mountains, on every side. Even from up here by the water tower where she could see over the range to the east, another serrated black line lay behind, like another row of teeth swallowing her whole. Like her job and life had swallowed her. She pulled out her phone. Parker answered on the first ring.

"You home?"

When she pulled up to his house, all his lights were off. Parker answered the door in different clothes from a few hours ago. Those hours felt like years. He stood in the doorway. Jean wanted to kill the space separating them.

"Did Moreno call you? Paul Henderson died—"

"No," Jean said, shaking her head. "Not now." She put her hand on his chest. He wrapped a hand around her back, pulling her inside with one arm and closing the door with the other. They stood in the dark, not needing the light to find their way. His hands reached up her back, his fingers in her hair. Small traces of him that she drank in small sips over the years deluged her. He smelled like soap—he had showered. His mouth was on hers. He tasted like fire.

After, she felt too guilty to go home. She drove to the station, where they kept a pullout cot in a spare office, not for times like these, exactly, but for other times like these. Except the light to her office was on. Turning the corner, she recognized the young man sitting behind her desk. Smith? Levi? What was his name? It was the blond rookie patrol, the Midwestern transplant she'd recruited to help comb the directories. His eyes were red like he'd been crying. Then she remembered Paul asking her to watch out for Josh. Remembered Moreno warning her that one of the baby patrol officers was family.

"The fuck are you doing in my office?"

My echo drags me farther down. The creek closes itself around me and so does the dark. It makes no sense—I know that it makes no sense—but I choke for air. This sensation of gagging—it's the same as hands closing around your throat. Like vines wrapped around each other, we descend. This is no creek. It's a chasm. And at the bottom, I can see her face clearly. At the bottom, our voices vanish.

I can't escape. The water is so cold. I try to wriggle out of her grip, but every time I move, she curls around me tighter. I think of Jo—maybe I can travel from here. I push the cold from me, push the vines tethering me to my echo and the dark. I picture our house—the tree swing. I picture the girls laughing. Daisy's blond curls, Jo's small, round face.

I gather the last of my breath as the girls come into sharper focus. They're no longer images of themselves—they're real. I'm standing in the ranch kitchen, washing up from dinner, watching them play from the window. A woman walks down the driveway. I can't make out her face, but she has incredibly short hair. Her skin as pale as a ghost. She's scared, but doing a good job of hiding it. The girls don't see her coming until the last second. They freeze. Jo sits on the swing, Daisy behind her, ten white knuckles gripping the rope.

I go to the door, ready to call to them that the woman is a friend. I've seen her before. But the old man who lives here walks past me, beating me to the door. Not being able to see through walls, the woman has no way of knowing he has propped his rifle against the counter. Right next to his fried egg sandwich. As I yell to warn her, something sharp pierces my side and I open my eyes, finding myself back in the creek. My face just above the water's surface. I gasp for air, filling my lungs in giant heaves. The pain ricochets up and down my side. She pulls me back into the chasm—going down, down, down.

LAURA

THE CLOSEST UBER, ACCORDING TO THE ONE BAR OF signal on Laura's phone, was 234 miles away. Laura tried to read the menu. Two grizzled men sat on stools by the counter. Laura imagined they held those stools every morning, and if you were to inspect the seats, you'd find perfect impressions of their asses carved into the cracked red pleather circles.

The sun glanced off the other side of the window, making her reflection appear opaque and solid. She hoped someone here would sell her a strong morning cocktail in a glass the size of her right thigh. The same waitress from the night before walked toward her table. Laura hoped she wouldn't recognize her.

"Hello again. Can't get enough of us?"

Laura had hoped wrong.

"Lumberjack special and coffee. You don't happen to have Bloody Marys, do you?"

"Afraid not."

Of course not.

The waitress took her menu and appeared less than a minute later with a pot of coffee. She filled Laura's fat white mug and disappeared into the kitchen. The coffee was bitter. They had let the pot sit on the burner too long. Laura overcompensated with sugar.

Laura retrieved Tami's notes and files, the one folder she had brought with her from the motel that morning. Tami the friendly Albuquerque librarian had been nice to her. Tami wouldn't have left her in a mountain town to fend for herself. Then Laura autocorrected. Jean had told her she was leaving in ten. As in, you want a ride back, have your ass ready. It was Laura who had put herself in this booth.

Laura flipped through the pages. Then she pulled out the list of cemeteries. Swiping away a new voicemail message from Kate, Laura opened a map on her phone. She pinned the address for the lake house, then pinned the locations of the barrels and the old church. One by one, she went through the list of cemeteries. It didn't take long. One stood out like the center of a wagon wheel, with each other point fanning out in an equidistant circle. An address in Silver Spring.

When the waitress returned a few minutes later with the lumberjack special, she found a twenty sitting under the sugar canister.

❁

IN EXCHANGE FOR A glowing five-star Yelp review and forty dollars, the motel owner had agreed to drive Laura to Silver Spring. Laura watched an old wrought-iron gate come into view as they got closer. What she had thought was an ornate pattern across the top was instead lettering.

Crown Ranch.

The motel owner asked again if this was the right address. There wasn't another mailbox, cross street, or any other sign of civilization as far as either of them could see.

"Yes," Laura said, praying it wasn't a lie.

Not wanting to drag or carry her bag down the gravel driveway, she tucked it behind the gate once the car pulled away. She kept her phone, a pen, and a notepad. From the road, Laura could see only the white farmhouse, made gray with time and dust, set way back at the end of the long driveway lined with trees.

She could have been the only person for miles, yet she felt a million sets of eyes on her, watching from the windows.

Normally, she would have knocked on the front door. But the front porch was filled with some sort of car engine, an old oscillating fan, a box window AC unit, and a small platoon of paint cans. Laura walked around toward the back of the house, figuring that if anyone still lived here, they used a side door for nonexistent trick-or-treaters, lost Girl Scouts selling Thin Mints, and nosy librarians wandering the desert.

Behind the house sat an ancient tree and an aging barn. A single swing hung from one of the branches. There was wind enough to rustle the branches overhead, but the swing stayed fixed in place as though someone were sitting on it.

Behind her, a door badly in need of WD-40 opened.

"Can I help you?"

An old man wearing denim overalls stepped through the door. His glasses were as large as the bottoms of Mexican Coke bottles. He looked like a Cabbage Patch Kid, wizened and brought to life.

"My name is Laura MacDonald," she said, defaulting to her professional voice. "I'm a librarian—" she paused. Normally she'd say where she was from, but she couldn't figure out how to explain what a research librarian from New Haven was doing in Silver Spring, New Mexico. "I'm looking for a county cemetery I had down as being here at your address."

"County cemetery?" the man asked.

"Yes sir," she said, mimicking the detective's manners. New Englanders were "yes" and "no" people, not "sir" and "ma'am" people.

"Well," he said, pulling off his glasses and rubbing them with a piece of untucked shirt. "I guess it *is* technically a county cemetery. Though it's mostly all these folks." He gestured behind him.

Laura did her best not to let her eyelids disappear under her eyebrows. She shifted from foot to foot, wondering how far and how fast she could make it down the driveway.

He laughed to himself. "Here, I'll take you round."

Laura kept her distance. The smell of eggs wafting from the man helped. Behind some trees, a small path cut through the brush. After another minute, they came to a metal gate, and the man stepped to the side, gesturing for Laura to enter.

Simple, unadorned white crosses rose from the ground, each one equidistant from the next. There was only enough room for the name, the date of birth, the date of death, and a simple description: mother, sister, wife, or father, grandfather, uncle. The ringing in her ears grew as she passed the first marker. Something was missing. No one had a last name. She walked around the cross to make sure she hadn't missed it. Then another, and another.

Harry, Mabel, Sylvia, James, Ned, Ernesto, Blair, Eugenia, Dorothea. No one had a last name. To construct their family tree, she would have to line up the dates and relationships; she couldn't follow patrilineal lines. Family plot or not, there should be surnames.

"They don't have last names," she said to the old man, the ringing subsiding with the sound of her own voice.

"No, I guess not," he said, as matter-of-fact as though she had commented on the weather.

"And these are all your family?"

"Yes, the Crowns."

"Okay," she said, thinking faster than her mouth could summon the questions that needed answering. "Is there anyone buried here who wasn't a member of your family?"

"Over yonder," he said, nodding to Laura's right. She had never heard someone say "yonder" before. A day of firsts.

A few rows of more traditional gravestones, all faces of angels and crosses and, in one case, a flower etched into marble slabs, filled the far corner.

"Do you mind if I take some pictures?" she asked.

"Not a problem," he said. "I got an egg sandwich I gotta clean up after, or I'll never hear the end of it. I'll leave you to it. You need anything, give a holler." He didn't wait for a reply before turning.

"Wait!" Laura called, louder than she meant to. He took his time in turning. "Have you ever heard of a Margaret Crown?"

He thought for a moment, scratching the patch of white hair above his left ear. "Don't think so."

"What about Peggy?" Laura asked, remembering Cynthia's message.

"Nope."

"Just a thought," she said.

When he turned again, a bit of wind picked up a stray branch, dragging its bony fingers across the dirt. A shiver ran along Laura's spine, and she checked over each shoulder, making sure she was alone. Then she got out her phone, swiped away a missed call from Kate, and began clicking. She had three days left before her flight. Three days left to figure out if any of these people were related to Jane Doe before heading back to her real life. The one where she had to answer her phone.

⁑

THE OLD MAN DROVE her back to T or C and dropped her off at the Walmart. Laura had two missions: get supplies and rob the police station, in that order. After her first stop, Laura called a cab and left the superstore with a roll of Scotch tape, canned wine, Post-its, pre-sharpened pencils, a prepackaged dinner of rotisserie chicken and mashed potatoes, and a two-pound bag of Twizzlers. Outside the police station, she begged the driver to wait for her, but she hedged her bets by stashing her bags behind a bush in case he took off.

It was half past nine. The desk officer remembered her, thankfully, and she signed in before heading back to Jean's office. She didn't know why, but she walked on her tiptoes, afraid to make a sound. By some miracle, the office door was open.

Laura flipped the switch, and light flooded the room. She turned on one of the desktops along the back wall. She sent the pictures of the graves to her email, then printed them. First goal, accomplished. Now the second.

Laura found an empty Bankers Box under the table and stacked the directories quickly. Using the printer seemed kosher, but removing evidence was another thing. Laura closed the door behind her, walking as quickly and nonchalantly as she could manage out of the station. She mouthed a thank-you when she saw the cab driver.

She opened the door and slid in the Bankers Box.

"The River's Edge Motel, please. And thank you for waiting," Laura said, wiping her forehead with the back of her forearm.

"You forgot about the bags in the bushes."

❄

LAURA SHOWERED, CHANGED INTO the bathrobe, and took out the plastic football-shaped container holding the rotisserie chicken. She tried to grip the side to pull the clear top off but couldn't. Her useless hands kept sliding off. Turning the chicken around for another way to open the plastic, she glanced at the ingredients. What was she doing? The chicken was probably full of hormones and God knows what other kinds of preservatives and chemicals. She couldn't eat this. They probably injected cancer directly into the chicken breast.

Then, like lightning, a shot ran through the entire length of her arm, beginning in her shoulder, curving through her elbow, and ending in the space between her ring finger and pinky. Laura swore and dropped the chicken, and thankfully, the plastic football didn't pop open. Involuntary tears filled her eyes as she cradled her useless right arm against her chest with her left. *It will pass*, she told herself.

Her phone buzzed again with another text, probably from Kate, and Laura turned her phone off completely. She ripped open the bag of Twizzlers with her teeth. These chemicals she would ignore, for now. With one red candy straw hanging out of the corner of her mouth, Laura focused her attention on the cemetery.

She taped each grave on the wall across from her bed in the same order as they appeared in the cemetery, hoping their positions would help indicate their relationships. Using the years as a guide, Laura began constructing the Crown family tree. By the end of her first can of wine, she had settled on the first and second generations. By the second can, the third generation. She downshifted to food to double-check her work, shoving cold mashed potatoes into her mouth.

Laura pulled out the non-Crowns who had been buried nearby. Hank Ohls, Mary-Pat Tiennan, Lisa A. Fulbright, and Alicia Cortez. Two other gravestones, out on the edge and facing the east, were so worn down that Laura couldn't make out the names.

The wind found its way through her window and brushed the curtains. Laura paced the room. The graves could be related family members, or they could be something else. How did she know they were all from the same family? The word of one old man? Laura heard the wind like a fist on the glass. A handful of papers lifted from the desk and fell on the floor like flat snow.

Laura turned to the old directories. Serrucho and Kirkland was the area where Margaret was found. The Crown Ranch was a good forty miles away. Maybe there was a connection.

Laura organized the leather directories by year, then checked one more time: still no Crowns. She eyed the names on the perimeter of the cemetery—the ones not related to the old man. Laura opened a spreadsheet on her laptop. As soon as she clicked the green icon and saw a new clean sheet of small gray rectangles open, she felt a sense of calm. She could do anything with a spreadsheet. Excel was her superpower.

Working through the first of the outside names, Laura found two Ohlses in the directories. She went one by one, copying names, addresses, years, and occupations into the spreadsheet. Together, they told a story. Generally, people appeared the first year they were married—or the first year they moved to town. Children came regularly, every two years or so. A large gap between the years that children appeared in the directory told a story: a child had died somewhere in those intervening years.

Nothing remarkable about the Ohlses stood out. The two families stayed at the same address in Kirkland—probably brothers. They each had four children: a large family by today's standards, but small for back then.

Laura moved on to the next family. No Tiennans in the Serrucho and Kirkland area. Lisa A. Fulbright didn't appear in the directories, but an online search pulled up a Las Cruces article: she had been murdered by her husband and—Laura winced— kids were involved. She stopped, reading the article. "Detectives Martinez and Parker arrived on the scene just after midnight." Was that *her* Martinez? Another strange coincidence? Laura moved on.

Afraid she wasn't going to find anything, Laura said a small prayer before turning to the last name: Alicia Cortez.

Laura turned, quickly, thinking she saw something across the room in the bathroom doorway. The room's silence had swelled and grown rigid, as though Laura could feel it sitting next to her. She shook her head. *What's wrong with you?* she wondered, and returned to the last name.

Alicia Cortez was in one of the directories, though not as a wife or head of household but as a child. Gonzalo Tomas Cortez and Helen Ruth Cortez lived on Horton Street in Kirkland. They had two children: Gonzalo Jr. and Alicia. They lived there for four years until the entry changed. In 1940, Helen Ruth Cortez was now listed as head of household with the notation *wid*. Gonzalo must have died the year prior—she was a widow. The following year, the family was no longer listed at Horton Street. Laura stared at the page where their name should have appeared.

Where had they gone? *Please have stayed local, please have stayed local*, Laura repeated to herself.

Laura returned to the directories, scanning for a Helen with two children and possibly a new last name and new address. Finally, she found Helen—listed as Helen Ruth Yates, married to Phil Herbert Yates, along with her children on Sweetwater Drive.

Laura thought she remembered that street name from somewhere, but she was too distracted by the children's names: they had each been anglicized. Gonzalo Jr. was now John Thomas Yates. Alicia was Alice. Laura ran her finger over the elder sibling—John. He had not only lost the "Jr." tying him to his father but had been forced to take his stepfather's surname—Yates. To make up for the loss, perhaps, he had taken his father's middle name, yet this too had been anglicized, with the addition of the *h*.

Then Laura saw a final child listed. Her finger hovered over the page, her eyes disbelieving the cluster of letters: *Dale*. Here was the missing brother of Gerry and Nancy. The taboo subject no one talked about. But why?

Laura studied the page, returning to the street name. *16 Sweetwater Drive*. She did know that name. Laura flipped to the

Tellefsen family. They also lived on Sweetwater, at number 12. Two houses down from Helen. Dale had been sent to live with a neighbor. Why? What arrangement had been made?

A cold patch of air hovered over her bed where Laura had laid out the directories. She shivered. When the cold intensified, she checked to see if one of the windows was open—it wasn't. Checking the AC, she saw it was off and turned on the heat instead. The thermostat was directly next to the dresser, and she found herself tethered to the spot, staring at herself in the mirror. Pulling down her shirt's neckline, she flexed her chest muscles, grimacing at her striated reflection. She shook her head, pushed the image of herself away, and got to work.

Laura didn't leave her room for another twenty-four hours, calling out for food and more canned wine. She didn't change out of the bathrobe either. She realized this was the longest she had gone without noticing pain in her arms. When she was done, she had mapped out the entire Cortez/Yates family, complete with birth certificates, marriage certificates, and death certificates.

After, Laura turned on her phone to check how many lunatic voicemails she probably had from her sister. She was surprised Kate hadn't sent out a welfare check on her. Laura would call back tomorrow. Then, the last message, a text, not a voicemail, from Jean. She showered, dressed, and ran out the door—but not before taking the directories, her stack of yellow legal pads with all her notes and family tree diagrams, and the picture of Margaret at Christmas with her.

JEAN

JEAN HAD PREPARED THE FILES—ALL THE FILES—
posting some to the whiteboards, leaving others in neat stacks on
her desk, for Laura's return. She had wanted to call the librarian
as soon as she had gotten to the station the night she spent with
Parker, but thought it best if they both cooled down first. She
had used the time to figure out exactly what she had and what
she didn't have. And to lambaste Patrol Officer Joshua F. Davis,
nephew of recently deceased detective Paul Henderson, who—
even after he retired, after he was moved to hospice—couldn't
put Jane Doe in a box. He had saved and copied some of his
files, bringing them with him when he left the force. But when
he gave his nephew the job of returning some files and gathering
different ones, things got confusing. The nephew had lost track
of which files he had returned and which new ones his uncle
wanted copies of, only taking one or two at a time. This was why
she had never seen the Florida lab report—it had literally gotten
lost in the nephew's shuffling. The kid also jammed the copy
machine every time he went to use it.

Unfortunately, stringing the rookie up by his thumbs was
frowned upon. Jean had to make do with a verbal thrashing that
left the kid's cheeks fifty shades of candy-apple red.

"Are you going to tell the commander?" he asked. His eyes were as red as his embarrassment. His uncle, who had been like a father to him, had died the same day as Ally. The same day Jean had taken a blowtorch to her marriage and ended up at Parker's front door.

"No," she said, feeling bad for the kid. "But I'll be on you like a hawk. You ever get the feeling you're not alone, feel like there's someone out of the corner of your eye, watching you—think of me."

The kid had nodded, nose running, shoulders hunched, and with his tail between his legs, headed for the door.

Once Jean had—finally had—all the files, she went back to the beginning, picking up the trail she had been trying to pick up from the jump. The land, the clearing where the bodies had been found. That slice of wild woods between the federally protected forest and the state-owned campgrounds and trail system, the acreage that used to be owned by Ironside Mining. The question she had never figured out the answer to: Why had Bjorn sold that tract of land off some ten years before the barrels were found?

The bulk of the files she never had access to—because she hadn't known they existed—were the company's financials. Another stack of spreadsheets. Balance sheets, income statements, cash flow, assets and liabilities. Jean hunkered down, locked her door, and pulled on her big-girl pants. Twenty-four hours later, ignoring texts from RJ, bleary-eyed and brain-fried, she had it. She texted Laura.

When the librarian arrived, the young woman looked how Jean felt. Run over by a freight train and eager for more. She held the box of directories and a stack of yellow legal pads.

"I'm assuming you got back okay," Jean said.

"The High Country Lodge now has a 5-star Yelp review, thanks to me," Laura said, as though this was supposed to make sense. She put the Bankers Box of directories on a free spot.

Jean bit her tongue. "I'm sorry for leaving you. I shouldn't have."

One side of the librarian's mouth curled down. "It was my fault. I was—I don't know what I was, but I have something to show you," she said, laying the yellow legal pads on the desk. "I found Dale."

Jean let Laura go first. The Tellefsens had lived on the same street as the Yates family. Dale, the black sheep, had been sent to the neighbors. John, Dale, and Alice, listed as siblings, lived at the Yates household on Sweetwater Drive. Gerry and Nancy Tellefsen—Dale's biological siblings—a few doors down. The librarian kept harping on the Yates kids' names.

"Gonzalo and Alicia Cortez—when their mother remarried, they're adopted by the stepfather, lose their biological father's surname, and their given names get anglicized as well."

Something about "Cortez" made Jean's stomach flip, but she couldn't place why. She left it for now. "Say that address again," Jean said, frowning. She went to her computer and did a property search. Her finger ran down the screen. "Alice Waddell and Susan Waddell, 16 Sweetwater Drive," she said, her jaw dropping an inch. She had never thought to look for Susan's name before. "Alice Waddell's maiden name is Alice Yates. I have that right?"

"Yes. But the name on her birth certificate is Alicia Cortez."

Cortez. It kept nagging her. Jean remembered what Susan had said about her mother. Susan had lived as a caregiver. The house they lived in together belonged to her grandparents. And her mother's brother lived up the street. But which brother—John or Dale? She did a reverse search in the directories, finding Sweetwater Drive in the back, then flipping to each entry for the street in the main section, organized by last name. Whatever house the brother lived in, it wasn't listed in the directories.

"We need to go," Jean said, throwing on her blazer. "Now."

There's no light down below. No light from the moon, or the sun—no trace of the night flowers and their sweet perfume. Maybe this is what I deserve. Sylvia can watch the girls. She has before. I belong to the dark. The pain in my side subsides.

"Open your eyes," the voice tells me.

The water is nearly black. I imagine that I can feel its edges along my skin, making me real again. We're deep, deep underwater.

"I need you to see something," she says.

In the drowned half-light, a collection of bones lies scattered.

"What is that?" I ask.

"It's me," the voice beside me says. "I told you, Peggy. I'm your echo. I'm what came after."

It is my fault. There: proof as hard as stone. I told myself he wouldn't do it again to shield myself. I hadn't been able to save my girls. I made a terrible choice. I couldn't allow myself to imagine the possibility he had done it again. The truth cuts me in two.

And I remember—I remember how I got here. I remember it like it was yesterday.

PEGGY

CURTIS HAD LEFT FOR TEXAS. A FEW DAYS LATER, ALICE left too, on a trip to buy supplies. It was only Dale and me and Daisy—we had never been alone, the three of us. Usually, Dale was busy—something always needed fixing or cleaning—but with Curtis gone, Dale was around. He never left my side, asking if he could dry dishes or sweep up.

I figured I would still make a proper dinner, even if it was only the three of us. We ate and played with Daisy. Normally, she grew quiet around dinner. She hardly ever ate a bite. But tonight, she ate everything I gave her, and we played checkers on the floor. Even though we all lived together, Dale rarely played with Daisy. But tonight, I saw a different version of my life playing out in front of me like a chapter I had missed.

We read stories, and when I put Daisy to bed, I remember her turning to me and asking if it could always be like this. I didn't know what she meant. Just us and Dale, Daisy said. I should have put it together.

The only thing I did put together was that I couldn't have a baby with Curtis. It was Curtis who had the temper. Curtis who had lost his license. Curtis who had forced me down, and got me to apologize after, as though it were all my fault.

The first time I ever had sex, I got pregnant. I wouldn't know for a few weeks if that afternoon with Curtis had made another life. But I knew I couldn't raise a baby with him. That time after the missing license, with a name I had never seen before, was the only time we had been together. Before, he had only ever used his hands. He said he couldn't sometimes. Sometimes turned into always. I should have realized what the real problem was.

I made a point of getting drunk, fast. I had been wearing one of Alice's dresses, loose along the shoulders, with one tie at the waist. I slipped off my bra after putting Daisy down.

Dale was talking about something, the pecan crop or a book he had read, I don't remember. I only remember feeling like I was wearing a layer of fire on my skin. I remember shifting in my chair, so my dress slipped off one of my shoulders. That was when he stopped talking.

"You're beautiful, you know that?"

I saw a different version of myself in his eyes. For the first time in a while, I felt like someone's center. I didn't have to go to him, he came to me. His hands were soft, finding my body, moving mine into his. I remember the candle's reflection against the windows. I remember thinking: *This is what it's supposed to feel like.*

After, he said: "I don't want you to get the wrong impression. I don't want this to be a one-night thing. I've wanted to do this for a long time." His fingers were in my hair, stroking it away from my face. "When they come back, we need to be careful. There's somewhere we can go."

I would have followed him to Jupiter.

When Alice came back, we acted as though nothing had happened. She didn't suspect anything. Dale made up a story about how his father wanted to do some repairs to a lake house he owned, a couple of hours south. Though every time I called it that, Dale corrected me: "It's technically a maar." He hadn't talked to his father in years; he saw this project as a way to repair the bridge between them. All the walls needed painting, a couple of floorboards needed to be replaced, things like that. He asked Alice if she thought it was a good idea for me to go help him. Told her how his father needed more help these days, with his other brother helping more with the business. Did she think I was up to the work? Didn't I seem lost, like I needed a project—a distraction?

It would mean I would have to make some trips down there. And I'd need a license, eventually. Until then, he'd have to drive me. Ideas are strongest when you let the other person think it was their own. She thought it was a good idea. One down, one to go.

When Curtis came back from Texas, with Jo beside him, I wanted to protect her, yes, but I also saw that I could leverage the situation. I knew, even then, there was a baby growing inside my belly. I placed a hand over my stomach.

"We can raise her, of course," I said. "Maybe, on the weekends, I could go help Dale with his family's lake house. It would be a good break from the kids."

All I wanted was something small for myself. Something that made me feel real, made me feel like a whole person. Dale gave me that.

Curtis replied: "I think it's a great idea. I'd be happy to watch the girls on the weekends."

After I died, that line would haunt me, forever.

LAURA

WHEN THEY PULLED INTO SWEETWATER DRIVE, JEAN put the car in park and turned to Laura, smiling.

"Why don't I go in first—make sure she's home. Then we can go in together," the detective said.

A car was parked in the driveway. A row of dolls sat behind the back dash. It looked like someone was home. Laura decided not to put up a fight. "Sure," she said.

"You have the picture of Margaret at Christmas?"

Laura pulled it from its folder and handed it to Jean.

"Don't know if I'll need it," she said. Laura could tell by now when the detective was bullshitting her. "Going to take your family tree too, just in case. Wait here," Jean said. "I'll be quick."

Before Jean got to the front door, Laura called out, "Remember, some people called her Peggy."

Jean nodded, then knocked. A woman around Jean's age answered. With her natural silver hair, turquoise caftan dress, and metallic bangles, she was a walking Home Shopping Network set. The door closed behind them.

After a few minutes, Laura got bored. She'd said she would wait. That didn't mean she had to wait in the car, right? She was the one who had found Sweetwater Drive. She was the one who had found Dale Tellefsen. She had found the Crown Ranch, all on her own.

Laura stepped into the street. Another road of packed dirt and sand. A few trees stood at the corner where Sweetwater met the main road in front of the Old Serrucho Bar and Store. Jean had gone into number 16, where the Yates family used to live. Farther in was number 12. That was odd, wasn't it? Normally, the numbers started small and then got bigger as you moved down the road. It wouldn't hurt to look.

After waiting a second to see if Jean would materialize, Laura walked down Sweetwater Drive, the calm blue desert sky above her, encouraging her on.

JEAN

WHILE SUSAN STEPPED INTO THE KITCHEN, JEAN
cleared the two bedrooms off the living room and the bathroom without her noticing. Jean returned to the living room
only a second before Susan returned, holding out a glass of
water.

"Thanks," Jean said, taking the cup. She had placed Laura's
yellow legal pads on the coffee table. Now, she picked them up,
finding the one she wanted. "Like I said, I have a few more questions. You were so helpful last time I stopped by."

"Whatever I can do to help," Susan said, sitting across from
her. She spread her turquoise dress across her lap.

"You said this house was in your family for a couple generations, right?"

"Yes," Susan said, now adjusting the bracelets on her forearm.

Jean handed her the yellow pad with the Yates family tree,
following lines and arrows to Susan's name, under her mother's—
Alice Waddell. Next to Alice was her brother, John Thomas.

"How do you have all this?" Susan said, uncertainty wrin-
kling her forehead. She studied the yellow page.

"A librarian, well, she's also a genealogist—she's waiting
outside in the car—helped out with our Jane Doe case. Your

mother's name came up in her research. Is her gravestone in a little county cemetery up in Socorro? Next to an old ranch?"

When Laura had described the cemetery, Jean knew it right away. It was the same place Ally and Eli's mother, Lisa A. Fulbright, had been laid to rest. How many times had Jean visited the place?

"She ever tell you why she wanted to be buried there?"

Susan's eyebrows furrowed. "She lived up there for a little while." Susan swallowed hard and straightened her bracelets.

"Anyone else live with them up at the ranch?" Jean asked.

Susan nodded before she answered. "An old family friend—Dale."

The sun hit low on the floor, reflecting off the bracelets on Susan's wrist and catching Jean's eye. A memory of another bracelet, of fingers gripping a woman's shoulder, hit her.

"Those are real nice," Jean said, nodding at Susan's wrist.

"What, these?"

"Help me out with this, but don't those bracelets look an awful lot like the ones this woman is wearing?" Jean said, pulling out the picture of Margaret, the baby, and the unnamed man at Christmas.

As Jean held out the photo in front of her, Susan went white, terror clawing her eyes. Susan's fingers moved to the interlocking bracelets on her wrist, hovering there, turning them over until she held the small plate with the engraved name between her fingers. She blinked hard, three times, trying to make the image in front of her come into view.

"How do you have a picture of Uncle Tommy?" she asked.

It was Jean's turn to go white, though she had better experience covering it.

"Ma'am, do you know the people in this picture?"

"That's my uncle Tommy, but I don't know who the woman and child are."

"Your uncle, is his full name John Thomas Yates?"

"Yes."

"He was your mother's brother?"

Susan nodded.

"And he went by his middle name. He had to change his name when he was young, after his mother remarried. Their birth name was Cortez. I think your uncle had people call him Tommy because it was the closest thing to Tomas, the last part of his father's name he was allowed to keep. But I bet he went by another name too. You ever hear anyone call him Curtis?"

Susan's arms began to tremble.

It had never sat right with Jean, that name in the margin. Curtis. So close to Cortez. Curtis, Cortez. A son and a father. Like Paul had said, he followed his father. With his name. The two rhymed, nearly. Like the slight dissonance in a call-and-response, or the warbling variation of an echo.

Susan didn't answer her question. "Who is that woman?"

"That woman was named Margaret Ann Washington." She paused, remembering what Laura had called to her. "Some people called her Peggy."

A tornado could have come through the living room and Susan wouldn't have moved from her seat. She stared at her wrist, slid the bracelets off, cupping her hand together to slide the smallest circle over her knuckles. A small silver rectangle, large enough for an inscription and nothing else, hung from the largest circle. When she handed the bracelets to Jean, Susan's fingers slipped, letting the chain fall. It swayed in the air.

"My uncle gave these to me," Susan said. "He told me he got these at an estate sale."

Jean took the chain of bracelets, gathering them back into a circle, and flipped the tiny rectangle over. There she saw the inscription: *To Peggy, Love Curtis*, etched in silver.

"That's her, isn't it," Susan said. "That's Jane Doe."

"Yes, it is." Jean told her mind to record the next part like a video—she knew she'd be returning to it.

"How was your relationship with your uncle, growing up?"

Susan crossed her arms over her stomach. "We lived next door to him for a few years, in this house. My parents split up when I was two. My mother would leave me alone here when she worked late. Sometimes he would come over to watch me."

"Did you like spending time with him?"

"No," Susan said. She sounded like she had been punched in the stomach. There was a reason this case never sat right with Jean. She had seen this movie before.

"Did your uncle ever hurt you?" Jean asked.

"He'd make me play games. Here or at his house. I wasn't supposed to tell anyone." She laughed to herself. "I never did."

She looked at the bracelets in Jean's hand.

"But I knew something was wrong. I mean, it was obvious. I didn't figure it out until I was older, and then it didn't matter anymore if I did tell someone."

"Where is your uncle now?"

Susan stood and went to the window, almost happy to have something to do with herself rather than stare at the bracelets. She moved a curtain aside. "I can't tell if his truck is there. He just got back from a camping trip."

Jean's eyes went wide as Susan surveyed the street.

"You mean he still lives here on this street?"

"He never left," Susan said, pressing her finger against the glass to point down the street. "He lives in his in-laws' old house. Well, in a camper behind his in-laws' old house." Susan glanced back toward her driveway. "Didn't you say you had someone waiting in the car? I don't see anyone there now."

PEGGY

IT WAS A FEW WEEKS INTO THE WET SEASON. CLOUDS appeared out of nowhere, then the rain came, hitting the roof like it would break through. Dale and I had to be more elaborate with our lies. I had my own car by then. I was supposed to be gone for a few hours. Dale had taken the baby with him on an errand. We were going to meet up. I had left the girls home with Alice and Curtis, but I turned around, afraid the road would get washed out.

When I got back to the ranch, I saw Alice's car was gone— she was supposed to be home. Then I saw, in the middle of the day, all the lights were on. In all the bedrooms. I should have listened to the fist in my stomach.

Once inside the door, I sensed possibility in the silence. Like something was waiting for me. Then I heard Daisy, under the rain, whimpering. And something else, like grunting. When I opened her door, it was like a can of black paint spilled out where her small body should be on her bed. My mind wouldn't let me see.

His hands clamped down on my shoulder. I knew what was coming. I didn't want Daisy to see. I had to get out of that room and ran to the door. It takes a long time for a person to die. It's a good thing. Your body is made to fight. It gives other people time to save you. I got as far as the living room, steps away from the front door. I tried to grab the doorknob—but he stopped me. I watched my hand, fixed in midair, inches away from the knob. He had me by my hair. Then he pulled me toward him. I felt his hands close around my neck. I kept waiting for the front door to open, for someone to stop him. But no one was coming.

I watched my crumpled body on the floor, and I knew I was gone. He stood over my body, and his sapphire eyes were somewhere else. He turned back to Daisy's room, and I was on top of him, clawing at his chest. We both heard it—tire tracks carving the wet gravel driveway. Someone else was home.

I was already dead, clawing at Curtis's back, trying to stop him. I ran to the window to see who it was, and Curtis went to the kitchen, where he kept the rifle.

I ran outside and screamed at the car window, pawing helplessly at Dale's face behind the wet glass. He had the baby in the back seat, asleep—car rides knocked her out. He must have been worried about flash flooding too and turned around.

Raindrops passed through my hands. Curtis stood on the porch with the rifle in his hands. Dale had only closed his eyes, no doubt catching a nap while the baby slept. He couldn't hear Curtis through the rain. Curtis took a step down, a second, looking for movement in the car. He came around to the side of the car. Dale's eyes were closed.

I did the only thing I could think of. I pictured the small black hole of the rifle. If I was nothing, I could fit inside. Curtis drew the gun, and I curled myself into the impossibly small hole, like a leaf burning. When he pulled the trigger, the rifle jammed.

Dale heard the click, somehow, through the rain. When he opened his eyes, he saw the rifle barrel staring him down. He put the car in reverse and flew down the driveway. It was the last time I saw him. And the last time I saw my youngest daughter.

Curtis turned to the house. I knew what he would do. The effort of twisting myself into a knot, blocking the rifle, had left me exhausted. The effort depleted all my remaining strength. He went into Daisy's room, then Jo's. Erasing each one like he did me. I knew there wasn't anything else I could do. I wrapped my invisible body around Daisy and Jo, whispering in their ears that I was here, it was going to be okay. Another woman's voice joined mine, saying over and over, *It's going to be okay.* Then we were together, on the other side. The woman who had whispered into my ear introduced herself: "My name's Sylvia." She was like us, a ghost. We all watched as Curtis went to the phone to make a call.

A little while later, we heard another car in the driveway, and I went to the window. A man I had never seen before emerged. He was broad through the shoulders, tall. I heard Curtis call him Gerry. He could have been Dale's twin, the resemblance was so strong.

I heard Curtis tell Gerry a story—*he'd* been the one to return to find Dale over our bodies. Dale had drawn the gun. The only true part was the ending: Dale drove off with the baby.

I watched Dale's brother—I could tell he wasn't sure what to believe, but it didn't stop him from helping. He left and came back with two barrels. They rolled our bodies inside. Jo screamed for her rabbit when Curtis put it in the barrel and poured a milky-white liquid over the contents—something Gerry had brought with him, probably from work. We followed the barrels in the truck bed. We were outside, in the woods. And there we stayed.

The only thing I brought with me from the house was my guilt. Instead of following Curtis to the car, blocking his rifle, what if I had gone straight into the house? If I had more time, could I have saved Daisy and Jo, somehow?

"Open your eyes," her voice says.

I heave, expelling great raking, wet coughs.

"Stop," she says. "You're fine."

I blink, twice, realizing we are at the creek side. Beside me sits a woman. I know her face, remembering a picture Dale kept on the little table next to his bed—of him, his brother, and his sister—his real brother and sister.

"I'm sorry for scaring you," she says.

"You're—you're Dale's sister. You're Nancy."

"Nancy Tellefsen," she says. She has drawn her knees into her chest. "Tom—he went by Curtis when he was with you—he moved back home after he killed you. Not that I knew. No one did. He told us all that Dale had run off after a bad breakup. I think he told my brother something different. If only Dale and my father—" She stops herself, shakes her head, letting something go. "I hadn't seen Tom since we were little. I always had a crush—the boy who lived next door. I had no idea what he was really like."

"And he—" The question's a cruelty I don't wish to bring on this woman. "He put you here?" I ask, blurring the truth.

"No," she says, pointing up the canyon. "Higher up that cliff-side. But I found you, eventually." Nancy picks at some feathered grass growing between rocks along the creek side. "I blamed you for what happened to me. I see now, it wasn't fair. You lost more than I did."

I peer into the water, knowing, without asking, what she means.

Her eyebrows rise in the middle, like canyon cliffs. "Two boys. He never touched them. Only me. He's the one who thought of their names. I went along with it. They're okay, mostly." She crunches her eyes closed. Her mouth presses into a sad, tangled line. She wipes her face with her forearm. "I think I'm okay too. Now that I know."

"What do you mean?" I ask.

"It wasn't your fault. Which means, it wasn't mine either."

Nancy stands and puts out a hand for me to hold on to. "Come on, I know the way. He lives with my younger son—out beyond my parents' old house." Nancy steps into the creek. By some magic, the water only comes to her knee. She bends down, cups water in her palms, and rubs it along her arms.

"They live on Sweetwater Drive."

LAURA

A SMALL, SQUAT ONE-STORY HOUSE SAT AT THE END OF Sweetwater Drive. The metal roof had rusted along alternating ribs as though the stripes of orange and sun-bleached blue were on purpose. The yard was a scattering of brush growing in upright, tufted clumps on the sandy ground. Two trees framed the front walk, but otherwise there wasn't a spot of shade around the house. The opposite side of the road was undeveloped, the brush higher here. Laura found a spot to crouch behind where she wouldn't be seen, she hoped.

It was the house that, on paper, belonged to John Yates— Nancy Tellefsen's second son with John Thomas Yates. It was strange, wasn't it? That the second son had been given the father's name? Even stranger that the son wasn't a Jr. They did, after all, share the same name.

According to the parcel map, 12 Sweetwater had the largest lot on the street. Trees and bushes and weeds colored the area green that continued along the lot line, giving the backyard privacy. Behind the house in the two-acre lot sat a line of cars in various stages of decrepitude. One was on cinder blocks; another was missing doors. Various abandoned push lawn mowers sat in a semicircle as though they were discussing town gossip. Behind scrap row, more abandoned machinery. The arm of a backhoe lay across a pile of metal sheeting. A small boat was tipped on its side, acting out a long-ago shipwreck. Behind this jumble, another building. Long and narrow—a lost Lego block, sitting alone in the desert carpet. The yard around this building was tidy. The building had a flat roof with generously wide eaves, blanketing each window in shade.

Odd, thought Laura, squinting to make out the farther building. It was the middle of the day, but it seemed the lights inside were on.

She ducked into the brush, wanting to check out the last building and also not wanting to go traipsing through the backyard.

Laura inched closer to the second house. On closer inspection, it was a mobile home minus mobility. A row of lattice separated the base from the ground. It was newer pine, as though it had been recently replaced. A faded brown pickup truck was parked along the far side of the house. She hadn't noticed it before, but there was a gap through the backyard-junkyard for an ad hoc driveway. The truck gave her pause. Someone was home.

She hesitated, studying each window. Her chest rocked steadily as her heartbeat took over. Was there a back door? Could someone be behind the house, out of sight? Maybe she should go back. But what if someone was there? It was better to know than to tuck tail, right?

Crawling farther down to get a view of the house's back, she saw it. The rest of the lot was a manicured, organized desert garden. Like pictures of English country estates with boxwoods organized into geometric patterns, except the rows here were succulents, cacti, and tall grasses she didn't know the names of. The square patch of desert a carefully tended stamp of green. Taller cacti cast shade in one of the corners. Paths of crushed white stone ran straight, then turned at sharp right angles at the corners. The whole maze differing shades and shapes of green.

Except for the trellis rising up the house's back wall. Brightly colored flowers with little trumpet-shaped blooms made a backdrop of reds and purples against the green floor.

When she reached back to pull her phone from her back pocket to take a picture, she felt a hand clamp down on her shoulder, tipping her backward into the brush.

"What are you doing?" Jean whisper-screamed. "Are you trying to die today?"

Laura rolled over, staying prone. Jean pulled her farther back into the bush. Together, they lay on the ground, propped on their elbows, peering at the house.

"That house belongs to our guy," Jean said, pointing to the mobile home and garden. "There are no property records, no deed. On paper, it doesn't exist."

"Who? Dale?" Laura asked.

"No—Dale wasn't involved. Wrong place at the wrong time." Jean pointed again, this time to the front of the lot. "The first house belongs to John Yates, Nancy's younger son with John Thomas Yates. This one," she said, indicating the house right in front of them, "belongs to his father. I spoke to the niece. Thanks for staying in the car like you promised, by the way. She identified John Thomas Yates as the guy in the Christmas photo. Uncle Tommy, she says, lived up in Socorro County, at an old ranch, with Dale, her mother Alice, and I'm pretty sure, with Peggy too. John Thomas Yates, her uncle, also went by Curtis, which explains a note the original detective made in the case file. I think when John Thomas was living up there, he was going by Curtis. The guy started his career on patrol in Socorro. He must have known John Thomas from when they were both living and working up there. That's why he wrote down 'Curtis' instead of his legal name. I think Yates was going by Curtis when he was younger, maybe to throw people off, but also as a nod to his birth name."

"You mean Cortez?" Laura asked.

The detective nodded.

"That's interesting," Laura said, thinking of other instances when surnames were turned into given names. It happened all the time. "But how do you know he's the—"

Jean grabbed Laura's forearm. The detective froze beside her. The back door had opened. From the narrow frame, a tall man, somewhere in his seventies or eighties, emerged. Faded blue jeans and a plain white T-shirt. The bottom half of a tattoo on one arm, the top covered by his short sleeve. Based on his age and what Jean had said, this was John Thomas Yates. Also known as Tom, sometimes Tommy. Also known as Curtis. Named Gonzalo Cortez at birth. A man with as many aliases as—Laura's train of thought was cut off when the detective spoke.

"I've seen him before."

JEAN

EVERY NERVE FIRED. EVERY INCH OF HER SKIN HUMMED. If the brush caught fire around her, she wouldn't have noticed. If the moon fell from the sky, she wouldn't have blinked. She knew this old man.

He had been the one resting alongside the trail when she first went to the clearing. The mottled skin, the sunspots—they were all the same. But his body language had changed. Before, when they crossed paths, he had been fumbling with his water bottle. He had lost his car keys, or so he said. It had been—she saw now—all an act. Down to the water dribbling from his chin. He wasn't a doddering incompetent. He was many things, a chameleon. He was a hiker, a hunter, and—now, Jean took in the full scope of the carefully tended succulents, agaves, prickly pears—a gardener. When she saw the waterfall of flowers covering the exterior, she blinked. Certain she was imagining the scene.

The entire yard spoke to one man's need to control his environment. To bend the natural world to his will. The crushed walkways of straight lines and hard turns. The succulents planted in evenly spaced rows. Even the flowers growing on vines up the trellis—they should, by their very nature, be tangled, woven randomly into each other and their wooden frame. Instead they had been pinned, inch by inch, in neat vertical columns of red and purple.

He strode to the corner of the yard in quick steps. Pulled out a watering can and filled it from a cistern and pump.

He began to water the flowers framing his back door.

With his attention focused, Jean glanced around, tried to wiggle backward another inch or two into the brush. Laura hadn't moved since he appeared. Good God, what had Jean been thinking? She had brought a stubborn, know-it-all, motormouthed librarian, prone to petty theft of Bibles and phone books, into the desert to die. Thinking of the civilian beside her, Jean reached behind her back, unclipping her .45. After nineteen years, today could be the day she discharged her weapon in the field. She didn't want it to come to that for a few reasons. Primarily, the only way they would get this guy for Margaret and the girls was to watch him, wait for him to slip up. He couldn't change his routines, couldn't know he was being surveilled. It would jeopardize her line of attack. He couldn't know they were here.

Next to her, Laura's arm shot out, hitting a branch. She grimaced, her face clenched in pain. She rubbed the spot on her elbow with her other arm. Mouthing to Jean the word *Sorry*.

The old man heard. Most people, when they heard an unexpected sound behind them, spun. An involuntary response from a nervous system programmed to fight or fly. He was wired differently. With the watering can in hand, he turned, inch by inch, slowly. As though he were simply moving on to a different patch of flowers that needed his attention. Jean watched, her palm now firmly around the .45's grip, as the man put the watering can down and stepped toward their hiding place in the bush.

She could announce herself. It would be over in a second. Unless the guy kept a weapon on him to water the flowers, they weren't in actual mortal danger. Although at this point, with a man who lived by himself out in no-man's-land, she wouldn't put it past him. But she couldn't announce herself. Jean's plan would never work. She didn't have him yet—a photo and a bracelet weren't enough. They were window dressing.

He stepped closer to them. Jean hated not having the upper hand: lying prone, stomach-down, in the dirt. The sun wasn't in her eyes—she had one thing going for her.

The only part of her body she was moving was her eyes, and she didn't dare take her eyes off him. Next to her, Laura had gotten the message. The young woman had practically stopped breathing. Jean had only a partial view of the librarian. Since her arm had jerked—Jean actually didn't know what had happened; she had seen the young woman rub her elbow the same way in Reserve—Laura hadn't moved. Terror turned her to rock.

The sound of his foot grinding the walkway closest to their hiding spot was like a dull knife running across a porcelain plate. A small blue-and-black bird hovered on a low branch, unmoving. Nature's alarm, itself too frightened, had failed. In the brush, the air was immovable. As though everything around her collectively held its breath, waiting to see if he would come any closer.

The hush was broken, not by sound but by light. A piercing white light flooded the bushes where they were hiding, as if someone had placed a searchlight directly on top of them.

Nancy leads me out of the clearing, through the woods. Unlike Jo, she doesn't snap herself from one place to another; she flies.

We are through the piñon—its needles cannot touch our skin.

We are over the canyon—its walls a poor barrier.

We are painted by the desert air—our invisible bodies leave silky waves in our wake.

Birds do not tremble, do not take flight as we fly.

We are everywhere, we are nowhere.

We are there.

The street sign declares this place Sweetwater. But I know different.

A small block of a house sits on hidden stilts covered with crisscross lattice above the desert floor. Rough brush out front, but the back—the back a desert garden. Why put all your care, all your work, hidden behind the house?

Because the garden is only for him.

There is my Curtis—Tom, to Nancy—standing in his garden, at its edge. I feel them before I see them, hiding in the rough brush flanking his yard. I know the fear of being hunted. I tried to put my body between my girls and his body before. It didn't work. I had drawn my own body away from him, trying—failing—to put space between him and them. It wasn't enough when I was alive. Maybe, today, it will be. After all, I started a fire to protect the hikers. I scan the yard, searching for something to use. There's nothing but a watering can.

Nancy takes my hand. She seems sure of herself. We stand, one in front of the other, placing ourselves between Curtis and the women. With our bodies stacked, the sun catches, refracts. Light explodes. I feel heat radiating through my chest and limbs.

Curtis raises an arm to cover his eyes. The women don't move. Good. He takes a step back, turning his head, back and forth, searching for where the light is coming from. As though we were a troublesome bulb to be turned back off. Nancy's hand squeezes mine. Insubstantial alone, together we make a shield.

Curtis stumbles, steps back, keeping his eyes pointed at the ground.

"Run," I say.

He takes another step, and his leg catches on a prickly pear's Ping-Pong-paddle-shaped leaf. Six needles pierce his calf, and he curses. I want to drive the needles deep into muscle. I lean toward him, but when I do, our light fades. Nancy grips my shoulder, pulling me back. Ignoring her, I press forward. I want to make him bleed.

The light dims, returning the backyard to normal. He picks his head up, looks around, peering back into the bush. Perhaps wondering if the light's source is hidden there.

"Margaret, don't," Nancy calls behind me.

I want to hurt him. Only a fraction of how he hurt me.

Nancy reaches for me, yanking one arm, but I stretch the other, clawing at him.

He takes another step toward the bushes, peering down.

Nancy wraps her arms around me, pressing me to her chest. We trip over each other and end up kneeling on the ground. She's behind me, her arms across my chest, her head pressed against my shoulder blade. The sun hits us again and forms a brighter, blinding white. Curtis is forced back on his heels and tumbles backward, like a beetle caught on its shell.

He turns himself over on his hands and knees, pushes himself up, and goes inside, limping on the way.

Nancy releases me. Behind us, the women start to breathe again. Can they sense us? See us?

"Margaret," Nancy says, pointing to his house. "Look what we did."

Along the back of his house, he has grown flowers. In shape, they're not unlike ours in the clearing. But these are smaller, colorful. Their heart-shaped trumpet petals open in the day. Our light hit the trellis. The outline of a man's body is pressed into the red and purple. Around his edges, the green leaves have turned yellow. The flowers' blooms have dried and turned to husky deadheads.

Behind us, the women have escaped. Their footsteps echo down the street. A car door closes; an engine starts. Our work here is done. The rest is up to them.

I have two questions for Nancy. When I was alive, I would stumble in insecurity. Hesitate. Never say the thing I wanted to say in the moment it needed saying. Today's different.

"Why don't you blame me for what happened? Back at the creek, you said it wasn't my fault. But it was. Not only what happened to me, but what happened to you and—" My throat catches. I don't want to say the next piece. I force the words out like bile. "And my girls."

"I wanted to blame you, at first. When I wasn't blaming myself. It was his greatest power because it let him get away with it, again and again. Him and every other monster like him. They make us believe it's our fault. Then they make others believe the same. What happened to me isn't your fault. It wasn't mine either." she says. I lean into the idea, trying to believe her. I could, perhaps. If it was only me. But I should have protected my girls. Endstop.

The second question, one whose answer I've longed to know and been afraid to know, all at the same time: "Is Dale still alive?"

"Yes," she says, and tells me where I can find him.

My stomach flutters at the idea. Dale, out there somewhere. I try to picture what he looks like as an old man. "Where will you go now?" I ask.

"Check on my boys. Then—I don't know. We'll see. Where are your girls? I never thought to ask."

"They're safe."

"You'll get them and go back to the clearing?"

Another time, I would have said yes. Now, I'm not so sure. There's possibility in not knowing. Sometimes having the answer is freeing. But certainty in one direction brings limitations in another.

"There's someone I should go see," I say. "I owe them a favor."

"Who?" Nancy says, her forehead creasing.

"Another echo."

LAURA

IT DIDN'T MATTER THAT JEAN'S OFFICE DIDN'T HAVE A clock. Laura had lost all sense of time. She had no idea how many hours in a row she had been up by this point, but there were several Chinese food container carcasses on the desk. Some were from lunch, some dinner, and some second dinner. Forget about counting cups of coffee. Come to think about it, she had promised Kate she'd call—what was that, yesterday? Had she remembered to tell her she wasn't coming home on her original flight?

Jean paced on one side of the room. The detective named Parker on the other. A younger guy closer to Laura's own age had given up completely and was sleeping with his head on his arms at the table next to her.

"He doesn't leave his trash out," Jean said. Laura had heard this sermon before. Entitled "The Number of Ways John Thomas Yates Is Not Cooperating with Our Surveillance and Patrol." Maybe Laura could put her head down too.

"He takes any trash, any recycling, straight to the dump. Always goes when it's busy—Saturday mornings. Doesn't use the town dump—no, no—why would he do that? Make it a little easier? Uses a private disposal company. Can't get in without a warrant. Can I get a warrant with a bracelet? Would I like every judge in Sierra County to laugh me out of their office?"

"He doesn't go anywhere," Parker said, ignoring the rhetorical question and moving on to the second way Yates was neglecting to hand over evidence.

"When he does, he doesn't smoke, doesn't throw out a cup," Jean said. "Doesn't go out to restaurants, bars."

"Maybe we could hire someone to give out little samples of General Tso's chicken in the grocery store aisle. Think a toothpick would be enough?" Parker asked, peering into a takeout container, armed and ready with chopsticks. He put the box down, his mouth a frown, chopsticks coming up empty.

"No," Jean said, pressing her fingers into the bridge of her nose.

"Look, we know the guy's in there. We know he's our guy. Let's go in there, get the biggest team we can—get SWAT from all the other counties combined—and go grab him," Parker said. This wasn't the first time he had made the case for force.

"No," Jean said. "We don't have a warrant. We don't have anything besides a bracelet. We need his DNA. Period. Even with his DNA, I can't link him to my victims. The only DNA of theirs left is maternal. This guy—this POS—there are more. I run him through the system, and I guarantee there are other open cases out there linked to him. He's done this before," Jean said, leaning over the table. "We run him through the system, we're going to get a hit. This wasn't his first and it wasn't his last. We get him on something else."

Parker sighed.

"Don't forget about the other daughter," Laura said, barely able to keep her head up straight. Laura had said, time and time again, that they had the baptism records for baby Amy. She could be the one who connected him to Margaret and Daisy. "If she ever had reason to upload her Ancestry or 23andMe results to one of the public platforms. If she ever got Ancestry or 23andMe in the first place. What about—" she said. Laura forgot what was supposed to come next. Jean and Parker studied her, waiting, until she finished with an apologetic, "Never mind." The guy taking a nap had the right idea. Her brain was full of cotton balls.

Laura put her head down, trying it out. Her face rested on an open map of the area. There were black dots for where they had been stationed in unmarked cars, watching Curtis's house on Sweetwater. Jean kept calling him John Thomas Yates. Laura, Curtis.

Because Curtis was the name Margaret had known him by. That was the name of the man who brought Laura to New Mexico. She supposed they all really should be calling him by the name on his birth certificate, Gonzalo Tomas Cortez Jr. Maybe it didn't matter. Maybe it did. An officer interrupted, showing up at Jean's door with a note in hand.

"Says I'm supposed to check on Laura MacDonald, age thirty, five foot six, short brown hair. Last seen by her sister going into Bradley International Airport, ten days ago. Was supposed to fly home yesterday, but never showed up. Kate Einhorn would like to know if her sister is okay. Any information would be appreciated."

Laura had done it. She had turned herself into a "Missing Sister" post.

Jean smirked. "Sounds like you should probably give your sister a call."

"Does that mean you'll take care of this?" the officer said. He was blond and acted more scared of Jean than Laura did, which she took comfort in.

"Yes, Officer Joshua F. Davis, I have it," Jean said. The kid nodded and skedaddled.

"Maybe he . . ." Jean started. Laura couldn't see it—the only things she could see were the backs of her eyelids—but Jean had crossed her arms over her chest. A chair's legs scraped the floor as someone sat down.

"Maybe we should call it a night," Parker said. He never said much to Laura. He said less to the other officer, who was now beginning to snore next to her. Lately, Laura was feeling like a third wheel. "I think we broke the young'uns."

Jean sighed.

Laura was going to protest being called both broken and a young'un, another word she never thought she'd say out loud, but as she picked up her head, the map came with it. Maybe some errant sweet-and-sour sauce had made a glue.

"I am not—" was as far as she got before the paper map demanded her attention.

"Do you know how ridiculous—" Jean started, leaning toward her. The paper was lifted away from Laura's cheek. When was the last time Laura had showered? Jean stopped mid-rebuke. She held the map out in front of her. Laura wiped her face with her sleeve.

"What are the names of John Thomas Yates's two sons with Nancy Tellefsen?" Jean asked. Laura knew she was talking to her and not Parker. She also knew Jean knew the answer; this was another rhetorical question.

"John and Reed Yates," Laura said. By now, she knew the family tree backward and forward.

"Why isn't John named John Jr.?" Jean said. Laura blinked, trying to figure out why Jean was smiling.

"I—" Laura stopped. "I don't know why. I had the same thought before. Back when I had intelligible thoughts."

"I'll tell you," Jean said, spreading the map on the table, avoiding any other spilled dipping sauce. "He isn't named for his father." Jean put her finger down on the map. "He's named for this mountain. Here, look."

Laura stood to see better. She peered at the map. Little curved lines for elevation ran parallel like miniature rivers across the peaks on the eastern side of the Gila.

"Moccasin John Mountain," Jean said first, her finger under the name. Then she drew her finger west, to another. "And Reeds Peak." The detective's eyes were wide, her smile wider.

"Parker," she said. "Tell Laura—would you rather be good or would you rather be lucky?"

"Lucky," he said. He was leaning back in his chair with his eyes closed.

"And why's that?"

If they were doing a bit, Laura didn't know the punch line. It sure sounded like a bit. Like they'd done this back-and-forth before. It was one of the reasons Laura was—she didn't like to admit it—growing jealous of Jean's former partner.

"Because I'm smart enough to know I'm not in control of any of it," Parker said.

"But what if you thought you could be? What if you thought you could control everything you touched?"

"Come again?" he asked.

Jean turned to Laura, who—she didn't like to admit it—was happy to have Jean's attention for whatever reveal was about to come next.

"I know how we're going to get him."

JEAN

IT COST A BUCK FIFTY TO RENT THE TRUTH OR CONSE-
quences Civic Center auditorium for the day. The clerk showed
Jean and Laura around the hall, which could be confused for
any multipurpose elementary school gym—raised stage, empty
wooden floor with stacks of folding chairs hanging on their
racks along the walls, ready for action.

"The stage fits up to sixty guests, per fire code," said the
woman who had showed them around. "The audience fits
another eight hundred. You said on the phone you were setting
up an auction?"

Jean nodded. "Are there tables we could put by the front
door? For people to sign in?"

"Let me check to make sure they're still in here," the woman
said, moving over to a double door at the back. Her head disappeared into the dark. "Yep, they're in here. How many you need?"

"Three or four in the front. Another one or two in here along
the side. For water bottles and snacks."

"We can set them up for you," the woman said, locking the
door behind her.

"And where are the thermostats?" Jean asked.

The woman pointed to the stage. "The one for in here is just behind that curtain. There's another out front. I can point it out to you."

"You have anything else scheduled for this month?" Jean asked.

"The next event is the annual Gathering of Quilts, which isn't until next year. So no," she said, unlocking a closet door off the main stage, peeking inside, and closing it again.

Jean exchanged glances with Laura. The librarian shrugged.

"We'll take it," Jean said.

"I never asked," the woman said. "What is it you're auctioning? Art? Paintings? Or—an estate?"

"Nothing like that," Laura said, half smiling.

"We have some land we're hoping to sell," Jean said.

JEAN PEERED OVER LAURA'S shoulder as she clicked through the pages they needed information for.

"First, description," Laura said, her fingers hovering over her laptop.

"Large property, directly off route—"

"No, no. It has to open with pizzazz."

"'Pizzazz'? What are you—eighty-two and hitting Friday church bingo? Even I don't say 'pizzazz.'"

"Look at this one," Laura said, clicking over to another tab. She read, "Incredible opportunity. . . Amongst the landscape of this Hancock County gem. . . Exceptionally well-managed timber—"

"He's not going to care about timber," Jean said.

"Or—Don't miss this outstanding opportunity," Laura said, trying another.

Jean massaged her temple and thought for a moment. "The last one wasn't terrible."

"Okay," Laura said, going back to the first page. She narrated as she typed. "An incredible opportunity to own a piece of heaven."

"Too much."

"An incredible opportunity to own a piece of nature."

"Fine. Keep going," Jean said.

"Ten acres of undisturbed wilderness adjacent to the Gila National Forest, perfect for—"

"Hiking, camping," Jean said, finishing the sentence. "Your own private rolling hills, creeks, and canyon views."

"Someone's getting into the spirit," Laura said, typing. "Now—the actual parcel details." She was silent as she filled these in. "And here—we upload the photographs." They had gone back to the clearing the day before to take pictures of the area.

"Anything else?" Jean asked.

"The Lands of America people said we could keep the listing up for eight weeks," Laura said.

"You put the auction details down?" Jean asked.

"Right here," Laura said, pointing to the screen. "We still think ten thousand?"

Jean nodded.

"What are the chances he's going to figure out this land isn't actually for sale?" Laura asked. She had brought up this point before. The Sierra County auditor had refused to post the information, saying that filing inaccurate property reports violated several state laws. The ten-acre parcel they had copied and pasted from the parcel information RJ helped Jean pull when she first reopened the case included the barrel site, the nearby creek and surrounding clearing, and a tract leading back to the road for private access.

"Even if he has a couple doubts, he won't care. He'll want it to be true. In his mind, it *is* his land. He won't be able to help himself."

"I hope this works," Laura said. "You ready to publish?"

"Go ahead," Jean said.

Laura clicked a button and sat back. "Now what?"

"Now, we make sure he sees it."

✾

JEAN ASSIGNED OFFICER JOSHUA F. Davis to come in the next day wearing business casual. She handed him a stack of flyers and a heavy-duty stapler. Told him which areas to cover. Laura bought targeted ads on Facebook.

"Think he's on MySpace or Tumblr?" she asked.

"Am I supposed to know what that means?" Jean said.

"Never mind. Facebook should be plenty."

✾

ON THE DAY OF the auction, they were all in place. Officer Davis and a handful of other detectives dressed the part, taking people's names, identification, and down payments in certified check.

"Explain to me again how this isn't entrapment?" Laura asked. They were hiding behind the stage curtain, watching the handful of people filtering in.

"We're not coercing him into committing a crime. There's nothing illegal about attending an auction for a parcel of land not actually up for auction."

"Can't someone sue us for fraud then?" Laura asked.

"Me, not you," Jean said. She pulled out the form she'd had Laura sign from her back pocket, bringing her into the official fold. Jean tore it in two and tossed it in the trash bin next to her. "You are no longer a volunteer deputy for the Sierra County Sheriff's Department. You are attending this auction in no official capacity and are here as a private citizen only. Probably as some podcast-bingeing true crime nut. You understand?"

"Got it," Laura said. She tucked in her shirt and straightened her hair.

"Now, remember: it'll be better if he's angry." She held out Laura's auction paddle. "Good luck."

Laura took the paddle and went out the side door behind the stage, heading back to the auditorium where she would blend in with the other attendees.

Jean studied the bottled water and coffee carafes lining the table alongside the far wall of the auditorium. She'd personally mix him a margarita, but bartending a land auction at ten in the morning would raise a couple of red flags.

When she saw him enter the double doors, wearing a pressed shirt and chinos with a crease ironed down the center over worn-out hiking boots, she pressed her finger to the thermostat, cutting off the air. In one hand he held the pamphlet they had put together on the various sites for sale, and in the other he held his auction paddle. He passed by the table of coffee and water, not taking either, and took a seat toward the front.

From behind the curtain, Jean watched as a few more people filled the seats. A couple of guys from the squad were filling in as auction attendees. Parker sat in the rear middle, pretending to scroll his phone. Laura had taken a seat directly in front of Yates.

Jean was about to give the nod to the auctioneer to begin when the doors opened a final time. In stepped someone she hadn't expected. Reed Yates entered, holding his auction paddle tentatively. She couldn't tell how the introduction of this wild card would affect the father. Maybe for the better. Maybe for the worse.

As Reed entered, he scanned the room, looking for someone. When he pegged the back of his father's head, he stopped. Jean waited, trying to predict whether he'd go sit next to him. When he took a seat on the other side of the room, Jean gave the signal for the auction to begin.

The challenge, as she had laid out to the cattle auctioneer brought in to run this phony land auction, was that they needed to stretch it out. Normally, these things took less than ten minutes. They needed more time. Even more so now that Yates hadn't taken a bottle of water or coffee to start.

As the auctioneer stepped to the podium, the soles of his cowboy boots clapped against the stage. He wore a plaid button-down, square glasses, and a gray handlebar mustache. A screen behind him showed the welcome slide they had prepared. Jean had pulled several other tracts of land and properties for sale around the county. If one of the non-undercover-police attendees actually bid on one of these sites, there would be an awkward conversation later.

"Welcome folks. We've got a special day today. Some down-right stunning pieces of property. We're going to begin in the southern part of the county and move our way north. To start, a tract of land outside Derry," the auctioneer began. Jean gave him the signal to slow down from the wings. "We have two hundred acres that can be subdivided into eight separate tracts. This is an absolutely fantastic opportunity for residential or commercial development. Investors, don't miss this chance."

Behind the auctioneer on the pull-down screen, a video played a montage of their photographs.

"Bidding will begin at—"

Before the auctioneer could finish, Jean pulled the projector's cord, cutting the feed. Jean hadn't told him her plan, only Laura. The librarian sat forward in her chair, then spun around to find the projector's source, feigning confusion.

"It looks like we're having some technical difficulties. Give us a couple minutes, folks. We'll get her back online and ready to go."

Some people pulled out their phones; others turned the pamphlet over, reading. Jean watched John Thomas Yates. He hadn't seen Reed yet.

"Get a drink of water," she whispered.

Jean watched as Laura reached into her bag, fiddling around for something. Then she pulled out something small—Jean couldn't see it—and turned to face Yates.

"What the—" Jean said. "Laura—" There was no point. The librarian couldn't hear her. She was talking to him. Jean's only view was the back of Laura's head. She was talking with her hands—she was nervous. By the man's face, he was uncomfortable, humoring her. Whatever it was she was saying, she wouldn't shut up. Then she put out her hand, offering him something. He took it. Jean watched as she opened a stick of gum, sliding one into her mouth. Incredibly, John Thomas Yates did the same, folding up the shiny silver wrapper and tucking it in a front pocket.

Jean stuck the projector cord in, halfway. The screen went fuzzy. She pushed it in all the way.

"Looks like we're back online—" the auctioneer began. He had been trying to make eye contact with her, but she'd been ignoring him, too focused on Laura's scheme. She hadn't yet turned back and kept yapping at Yates. Jean pulled the cord a second time. Laura threw her hands into the air, said something else, then stood, leaving her bag on the chair. She went to the table and got two bottles of water. Jean watched as she offered one to Yates. He took it, twisted the cap open, and took a sip. Jean slid the cord back into place.

"There we go," the auctioneer said. "Now—we were just getting started with bidding."

One of the decoy detectives bid on the Derry property. The auctioneer moved on to a second property, this one a sprawling cattle ranch up for sale. Another decoy bid on this one. Then the slide changed to a wooded forest floor.

"This next one is truly something special. This tract of land abuts the Gila National Forest. Perfect spot for your own cabin, a home away from home. The land includes a creek, and some stunning views of the surrounding canyons."

He continued. The footage, like the others, started at the ground level. Jean had hired the photographer because he swore he could get video of the area from a remote-controlled camera. It looked like a miniature helicopter when he had set it up in the clearing. She had led him there herself, at dusk, to capture the footage. The video didn't have any audio. Late afternoon sun honeyed the trees and canyon walls. The camera hovered over the tree line, capturing a bird's-eye view. Jean watched Yates. He sat forward in his chair, his jaw motoring on that stick of Wrigley's. He took another sip of water and placed the bottle on the floor by his feet.

"Bidding will start—" The auctioneer hadn't had a chance to finish before John Thomas Yates's paddle was in the air. "We have our first bidder. Ten thousand, bidding starts at ten thousand and I have the gentleman up front," he said, nodding at Yates. "Is there another?"

Reed Yates raised his paddle.

"And I have a second, do I have eleven? I do. Eleven thousand in the back. Do I have twelve?"

John Thomas Yates signaled yes. Then turned, ever so slightly, to see who was bidding against him. When he saw his son, his face remained stony.

"I have twelve. Twelve is the current bid. A generous bid for a generous piece of land. Is there thirteen? I have thirteen. The young man in the back has thirteen. Do I have fourteen?"

They went back and forth. Laura hadn't gotten involved. She must have seen there wasn't a need to. Each time he had to raise his paddle to outbid his son, John Thomas Yates turned another shade of red. They got up to sixteen, then seventeen. Jean didn't care who won any longer. She wanted it over. She had what she needed. Now, she had to find a way to get it.

"Eighteen! I have eighteen to the man in back. Is there nineteen? Anyone have nineteen?" The auctioneer was either getting carried away or it was part of his shtick. Probably the latter.

"Twenty-four," someone new called out. Jean knew that voice. Laura had stepped into the fray.

"Twenty-four to the young woman in black," the auctioneer said, smiling at Laura.

Reed didn't counter. John Thomas Yates's face had gone purple. He didn't have the money. It didn't matter, but he didn't know. He thought he was losing his domain.

"Anyone have twenty-five? Twenty-four to the young woman in front! Congratulations young lady, the land is yours."

John Thomas Yates stood. Jean signaled to the detective closest to Laura to move in, but he didn't see her. Yates looked like he could pick up a metal folding chair and bring it down on Laura for taking his toy at the playground. Jean could imagine him whining, *That's mine.* Instead, he did the next most childish thing she could have imagined. He spit on the back of Laura's head.

Laura tucked her chin to her chest but didn't dare turn around. John Thomas Yates stormed out of the auditorium, ignoring his son as he found the exit doors. A square of sunlight backlit the auditorium before the doors slammed shut. Jean signaled to the auctioneer to wrap it up.

"That will do it for the day," he said. "Please see the handy people up front who will help you arrange your final payments for those who won. Y'all enjoy the rest of your day."

Jean took the steps down in two giant leaps. The detective closest to Laura had his arms out, in case anyone should try to come closer. Laura's hands hovered over her hair. She had her neck at a crooked angle, her mouth undecided between a smile and a frown. Jean had gloves on by the time she stooped to bag Yates's discarded bottle of water. When she saw the back of

Laura's head, she had to stop herself from smiling, remembering how Laura was trying to grow it out. She'd have to buzz the back of it. Yates had spit the piece of gum Laura had offered him. The shiny piece of white, the color of dirty cauliflower, clung to the librarian's inch-long brown hair.

Everything about the clearing looks different now that we're leaving. There's possibility between the trees. Space where there used to be permanence. For the first time since I can remember, it feels like there's another world waiting for us beyond the canyon walls.

I got the girls from Sylvia, thanking her profusely. Then brought them here. They'd want to say goodbye before we left for good.

I sit next to Daisy and put an arm around her. We're sitting by the creek, listening to it murmur. Nancy is gone. She won't be back.

"I'm sorry for everything that happened," I say to my oldest daughter. "I should have known, and I should have protected you."

Daisy wraps her small arms around me, squeezing my middle. Jo joins us, holding Mrs. Philip-Shandy under her arm. I pull her in close to me. "You did your best, Mama," Daisy says. Her voice breaks me in two.

Before Jo can say anything, yipping comes from behind some bushes; then a woman curses, trips. Sylvia pushes through some brush into the clearing, the fat Chihuahua pulling her along by a thin leash.

"He hasn't shut up since you left," she says. "I was hoping you'd still be here." She lets go of the leash, and the dog runs to the girls, licking their legs and crawling up their knees.

"Does he have a name?" I ask.

"Bob," Jo says.

"Bob the dog?"

"What's wrong with that?" Daisy asks.

Bob runs after a squirrel, and the girls race after him, reaching for his leash.

"I hope you don't mind," Sylvia says. "I didn't think you would. We're leaving too. My grandson passed last night. He didn't have any children of his own. He's the last of us. It's time for us to move on.

"Before I go," Sylvia says, sitting next to me. "There's something I've been wanting to tell you. I didn't know you before, but I watched you with those girls when you were at the ranch. You couldn't see what was happening, but I did. I was there, the entire time. He was many things, but first and foremost, he was a liar. He spun you around and around so many times, you didn't know which way was north. If you had known, he would have ended it sooner. The only person to blame is him."

"But the last night, I could have—I wanted to—the baby—" I can't bring myself to say the words.

"No," she says, as firmly as I've ever heard her. "You did the only thing you could."

A pain that runs through my shoulders, up into my neck, releases.

"Thank you," I say.

The girls, leash in hand, run back to us with fat Bob trailing behind them, panting and hacking like he's going to cough up a lung.

"You're all going to be okay," Sylvia says, echoing what she whispered to me that night, when she was a ghost, and I was yet to be. She hugs each of the girls, smiles at me a final time, and, as she walks away, evaporates, like a mist dissolving in the morning heat.

"Where'd she go?" Daisy asks.

"To the place to go when you're ready," I say. "I had a couple ideas about where we could go next, but I wanted to ask you girls first. Jo—" I say. Her brown eyes rake the ground, refusing to meet mine. "Jo"—I start again—"who taught you to travel?"

Jo's cheeks flush.

"Was it your mother? Your other mother?" I ask gently.

"Don't be mad," she says.

"I could never be mad at you," I say, kneeling at her side. "Is that where you've been going? Have you been going to see your mother?"

She nods. "And my gramma." She takes a gulping breath. "Does that mean you don't want me anymore?"

"Never, never ever in a million years."

Jo gathers courage to explain. "The first night, she came to find me. She wanted to make sure I was—" Her small voice catches. "When she died, there was a voice in my head, telling me I'd be okay. It was her. When we died, she came. She told me she never forgot about me. She wanted me to stay. She always wanted me to have a sister. So instead of going with her, sometimes I went to visit her."

"I'm glad you did," I say.

"Is that where we're going?" Daisy asks. She's holding the leash and the dog has calmed, plopped at her feet like a rag doll. "Are we going to see Jo's other mother?"

"Yes. But if it's okay with you, I have someone else I want to see first."

I take the girls' hands and follow Nancy's directions. Outside the city, there's a sprawling one-story building. I don't dare take the girls inside. Instead, we peer through his window.

He's an old man now. Crepey skin hanging along his forearm. Age spots along his neck. I should wear these time stamps too. I should be on the other side of the glass, holding his hand. There's a TV in the corner. A twin-sized bed centers the room. A shelf holds a row of carved wooden figurines. Across the room, a door opens. A woman steps through. This is the part I was most afraid of. She's so old—so much older than when I left her. Her age confirms the years I lost. She has natural silver and gray hair.

"Mama, who is she?" Daisy asks.

"Your little sister," I say. "Do you remember her? She was only a baby."

Daisy nods. "I remember. She liked to chew on her toes."

"I remember too," Jo adds. "She smelled like milk."

My youngest daughter smiles at the old man. Places a blanket across his lap. He acts as though he doesn't recognize her, but he has to. Time can't erase the person you spent your life saving.

It's enough to know they're here.

I'll come back when they're ready.

For now, we have other adventures and other debts to pay.

"Where do you go to meet your mother?" I ask Jo. Her face breaks into a wide smile.

We hold hands again and picture a golden field halfway across the world. We are in the air and above the earth, floating. Our bodies are diaphanous vapors stretched across the sky. I feel the ground stop spinning below me, and in the distance stands a row of tall cypress trees.

When the ground rises to meet us, we're standing on the edge of the field. A small village sits behind us, filled with flavored ices and treats. The girls run out, their fingers dancing through the tall grass, laughing. I see two women standing by the tree line, waiting. One with hair as dark as Jo's with her arms outstretched, and the other with a smile as broad as her granddaughter's.

The air is like the ground—golden and warm. Along the tree line, birdsong whistles between the leaves. Someday, when we are done with these invisible bodies, when my last daughter has joined us, perhaps I would like to be a bird too.

SIX
MONTHS
LATER

LAURA OPENED THE BACK DOOR OF HER THREE-bedroom in the center of Truth or Consequences to let Bella out. It wasn't her normal time, but Laura would be gone the rest of the day. They had learned the hard way when the stone yard was too hot for Bella's paws. When the red-nosed pit mix went out for the first time after they had moved in, during late afternoon, she had picked up her paws as though she were stepping on broken glass. Then she lay down, rolling over on her side, waiting to be rescued. It wasn't until Laura went out with her own bare feet, burning her soles, that she figured out the problem.

The kid next door was weed whacking the tufts of grass sprouting along their driveway. Next to them was the only house with a lawn in her neighborhood. Laura couldn't imagine what the water bill was. She could water her plants Wednesdays, Fridays, and Sundays, but not between the hours of ten in the morning and six at night. She had learned when another neighbor came by and reminded her while she was watering the primrose she planted outside her windows. Waist-high native grasses grew along the fenced yard's borders. Otherwise, the yard was all stone, like most in the neighborhood.

Laura let Bella back in, locking the door behind them. She had an appointment for security cameras later in the week. Kate had insisted, and for once, Laura hadn't put up a fight.

It had been a few weeks since Laura and Bella made the move. Right after Jean shaved the back of her head, Laura had gone back home to wait for the DNA to come back. She had been refreshing her email every fifteen minutes and looking at her phone nonstop until, one day, it rang with a 575 area code.

Jean hadn't bothered with hello. "I haven't heard anything yet, but is there any chance you'd consider relocating? I took a job with the state. And I get to pick my own people."

New Mexico, seeing the need for renewed investigations into open cold cases, had created a new department. The county was cutting its cold case budget because the state would be expanding its own. Jean had been given one of its slots, which she agreed to, on the condition that she could bring in her own people and choose her own cases. Also, that she took every Tuesday and every other Friday off in exchange for working a few Saturdays. There was a stroller she planned to get out of her attic and an old crib to set up in her guest room for a certain newborn.

"What happened to retiring?" Laura had asked.

"Don't have it in me," she said. "I promised my husband I'd go on a cruise with him. If I make it back alive."

By the time Laura had packed up her things and driven them two-thirds of the way across the country with Bella riding shotgun, the results had come back. But Jean, she hadn't. She'd never left.

"How was the cruise?" Laura asked on her first day.

"Couldn't tell you. I never went. I'm not a cruise person after all."

Laura didn't ask when she noticed the detective wasn't wearing her wedding ring anymore.

"But I figured out our mistake," Jean offered in place of personal details. "We spelled Amy wrong. Or rather, the priest did."

Once they had John Thomas Yates's DNA, Jean had run it through CODIS, the federal DNA database, and GEDmatch, an open source ancestry site. CODIS told them he was a match to a single rape kit from a little town in West Texas. A mother had brought her ten-year-old daughter in, claiming she had been raped by a man working near their property. A DNA sample had been taken, but no match had ever been found. Until John Thomas Yates, aka Curtis Yates, aka Gonzalo Cortez, and any other aliases they hadn't found yet. Jean hadn't been surprised.

"The case picks the cop," she had told Laura over the phone.

GEDmatch, on the other hand, reported his cousins, four and five times removed, nieces and nephews. Jean didn't have the training to sort the results herself, but even she could understand the top hit: a daughter.

They had an appointment to meet the daughter later today.

Laura went out to her car with a towel in hand. She put the towel over her black seat and opened the windows, which she'd leave down until the AC kept pace with the heat. She now understood why everyone around town seemed to own a white car, and she had a call in to a handyman to repair her leaning carport. She put in the address in Albuquerque and headed north.

✵

EVENING STAR WAS A chain of memory care assisted-living facilities, and Jean was already parked outside when Laura pulled in. They would have driven together, but Jean had to meet with an attorney in the city earlier.

In the few minutes she had been standing in the parking lot, going over their plan, a thin layer of sweat coated Laura's stomach. The temperature drop when they stepped into the air-conditioned lobby felt like a slap.

Inside Evening Star, clusters of traditional maroon-and-beige-striped couches and armchairs surrounded mahogany coffee tables. The lobby could have been in any chain hotel—except for the faint, stale smell of rubbing alcohol and grandma's heavy floral perfume. Jean went to the corner, where she had a view of the parking lot and front door. Laura milled around, waiting. A couple closer to Jean's age, dressed to play golf, entered. A nurse led them back. The hall doors all had locks. Couldn't have grandma wandering out into the parking lot.

Another woman entered next. Her hair was silver and gray, naturally wavy. She wore a full maxi skirt and a denim jacket. She looked like a cool retired art teacher. Jean approached her, putting out her hand.

"Detective Sergeant Jean Martinez with the state. Are you Aimee Burns?"

The art teacher stunt double nodded as Jean introduced Laura. "Aimee, this is Laura MacDonald, our genealogist. I believe you two spoke on the phone." It was strange to hear herself introduced as something other than a librarian.

"It's nice to meet you in person," Aimee said. Her smile was for show; Laura had seen it before. She was Alice falling down the rabbit hole. The picnic she'd left under the shaded tree? A story. A hoax. A lie. "You do those stupid tests thinking you'll find out about a couple lost cousins, or find out you're 3 percent Sephardic Jew or something. Not, your dad isn't your dad. When I got my results, I never asked him about it. I was too scared it would change our relationship. Now, it's too late to ask." She bit the inside of her cheek.

"I brought hard copies of the files I emailed you," Laura said, opening her bag. "We can go over them again in person. I want to make sure you understand everything."

"Can we do it later?" Aimee said. She checked her watch. "He's best in the morning. If he's having a good day, I don't want to miss it."

Jean and Laura nodded. "Of course," Jean said.

"Let me tell them at the desk we're ready to go back," Aimee said, leaving them.

A nurse joined them. Laura sized up every nurse she met, deciding whether they could handle an oncology department or an ICU. This one couldn't. She brought them through two sets of locked doors, leading the three women to room 62. The name, typed and printed on white cardstock and slipped under the door's number, declared the room home of Dan Burns, memory care patient.

"Here we are," the nurse said, opening the door and standing to the side.

Before they went in, Aimee said, "I hope it's a good day. By the way, he keeps calling me Peggy, just so you know. And he insists we call him Dale. I'm still not sure why. Just go with it or he gets upset. It's like he's living in the past. Or some confused other dimension."

Jean turned to Laura, who said only, "Time loop."

Morning sunshine flooded the room. A large rectangle of light like a rug across the floor. The windows looked out to some tall grasses and cacti. An older man sat hunched over in a chair next to his bed, a thin blanket draped over thinner legs.

"Mr. Burns? You have some guests today," the nurse called. She brought two chairs in from the hall, and Jean and Laura took seats opposite the man. Laura studied how he reacted to the introduction of strangers.

"The name is Dale. Dale Tellefsen, how many times do I have to tell you people?" The man turned and stared blankly. Aimee went over, kissing him on the cheek before sitting on the bed. "Dad," she said, "these women have a couple of questions about an old friend of yours."

"We should ask Peggy first," he answered. "I don't know if Peggy would like it."

"Dad, I'm Aimee," she said. Her voice caught. She swallowed. Said to Laura and Jean, "Sorry. This may not work."

"My mother has dementia. I get it," Laura said. "She's actually at another Evening Star."

"Small world," said Aimee.

"Very."

This seemed to make Aimee feel better. She visibly relaxed her shoulders.

"Mr. Tellefsen," Jean said. "My name is Jean Martinez. I wanted to talk about a couple old friends of yours." She pulled out the picture of Margaret and Daisy at Christmas with Curtis Yates. "Do you remember this woman? Do you recognize her?"

Laura kept watch on the old man's eyes. If he knew the people in the photo, he wasn't giving up any clues. The man with a license with the name Dan Burns turned, staring out the window. A hummingbird was on the other side, floating. Maybe she was staring back. Maybe she was admiring her reflection.

"Do you remember a woman named Margaret Washington? She may have changed her name to Margaret Crown, and we think all her friends called her—"

"Peggy," the man said. "Peggy loved hummingbirds." He turned back to Aimee, cupped her soft hand in his two. They were bony cages, holding her still. "Peggy loved you."

The woman blinked, rapid-fire. Shook her head, pushing the pooling tears to the corners of her eyes. "I—I'll be back," she said, making a quick move for the door.

Laura shrugged at Jean. "It's normal," she said. "It's a lot."

Jean brought out the photo again. "Do you recognize this man?" she asked, her finger under Curtis's face.

"Just like his father," he said.

"What do you mean?"

"His father was mean, cruel. His real father, Gonzalo, beat him and his mom. One day, she had enough. Mother made him change his name when she married that Yates man. John Thomas, she called him. I always called him Cortez. He wanted me to. I lived with them, when I was young. My mother couldn't handle me. He was like a brother. We moved to California later. He started going by Curtis instead."

"And sir, are you saying John Thomas Yates's mother—Helen Ruth—are you saying she killed Gonzalo Sr.?"

"It's what he told me," he said. He rocked slightly in his chair. "He said his mother didn't want him to follow the father."

Laura asked the next question. "Dale," she said, slowly. "Do you know what happened to Peggy?"

He pressed his eyes closed. On the other side of the window, the hummingbird's wings were like angel wings, blurred and ghostly. There, and not there, all at once. "Curtis," he said. "I had to take the baby. I couldn't get the girls." His head rocked back.

"Dale, we think Curtis might have also—" Laura stopped. Jean's fingers pressed against her forearm.

"There's no point," Jean said.

"It's better to know the truth," Laura said, thinking of her own mother and what she'd kept from her. "Dale, we think Curtis also killed your sister, Nancy. After you left with the baby, did you ever talk to Nancy?"

He shook his head. "Nancy's gone?"

"Yes, Nancy's gone. Did you ever talk to her after you took Aimee and moved away?"

"Nancy's gone?" he asked, repeating himself.

Laura nodded, slowly.

"I tried to keep her safe," Dale said.

"We know," Jean offered.

He peered out the window again. The hummingbird hovered on the other side of the glass. Dale's face smoothed, the wet streaks ill-fitting on a now-smiling face. "She likes hummingbirds," he said again.

"Yes sir," Jean said.

Laura could tell they were done with the questions. Dale Tellefsen had gone by Dan Burns ever since he took Aimee Gloria Crown, given a made-up surname because her stepfather, or adoptive father, Laura wasn't sure which applied here, was trying to keep her from the truth of her biological father: John Thomas Yates. Dale was showing signs he was done for the day. Unfortunately, they weren't done with him.

"Mr. Burns," Jean said, using the name he was more likely to associate with medical procedures. "We have Aimee's permission to take a saliva sample from you." She already had her gloves on and the long swab ready. "Would you mind opening your mouth for me?"

As Jean was finishing, Aimee returned to the doorway. "Any luck?" she asked.

"We got what we needed," Jean said. "Is there someplace you'd like to go? We have a few things we want to go over with you."

"Anywhere but here. There's a taco place around the corner. If it's okay with you—I need a drink."

❀

THE THREE WOMEN SAT around a small square table acting as a pedestal to a bowl of tortilla chips the size of a baby elephant. They were fresh. They had a thick layer of salt. They were perfect. A TV in the corner played soccer. A few men taking an early lunch sat at the bar.

Their drinks came, and Laura did her best not to gulp down her margarita. When Jean gave her the evil eye, she put her drink down and got out her paperwork.

"This is what we know for certain," she began. "Your biological father is Gonzalo Tomas Cortez Jr. When his father died, his mother, Helen Ruth, married Phil Herbert Yates. When she remarried, she had the children change their names. Alicia, the daughter, became Alice. Gonzalo Tomas Cortez Jr. was now John Thomas Yates. Their family moved down the street from Bjorn and Anete Tellefsen on Sweetwater Drive in Serrucho. The Tellefsens had three children—Gerry, Dale, and Nancy. Dale was a wild child. His parents couldn't control him and didn't know what to do with him. Helen and Phil must have offered to raise him, because he's listed as a child in their household in certain records.

"Around the same time, across the country, Margaret Washington is the second oldest of five girls. When her parents divorced, the oldest two stayed in Connecticut with their father, a naval operator. The youngest three went with their mother to Southern California, where she was from originally. While she's in college, Margaret finds out she's pregnant with a little girl, Daisy—"

"My sister," Aimee said.

"Technically, your half sister."

Aimee nodded. Laura continued. "When it's discovered she's pregnant, Margaret is sent to live with her mother in Los Angeles, which is where Daisy is born. At some point, she meets John Thomas Yates, though by now he has picked up a new nickname: Curtis. We think because it reminds him of Cortez. Though he may have also started adopting nicknames to cover his tracks.

"Curtis had moved to LA with Dale and Alice. The three were something like siblings. Curtis and Alice were actual brother and sister, but Dale had lived with them most their lives. Margaret and Curtis met and began a romantic relationship, probably in the months after Daisy was born. Margaret introduced Curtis to her family as a boyfriend at a Christmas party. Shortly after, she moved to New Mexico with Curtis, Dale, and Alice. Margaret brought Daisy with her. Margaret has a driver's license from the state, and another daughter,

Amy Crown, has a baptismal record at a local church. However, we believe the baptismal record to be in error. Crown was a last name Margaret had picked up based on the ranch they were living at, and she used a less common spelling for her daughter's name."

"My name," Aimee said.

"Yes," Laura said, nodding.

"And Curtis, my biological father, killed Margaret and Daisy," she asked.

"We think so," Jean said, leaning in. "His DNA is a match to other violent offenses back in West Texas. Those were the ones we were able to arrest him on. God bless Texas, they don't have a statue of limitations when it comes to children. He's going to get anywhere between 25 to 99 years. I may personally mail him a monthly package of multivitamins to make sure he doesn't miss out."

"And Curtis, or John Thomas, or whatever he was called— that's—he is for certain my biological father?" Aimee asked again, perhaps hoping for a different answer.

"Based on your DNA sample you uploaded to Ancestry and GEDmatch, yes. If you hadn't uploaded your results to GEDmatch, we never would have found you. Ancestry doesn't share their results with police investigations, but GEDmatch does. When we uploaded Yates's DNA there, you came up as his daughter. He also had two sons—your half brothers—with Nancy Tellefsen. When you're ready, they both said they'd like to meet you."

"And Nancy was another victim," Aimee said.

"Yes," Jean said. "He was going by Curtis then. He and Margaret were in a romantic relationship while they lived at a ranch up in Socorro County. Dale Tellefsen and Alice Yates were also living there. Margaret became pregnant with you, and shortly after you were born, Curtis killed her, Daisy, and another little girl who had been living with them."

"That's what I don't understand," Aimee said, pressing a finger to her forehead. "Who is the other little girl they found in—" She couldn't bring herself to say the word.

"Curtis, unfortunately, had a pattern. He preyed on single mothers in order to victimize their daughters. We believe the other little girl was another one of his victims, and her mother, likely another victim as well."

Aimee kept her eyes pinched closed. "But you don't know the other little girl's name?"

"Not yet," Laura said. "In genealogy you learn, for every mystery you solve, ten more take its place."

"But Nancy wasn't part of the pattern," Aimee said.

"No, she wasn't," Jean said. "I can't confirm this, but my sense is he needed to keep the Tellefsen family close. I don't believe he could have moved those barrels by himself. I think he called Gerry Tellefsen for help. They knew each other growing up, and the barrels ended up on a piece of land the Tellefsen mining company owned. He not only needed to keep the Tellefsens close, he wanted to keep the barrels close."

"And my father, Dan Burns, isn't who he said he is," Aimee said.

"With the sample we retrieved from your father today, we'll be able to confirm if he's really Dale by comparing his sample to John and Reed Tellefsen. If he is related, they'll share autosomal DNA. And as I explained on the phone, the only DNA left in Jane Doe's remains were mitochondrial, linked to the mother's side. You were a direct match to her profile; you are her biological daughter. It doesn't change anything about your father, Dan Burns. He's still the man who loved you and raised you. It's very likely that had your father not taken you—you would have become another one of Curtis's victims."

"I know, I don't—" Aimee said, waving a hand in the air. "It's just—" She shook her head and laughed. "Knowing a man like that—a man who could hurt little girls. Knowing that man is half your DNA? It's like—"

"It's like he's a cancer," Laura said.

"That's exactly right," Aimee said, pressing her hands to her chest. "That's what it feels like. Like half of me is diseased." She paused. "Could you show me the spot where they were found?"

"I can, but it looks all different now. After we brought him in, a late-season wildfire came through the area, wiping it clean."

"I'd still like to see it," Aimee said.

"I can show you," Jean said.

"You also have an aunt—Margaret's half sister, Cynthia—who would like to meet you. If you're up for it," Laura said.

"One thing at a time," Aimee said, running her fingers through the condensation on her glass. "But yes, tell her I'd like to meet her. I may need a little time."

LAURA PULLED INTO HER driveway several hours later. She had some work to do back in the office, and she had stopped by the outdoor store on Broadway. It was about time she had a good pair of hiking boots if she was going to live surrounded by mountains.

It was nearing seven, and the sun was beginning to fade. Unlocking her front door, she held it open for Bella, who joined her outside.

"You wanna go for a walk?" she asked.

Bella's tail thwapped yes.

Laura unhooked her leash, and together they walked to the end of their street. This late in the day, the pavement had cooled enough for Bella's sensitive paws. Maybe there were little doggie booties she could buy for midday treks.

At the end of their street, Laura turned a corner, heading down the dead end whose sign warned No Through Way.

Here, where streets ended, the wild began. Laura and Bella had a route that took them beyond the neighborhood's borders. They passed through brush with the terra-cotta-colored mountains behind them. New Mexico was greener than she ever could have imagined. The dirt was the color of baked clay, and if the wind picked up, you'd get a taste of it on your tongue. But there was so much green in the trees and grass and brush.

Laura wouldn't yet let Bella run off leash, afraid she'd get bitten by something lurking. They paused. Laura arched her back, leaning into the Southwestern sun. Her face warmed. She ran her hands through the back of her hair. It had grown out more. With each day, she felt a little bit more like herself, and a little bit less like the person waiting on an exam table. She still had checkups and more rounds of immunotherapy, but she could see a time where cancer wouldn't color every day and thought.

Maybe.

They waited until the sun sank a little lower, threatening darkness. Somewhere, birds called, their voices sounding almost like cats meowing.

Together, they walked back.

When they got to the front of their house, Laura saw her mailbox hanging open like a fish's gaping mouth caught on a line. She reached in, pulling out a package. Reading the return label, she knew it held her most recent eBay purchase. She tore open the strip, revealing a faded pink rabbit with a black-and-white checked bow around one ear. It wasn't the same one from the barrel, but another that looked just like it, from an antique store outside Beaumont, Texas, near where the other little girl had been born. The girl Laura thought of as the second daughter. Laura would find her name. Maybe there was one more piece of truth to be discovered.

ACKNOWLEDGMENTS

WRITING IS SOLITARY. PUBLISHING TAKES A VILLAGE. To Rachel Ekstrom Courage, thanks for your belief, and to Masie Cochran, thanks for your wisdom. Thanks to the entire team at Tin House: Craig Popelars, Nanci McCloskey, Beth Steidle, Alyssa Ogi, Elizabeth DeMeo, Becky Kraemer, Anne Horowitz, Allison Dubinsky, Jae Nichelle, and Alice Yang.

Thanks to early readers: Megan Holzman, Heather Shaw, Nicholas Thomas, Christopher Spencer, Emily Hitchcock, Ian Moeckel, Elizabeth Staple, Genoveva Dimova, and Re Marzullo. Thanks to Hilary Davidson, Jane Pek, Vanessa Cuti, Katie Gutierrez, and Katy Hays for your kind words.

This book would not have been possible without *Forensic Genealogy* by Colleen Fitzpatrick, PhD. Also: Barbara Taylor's course, Intro to DNA 101, available online through DNA Adoption, Philip Varney's *New Mexico's Best Ghost Towns*, and the Bear Brook Podcast by Jason Moon at NHPR. Go listen if you haven't already. Thanks to Colleen Smith for confirming medical details. All mistakes are my own. Thanks also to Megan Sheeran who graciously gave me her time to ask questions about her work in the Genealogy Department at Columbus Metropolitan Library. Same mistake disclaimer here. And though we haven't met, thanks to librarian Rebekah Heath, and genealogist Barbara Rae-Venter for their work. You are an inspiration.

My Peggy is not Marlyse Elizabeth Honeychurch, but her name is worth stating here too. To Marlyse and her daugters, Marie Elizabeth Vaughn and Sarah Lynn McWaters, and the still unidentified middle child, your names matter. More than 600,000 people go missing every year. In addition, there are an estimated 4,400 unidentified bodies found each year, and each year, 1,000 of these people remain John or Jane Does. Please consider the National Missing and Unidentified Persons System (NamUs), the Doe Network, the National Center for Missing and Exploited Children (NECMEC), and the Black and Missing Foundation (BAMFI) in your giving. While we're here, if you have ever purchased a kit through Ancestry, 23andMe or any other private genealogy site, please head over to GEDmatch and upload your results. It only takes a few minutes.

To my family: thank you for your support and belief. To my parents: thank you for always taking me to the Needham Public Library and to our local bookstores. I was blessed. Thanks to my nurses and doctors at Yale, especially Dr. Andrea Silber, my oncologist. I was lucky. To cancer patients and survivors, this book is also for you.

Last, thank you to my husband and partner, Ryan. None of this is possible without you. Thank you for our life together.